677668

SHARED TOMORROWS:
Science Fiction in Collaboration

SHARED TOMORROWS:
Science Fiction in Collaboration

Edited by
BILL PRONZINI and BARRY N. MALZBERG

St. Martin's Press New York

Copyright © 1979 by Bill Pronzini and Barry N. Malzberg
All rights reserved. For information, write:
St. Martin's Press, Inc., 175 Fifth Ave., New York, N.Y. 10010.
Manufactured in the United States of America

1st Edition

Library of Congress Cataloging in Publication Data

Main entry under title:

Shared tomorrows.
   1. Science fiction, American. I. Malzberg,
Barry N. II. Pronzini, Bill.
PZ1.S4997   [PS648.S3]   813'.0876   79-16344
ISBN 0-312-71637-0

ACKNOWLEDGMENTS

TIGER RIDE, by James Blish and Damon Knight. Copyright © 1948 by Street & Smith Publications, Inc. First published in *Astounding*. Reprinted by permission of Damon Knight.

DARK INTERLUDE, by Mack Reynolds and Fredric Brown. Copyright © 1950 by World Editions, Inc. First published in *Galaxy*. Reprinted by permission of Scott Meredith Literary Agency, Inc., 845 Third Avenue, New York, N.Y. 10022.

BEASTS OF BOURBON, by L. Sprague de Camp and Fletcher Pratt. Copyright © 1951 by Fantasy House, Inc. First published in *The Magazine of Fantasy & Science Fiction*. Reprinted by permission of L. Sprague de Camp.

SOUND DECISION, by Randall Garrett and Robert Silverberg. Copyright © 1956 by Street & Smith Publications, Inc. First published in *Astounding*. Reprinted by permission of Scott Meredith Literary Agency, Inc., 845 Third Avenue, New York, N.Y. 10022.

GRATITUDE GUARANTEED, by R. Bretnor and Kris Neville. Copyright © 1953 by Fantasy House, Inc. First published in *The Magazine of Fantasy & Science Fiction*. Reprinted by permission of the authors.

MARY CELESTIAL, by Miriam Allen deFord and Anthony Boucher. Copyright © 1955 by Fantasy House, Inc. First published in *The Magazine of Fantasy & Science Fiction*. Reprinted by permission of Curtis Brown, Ltd.

THE QUAKER CANNON, by Frederik Pohl and C. M. Kornbluth. Copyright © 1961 by Street & Smith Publications, Inc. First published in *Analog*. Reprinted by permission of Robert P. Mills, Ltd.

ELEMENTARY, by Laurence M. Janifer and Michael Kurland. Copyright © 1964 by Mercury Press, Inc. First published in *The Magazine of Fantasy & Science Fiction*. Reprinted by permission of the authors.

THE LOOLIES ARE HERE, by Ruth Allison and Jane Rice. Copyright © 1966 by Berkley Publishing Corp. First published in *Orbit 1*. Reprinted by permission of Robert P. Mills, Ltd.

MURPHY'S HALL, by Poul and Karen Anderson. Copyright © 1971 by Lancer Books, Inc. First published in *Infinity 2*. Reprinted by permission of Scott Meredith Literary Agency, Inc., 845 Third Avenue, New York, N.Y. 10022.

FACES FORWARD, by Jack Dann and George Zebrowski. Copyright © 1975 by Roger Elwood. First published in *Dystopian Visions*. Reprinted by permission of the authors.

PROSE BOWL, by Bill Pronzini and Barry N. Malzberg. Copyright © 1979 by Mercury Press, Inc. First published in *The Magazine of Fantasy & Science Fiction*. Reprinted by permission of the authors.

CONTENTS

INTRODUCTION	xi
TIGER RIDE	
by James Blish and Damon Knight	1
DARK INTERLUDE	
by Mack Reynolds and Fredric Brown	17
BEASTS OF BOURBON	
by L. Sprague de Camp and Fletcher Pratt	28
SOUND DECISION	
by Randall Garrett and Robert Silverberg	41
GRATITUDE GUARANTEED	
by R. Bretnor and Kris Neville	83
MARY CELESTIAL	
by Miriam Allen deFord and Anthony Boucher	109
THE QUAKER CANNON	
by Frederik Pohl and C. M. Kornbluth	130

ELEMENTARY
 by Laurence M. Janifer and Michael Kurland   *157*

THE LOOLIES ARE HERE
 by Ruth Allison and Jane Rice   *171*

MURPHY'S HALL
 by Poul and Karen Anderson   *178*

FACES FORWARD
 by Jack Dann and George Zebrowski   *196*

PROSE BOWL
 by Bill Pronzini and Barry N. Malzberg   *202*

BIBLIOGRAPHY   *233*

INTRODUCTION

To write fiction is a profoundly individual act: intensity of vision, clarity of focus, idiosyncrasy of approach, and so on (painting, classical music composition, and sexual fantasizing fall, perhaps, into a similar category). So it is not surprising that no more than a small percentage of novels and short stories have a shared by-line. What *is* remarkable is that the genres–and particularly science fiction–have had a substantial amount of collaborative work of at least good quality. In fact, two sets of collaborators in science fiction, Henry Kuttner/C. L. Moore and Frederik Pohl/C. M. Kornbluth, are better known for what they've done together than what they've done individually.

Writers of major stature have worked together and with any number of minor writers almost from the field's beginnings. As early as 1919 E. E. "Doc" Smith, while writing his famous space opera *Skylark of Space* (it was not published until 1934, which is an example both of perseverance and of short-sightedness among the editors of the time), secretly brought in a woman collaborator to do the romance passages because he felt uncomfortable with them. In the twenties, in the allied category of fantasy/macabre, H.P. Lovecraft co-authored several stories, not always with a shared by-line, for *Weird Tales*. In the thirties, works by collaborative teams became an established if not frequent occurrence in the pages of the genre's pulp magazines: Nat Schachner and Arthur Leo Zagat, Edwin Balmer and Philip Wylie, Earl and Otto Binder, August Derleth and Mark Schorer, in the early years of that decade; the industrious, ambitious, and literarily incestuous group of New York writers who called themselves the Futurians–Pohl, Kornbluth, Isaac Asimov, Robert W. Lowndes, Donald Wollheim, Richard Wilson–in the latter 1930s.

The forties. Kuttner and Moore were married and began writing most of their important work together, a good portion of it under the pseudonym of Lewis Padgett. Ray Bradbury made his first sale in partnership with Henry Hasse; Poul Anderson made his first sale with F. N. Waldrop. L. Sprague de Camp and Fletcher Pratt joined forces. So did some of the field's earliest and best anthologists: Raymond Healy and J. Francis McComas with their landmark *Adventures in Time and Space* in 1946; Leo Margulies and Oscar J. Friend with *From Off This World* and *My Best Science Fiction Story;* Everett Bleiler and T. E. Dikty with the first of their long-running series, *The Best Science Fiction Stories of the Year*. And so did Anthony Boucher and J. Francis McComas to co-found *The Magazine of Fantasy & Science Fiction.*

The fifties. Pohl and Kornbluth produced the bulk of their superior novels and short stories. Randall Garrett teamed with Robert Silverberg and Laurence M. Janifer. Mark Clifton teamed with Alex Apostolides. Fredric Brown teamed with Mack Reynolds.

The sixties and seventies. Michael Moorcock's circle of writers in England collaborating for *New Worlds*. Harlan Ellison doing one-shots with more than a dozen of the biggest names in the field. Harry Harrison and Brian W. Aldiss co-editing a series of present-day and retrospective anthologies. Gregory Benford and Gordon Eklund writing the Nebula-winning novella, "If the Stars Are Gods." Larry Niven and Jerry Pournelle producing *The Mote in God's Eye, Inferno,* and *Lucifer's Hammer* . . . .

No more than a small percentage, really, of the total output in science fiction over the last six decades. And yet, on the other hand, quite a few talented writers working in tandem, quite a few works of interest and quality published in the short story form alone.

An anthology of this type, therefore, would seem long overdue. Science fiction is perhaps the most heavily anthologized of all fields of literature past and present, and in recent years almost every aspect of it has been explored; but until *Shared Tomorrows* there has been no gathering of collaborative stories.*

It is perhaps fitting that the first anthology of science fiction in collaboration should have been put together by an active collaborative team. We like to think so, anyway. We write novels and short stories together; we have edited other anthologies together. Why not a co-edited anthology of co-written stories? one of us said some time ago. Good thinking, the other one said. Like all ongoing collaborators, we always agree with each other.

Which leads us to a few words about the art of collaboration.

Ideally it should be a fusion of talents toward a third voice and thus result in a story beyond the skills or vision of either of the individual writers. In the best cases it is; in others it becomes a gimmick, a species of play, a party activity somewhere between bitching and parlor tricks as a means of passing the time. (Not that we mean to derogate time-passing, you understand. Writing, as has been pointed out on many occasions, is a lonely business. You take your companionship where you can, and collaboration, while it may double the work–it sometimes does for us–can at least halve the loneliness. Collaboration in the novel form is hard or harder work; in the short story it can be almost pleasant.)

But just how *do* writers collaborate?

We have been asked that question dozens of times (almost as often as we've been asked if we've ever had anything published, what names we write under, where we get our ideas). What we usually tell people is that one of us does the action and one does the introspection; one does the dialogue and one does the de-

---

* *Partners in Wonder*, Harlan Ellison's collection of his co-written stories with various personalities, was published in the early seventies. But Ellison is a circumstance unto himself and the book a function of his individual vision; it did not go afield.

scription; one does the upbeat stuff and one does the despair. The truth is: it all depends.

In our case we most often rewrite each other's material, although we have also written fiction consecutively (one moving in when the other raises the flag), and by one working out a fragment given him by the other, and by one revising an unsold story created by the other. X and Y used to get drunk in a hotel room for three weeks while they wrote a novel in alternate savage bursts at the typewriter. B would create a detailed plot outline and C would write the prose. Pohl and Kornbluth lived in Pohl's house in New Jersey and wrote two drafts of everything, one doing the first and the other the final and polish. Kuttner and Moore literally wrote as one: they were so involved in the personal sense and had such similar styles and visions that they could not later tell where one left off in a story and the other began.

Like we said–it all depends. In this most idiosyncratic of businesses, even the joint efforts are bound to be idiosyncratic.

Anyhow–

A dozen examples of collaboration in science fiction follow, including one of our own. If you don't like any of them, blame one of us: he selected half the stories and his taste is sometimes suspect. Or is it the other one whose taste is suspect?

I don't know.

Neither do I.

See? As collaborators we always agree on everything.

–Bill Pronzini and
Barry N. Malzberg
January 1979

SHARED TOMORROWS:
Science Fiction in Collaboration

TIGER RIDE by James Blish and Damon Knight

"Tiger Ride" was written in early 1948 when both James Blish and Damon Knight were employed at a New York literary agency. It appeared in Astounding (where Knight was to sell only two more stories in the next thirty years), and is their only collaboration. In fact, it is Knight's only collaboration, period, and Blish's only joint effort in the short story form (he did do a pair of novels with the late Norman L. Knight in the sixties).

Blish (1921-1975) and Knight (b. 1922) had oddly parallel careers nonetheless. They began in publishing at the above-mentioned literary agency, and in the early fifties emerged, simultaneously, as the first serious critics of science fiction as a literary form–Blish with Issues at Hand and More Issues at Hand, both under the name of William Atheling, and Knight with In Search of Wonder. They also began to publish important novels at about the same time: Blish with Seedling Stars (1957) and the Hugo-winning A Case of Conscience (1958); Knight with A for Anything (1956). In the years before his death, however, Blish unfortunately confined himself to publishing Star Trek novelizations and now seems to be a somewhat forgotten figure in the mainstream of the field. Knight, on the other hand, while he does little fiction these days (only two stories in the decade), remains a substantial figure by virtue of collections, numerous anthologies of high quality, and his autobiographical account of The Futurians (1977).

A sophisticated story for its time, "Tiger Ride" holds up remarkably well–as does almost all of the early Knight (he was perhaps the most stylistically gifted writer of his generation) and some of the early Blish–three decades later. It's too bad that the whim of two young men did not persist for at least a few more collaborations.

TIGER RIDE

By James Blish and Damon Knight

2/4/2121

Tested the levitator units this morning. Both performed well with the dummies, and Laura insisted on trying one herself–they were tuned to her voice, anyhow. Chapelin objected, of course, but his wife overrode him as usual. I believe she was actually hoping there would be an accident.

Laura Peel said: "Just the same, I'm going to do it."

The wind was in her fair hair and pressing her clothes gently against the length of her slim body. She looked uncommonly beautiful, Hal Osborn thought. He wondered, what the devil does Chapelin see when he looks at her?

Chapelin's big blond face was a study in prudence and responsibility. He said: "Now, let's not be unreasonable, Laura–"

Niki Chapelin's voice cut him off. "Oh, why not let her? It's perfectly safe, isn't it, Hal?"

"Nope," said Hal. If anything did happen, he thought, all she'd have to do would be to remind everybody, "But Hal said–"

Her small mask turned toward him, and the basilisk eyes drilled holes in his forehead. He felt again the rising urge toward murder which often shook him these days; the isolation was beginning to tell on them all, and sometimes Hal thought he would abandon Laura and ultronics and all the rest for a chance to leave this God-forsaken tomb of a planet.

No, he corrected himself, not a tomb; a ghost, and the brother of a ghost. Styrtis Delta III was the satellite of a huge planet, which in turn swung around a Gray Ghost–a star so huge and rarefied that it gave no light. Luckily there was a yellow companion star which provided almost-normal days for half the year; the nights, rendered deep, livid blue-green by the reflection from the methane-swathed giant planet, were not normal, but they were bearable.

And the whole complicated system was in a corner of the galaxy where no possible explosion, no matter how titanic, could injure the works of man–in a limb of stars which man had never before visited, and had scarcely mapped. The Earth Council had awarded this planet to the ultronics group, and given them the period of "summer" at Council expense to work out their discoveries. When the yellow sun was eclipsed by the Gray Ghost, Styrtis Delta III would have a winter that might have made even Dante tremble.

The people who had once inhabited this planet must have been unique; the seasonal changes they had had to withstand were terrific. Whatever had killed them off, it hadn't been the weather, for the ruins of their cities still showed the open spaces and wide-spanned architecture of a race as used to storm as to quiet. Maybe they'd killed each other off; storms of emotion could destroy things untouchable by Nature.

Luckily, Niki could spare Hal only the one look. Chapelin was beginning to repeat all his arguments to her, and she had to turn on her heavy artillery: Mark IX, the look of bored impatience.

The levitator was an entirely new device, said Chapelin, it was new even in the hundred-kilo lab stage, let alone belt-size. It wasn't just the danger of falling, he said, there was a thing made of platinum called a governor that was only three mm long, and if that went, Laura could find herself digging a hole in the ground with two Gs behind her. There were good reasons for never testing a new ultronic device in person before it had had at least fifty hours' run on the dummies–dummies don't experiment with unfamiliar equipment, they don't move of their own accord in flight and disarrange things, they don't miscalculate and release the total ultimate energy that could consume a whole group of suns.

Niki was swinging her riding crop against her skinny tailored thigh. She had come because she was Chapelin's wife, and because Laura was coming. Ultronics interested her mildly, sometimes.

Hal stole a glance at Laura. On the other side of her, little

Mike Cohen was chewing his pipe, watching and saying nothing. Hal met his speculative gaze, and looked away guiltily. Laura's mouth had had that hurt, childish down-curve, the same as it always had when she was watching Chapelin unseen. Her spine was as straight as ever, though. She's licked, he thought, she always gets licked. She'll go through with it out of sheer defiance.

A star-shaped shadow passed slowly between Hal and the Chapelins. He looked up.

"Wind's blowing them toward the edge of the plateau," he said. "Better pull 'em back."

Everybody looked. High over their heads, the two seven-foot mannikins were canted slightly, their blank heads pointed toward the distant Killhope range. "Wind's pretty strong up there," Chapelin said uncomfortably. "You might as well bring them down, Laura."

Niki said: *"That's* better, dear. You're so much nicer when you're not stubborn."

Chapelin turned back to her. "Wait a minute," he said, "I didn't mean–"

"I'm going to do it anyhow," Laura said clearly, "whether you let me or not." Her lips compressed. She watched the dummies and said: "Right. Right– Enough. Down."

"Well," Chapelin said, "be careful."

Hal felt the surge of hatred again. Chapelin, can't you see she loves you? Won't you put up any kind of a fight, make her see that you're worried about her? If you'd show the slightest interest, you could persuade her not to try it–

The dummies floated down until the tips of their legs touched the ground. They hung there, swaying gently. Laura said: "Stop," and they sat down abruptly as if their strings had been cut, then flopped over and lay sprawled on the sun-caked turf.

Chapelin had drawn his wife a couple of meters away and was talking to her earnestly. Niki was listening to him with no sign of impatience, which meant that she was amused.

Hal choked and walked over to the dummies. Laura was kneeling beside one of them, taking off its belt. She got up as he approached, her bare knees dusty.

"Let's have a look at it," Hal said. "That landing was a little rough."

She put the articulated silver band around her waist, leaving the one she'd been wearing on the ground. "Let me alone just now, Hal," she said in a barely audible voice. She stepped away and said: "Up."

The belt took her up.

Hal watched her go, squinting his eyes against the lemon-yellow sky. She went straight up, with a halo of saffron light on the top of her blond head, and stayed there until he was beginning to wonder if she was ever coming down again. Then she dropped swiftly, turned, and swooped over their heads.

Hal swore. Laura didn't know what "careful" meant. He was angry at himself for failing to try to stop her, and angry at her for taking out her feelings about Chapelin on them all. If that governor cut out, they might all die–the whole crazy solar system, the whole ridge of stars could be annihilated under certain conditions.

She was up high again now, so high she could barely be seen. Despite the hot sun on the plateau, it was cold that high up, cold and blustery with the ceaseless blast of this planet's rapid revolution. Then she began to drop again, faster than she should, as if under power.

At the lip of the plateau, Laura seemed to see that she was going to miss it, and reversed the controls. The belt jerked her slantwise back toward them, and burned out in a flare of copper-colored energy. Everyone but Hal hit the ground and waited for the world to end.

Hal stayed on his feet, his mind a well of horror. Laura's body tumbled over their heads and struck just beyond them.

Then everyone was running.

Oh, yes; we buried old Jonas today. He was a quiet, pathetic little guy, but he wanted to go home like the rest of us; I wish we could have had his body shipped back, but twenty-five thousand volts doesn't leave much to ship. Besides, the accident with Laura rather took our minds off him.

In the shack Hal shifted his weight uncomfortably on a drum. Mike Cohen was talking quietly, but Hal only half heard him. Laura lay on one of the cots, seemingly without a single bruise; but she was not breathing. Chapelin sat beside her, wringing his hands in a blind, stupid way. Niki had the good sense to be absent, out in the generator shed, congratulating herself, Hal supposed.

"I still think she's alive," Mike Cohen went on. "We know so little about ultronics—every accident's a freak at this stage."

Hal stirred. "The belt wasn't hurt," he said numbly. "At first I thought it'd sliced her right in two." He looked at the gleaming, jointed thing, still clasping Laura's waist. They had been afraid to touch it—if there were still a residue of energy in there, and the governor gone—

"That's right. And the fall should have broken all her bones. She hit hard. But . . . I don't think she really hit at all. Something took up the shock."

"What, then?"

A strangled sound came from the cot. Hal started and stood up, his heart thudding under his breastbone. The sound, however, had come from Chapelin, who was also standing, bending over Laura.

"Chapelin? What is it?"

"She's breathing. She started, all of a sudden. I—" His voice broke, and he stood silent, hands working at his sides.

But it was true. Laura's breast was rising and falling regularly, naturally. There was still no color in her face.

Even as Hal noted that, a faint tinge of pink crept in over her cheekbones.

"Thank God," Chapelin muttered. "She's coming around." He looked at Hal and at Mike Cohen, meeting their eyes for the first time since the accident. "It was funny. I heard a sort of sigh, and when I looked, she was breathing just as if she'd been asleep. Shall we try to get the belt off now?"

"I don't think we should." Mike said. "It may still be in operation, and it's tuned to her. Best wait 'til she tells it to turn off."

"How do you know it's still on?"

"It must be. That flash of copper light—it was only an electrical short, or we'd none of us be here now. We've never been able to overload an ultronic field before, and *something* must have shielded her during that fall."

On the cot, Laura whispered, quite clearly: "Is that you, Mike? Where are you? I can't see you."

Chapelin bent over her. "Laura," he said huskily. "How do you feel? Can you move a little?"

"I'm all right, but it seems so dark. I can just barely make you out."

Mike Cohen chuckled, a small, joyous sound. "You're O.K., Laura. We were too busy to remember about such little things as sunset." He trotted quickly across the room and turned on the lights. Laura sat up in the fluorescent glow and blinked at them.

For a moment no one could speak. Then, from the doorway, Niki Chapelin's voice said: "Why darling! What a *relief!*"

2/5/2121

Laura's not hurt, but naturally somewhat shocked emotionally. We were all anxious to look at the innards of the belt, but she won't give it up; claims that it saved her life now and that it goes with her uniform. It is decorative, at that.

It was very quiet in the little laboratory; only the sound of Hal's breathing and the minute-ticking of the device upon which he was working broke the stillness. Outside the window, a silent landscape lay bathed in deep blue-green, like a vision of the bottom of a sea.

There was a modest knock on the door, and a dial on the table moved slightly. That, Hal knew, would be Laura; no one else would be carrying or wearing anything which would disturb an ultrometer, especially not at this hour. If only she'd surrender that belt! He wondered what she wanted of him.

The knock sounded again. "Come in," Hal said. The girl slipped past the door and closed it carefully.

"Hello, Hal."

"Hi. What can I do for you?"

"I got to feeling a little depressed and wanted company. Do you mind?"

"Chapelin's still up, I saw the light in the shack," Hal said sullenly. The next instant he could have bitten off his tongue; but Laura did not seem to react at all.

"No, I wanted to talk to you. What are you doing?"

He said wonderingly: "The same as always–trying to get enough of a grip on the ultronic flow to disrupt it. The little ticker here records the energy flux. If I can cause it to miss a beat now and then, I'll know I've managed to interfere. So far, no soap; we can direct the flow, but not modify it."

"Watch the blast limit."

Hal shrugged. That was the problem, of course. This energy was strictly sub-subatomic; somewhere nearby there was a nexus where the fields met, a nexus where cosmic rays were created, out of some ground energy called ultronic as a handy label. Chapelin thought there must be billions of such nexi in every galaxy, but they had been indetectable by their very nature until just recently. The Earth Council had been scared to death when Chapelin had reported the results of his first investigations, and had quarantined the whole group. Unless they could learn how to modify the forces involved–

"We've done well so far, all things considered," Hal said. "The moment we do badly, it'll be all up for us, and this whole corner of the universe."

Laura nodded seriously. Hal looked at her. As always, her loveliness hurt him, made it difficult for him to concentrate on what he was saying.

"But you didn't come here to talk ultronics, surely. Isn't there–"

She smiled, a little wistfully. "I don't care what we talk about, Hal. That accident–you don't go through a thing like that without being forced to think about things. I remembered your asking to see the belt before I went up, and how you tried to look out for me, and a lot of things you've done for me–and I knew all of a sudden that I owed you a lot more than I'd been ready to admit."

Hal made an awkward gesture. "It's nothing, Laura. I've made no secret of how I feel. If you don't share the feeling, those little attentions can become a nuisance, I know."

"That's true," Laura said. "And I realize now how careful you were not to . . . to force anything on me. Not everybody would be that considerate, so many parsecs from any sort of civilization. It's given me a chance to find out how I really do feel–that, and the accident."

Hal felt his heart begin to thunder against his ribs, but he kept seated by sheer will-power. "Laura," he said, "please don't feel that you have to commit yourself. It's really the parsecs that count the most. When six people–five, now–are marooned, in close quarters, for so long, all kinds of unnatural emotional tensions develop. It's best not to add to them if there's any way to avoid it."

Laura nodded. "I know. But most of the tensions that are already here are my fault. Oh, don't deny it, it's true. Niki wouldn't be here if it weren't for me, and the way I felt about Chapelin. I've been a useful lab technie, but emotionally I've always been in the way. It's different now. Chapelin–he's a sort of timid moose, isn't he? I've been pretty blind. I flatter myself that I can see, now." She toyed with an amber-handled, tiny screw driver on the workbench. "That's–why I'm here."

The blood roared in Hal's temples. He said: "Laura–"

After that it was very quiet in the little shack.

2/8/2121

The Council survey ship came by yesterday, and we had a good report to make; if they could have landed, we'd have been able to show them things that would have made their eyes bug. But they weren't going through our area, and only inquired in a routine way; Earth's still scared green of ultronics. One funny business: when I reported Jonas's death–expecting all kinds of hows and whens and whys–the Ship's Recorder didn't seem to know what I was talking about. "Jonas who?" he said. "Did you have a stowaway?" Evidently Earth has already forgotten us, and can't be bothered over whether there were five or six or thirteen in the group.

For a while things seemed to go along well enough; but Hal could not rid himself of the sensation that somewhere there was something radically wrong, if only he could find it. Oh, there was Chapelin to account for some of it. The accident, for which he could not help but hold himself responsible, seemed to have jarred some long-dormant cells to activity in Chapelin's mind. For the first time he seemed to be looking at Laura as something besides a competent laboratory assistant. They were all aware of it, Niki most of all, of course–for Niki had suspected it even when it didn't exist–but it was marked enough to worry even Mike Cohen.

That caused tension, but it was the old, familiar kind of tension. This other thing was–strange. Hal couldn't pin it down; it was a general uneasiness, strongest when he saw the belt gleaming enigmatically about Laura's slim waist, and when he reviewed certain entries in his journal. It was as if he were awaiting some disaster he could not describe, and it kept him up late every night, crouched over the ticking little modulator.

Even there, he had enough success to make him hopeful; within three nights he was able to modulate the steady ultronic flow, and on the fourth night he discovered, all at once, a chain of improbable formulae describing the phenomenon–a chain which showed him that his next step would have triggered the blast whose echoes they all heard in nightmares.

It was as if there was a silent conspiracy afoot, a conspiracy to convince Hal that Everything was going to be All Right. He looked at the equations again; they were new, a brand of math he seemingly had invented on the spot–and he had "discovered" them about ten minutes before he would have set off an interstellar catastrophe.

There was one kind of math Hal knew as well as he knew his own name: permutations and combinations. A few sheets of paper later, he had worked out the chances against his making this particular discovery at this particular time. The result: 3×10^{18}. Such coincidences *did* occur, but–

He shut off the detectors, and discovered that his hand was shaking a little. If only he could pin down this irrational dread! Well, if he were that unsteady, he'd better cut the generator that fed his lab, or there'd really be a blow-up, miracle or no miracle. He stood up, stretching cramped muscles. The modulator glimmered up at him from the bench. He put it in his pocket and went out into the green gloom.

The spongy, elaborately-branched moss effectively silenced his footsteps. When he jerked open the door of the generator shed, Chapelin and Laura were still locked together.

Hal gagged and tried to step out again, but they had heard the door open. Chapelin broke away, his big face turning the color of old turnips in the greenish light. Laura did not blush, but she looked–miserable.

"Sorry," Hal said, his voice as harsh as a rasp. "However, as long as I'm here–"

He strode past them and yanked the big switch from its blades. Laura said: "Hal . . . it isn't quite what–"

He spun on her. "Oh, it isn't, eh?" he said grimly. "I suppose Everything Is Really All Right?"

"Now, wait a minute," Chapelin blurted. "I don't know what right you have to be taking that tone–"

"Of course you don't. Probably Laura just said she's been thinking and wanted to talk to somebody–or don't you use the same line on us all, Laura?"

Laura raised her hand as if to ward off a blow. Inside Hal's chest a rusty can opener ripped at his heart. He said: "You're, on the spot now, Laura. You can be all things to all men if you try, but not to more than one man at a time! Your story can satisfy either Chapelin or me–but not both of us at once. Want to try?"

Laura's lips thinned a little. "I don't think I'll bother," she said, walking toward the door. "I don't like taking orders."

Hal caught her wrist and forced her back against the now-silent generator. "Clever," he said, "I forgot the outraged-virtue act; it's good–almost good enough. But it won't work with me, Laura. I think I know the story now."

"What's going on here?" Mike Cohen's voice said from the doorway. "If you'd open a window, they could hear you all the way back on Earth."

"Hello, Mike," Hal said, without turning. "Stick around. I'm either making an ass of myself or staging a showdown, one or the other. Niki with you?"

"Naturally," Niki's voice said. The cold fury in it was appalling; Niki did not yet know what had happened, but in any such situation she had only one guess to make.

"What's the story?" Mike said.

"You know most of it. The crux of it is that belt of Laura's. It's still in operation, we know that; and I think it's somehow invaded her mind. The way she's been acting since the accident isn't like her. And the effect she's had on events outside her own personal interests has been too great to shrug off. It includes creating a body out of nothing."

"A body?" Niki said. "You mean–she killed Jonas? But we all saw him electrocuted while we were a long way away from the generators–"

"You're close, Niki, I think she *created* Jonas–or the belt did."

Chapelin said: "Maybe you'd better go to bed, Hal."

"Maybe. First, you can explain to me why we haven't a single record in this camp which mentions 'old Jonas' *before* the accident happened. Check me if you like. Odd, isn't it? The first time he's mentioned is when we buried him. And the Council ship had never heard of him. To top it off–there are only five acceleration hammocks in the stores. Where's Jonas's? Did he come here in a bucket?''

"We buried him in his hammock," Laura said in a small voice.

"Did we? We only had five hammocks to begin with, the QM record shows it. It also shows rations for only five. With one less person, we should be accumulating an overstock of food, but we aren't, though we're eating exactly the same menus we've always eaten."

"Suppose it's so," Mike Cohen said. "Suppose there never was any such person as Jonas–it's a fantastic assumption, but your evidence seems to prove it–what's the point of such a deception?"

"That," Hal said, "is what I mean to find out. I also want to find out why I got about a century's worth of advanced ultronic math shoved into my cranium tonight, all at once, just at the moment when I would have blown us to kingdom come without it." He took the modulator out of his pocket. "This is the result. Knowing how *not* to blow us up fortunately includes knowing *how* to. Hand over that belt, Laura–or I'll disrupt it!"

Laura said, "I . . . I can't. You're right, Hal. I can't make everyone happy at once, so I have to admit it. But I can't give up the belt."

"Why not?" Hal demanded.

"Because . . . *I am* the belt!"

Chapelin gasped: "Laura, don't be insane."

"It was Laura that you buried. She was killed in the accident. As Mike says, there was never any such person as 'old Jonas.' I instilled his memory in your minds to account for the corpse, which was unrecognizable after . . . after what had happened to it."

The knife turned deeper in Hal's heart. Every curve, every coloring, every sound of the voice was Laura's–

Mike said softly: "We've done Frankenstein one better."

Tiger Ride

"I don't think so," Hal said steadily. "I think we've just re-enacted a limerick. Remember the one about the young lady from Niger? She smiled as she rode on the tiger—"

"They came back from the ride with the lady inside," Mike whispered, "And the smile on the face of the tiger."

"Yes. I don't think this is one of our belts. Ours weren't complex enough to pull off a stunt like this, no matter how they might have been deranged."

The girl looked steadily at Hal; it was quite impossible to imagine that she was changed. "Hal is right," she said. "When your belt burned out, there was an instantaneous ultronic stress, a condition we call inter-space. The mathematics are difficult, but I can teach them to you. The results, roughly, were to create an exchange in time; your belt was sent a hundred thousand years into this planet's past, and replaced by this belt—myself."

"The people here knew ultronics?" Chapelin asked.

"Very well. Their belts were at first much like yours—simple levitating devices. But as they learned more, they found that they could travel space without spaceships; new belts made a protecting envelope, manufactured food and air, disposed of waste. As the centuries went by, the belts came to be the universal tool; there was nothing they could not do; eventually they were endowed with some intelligence and with the ability to read minds—to meet their owners' needs, and even anticipate them."

"What," Hal said, "happened to the people?"

"We don't know," Laura's voice said. "They died. More and more of them ceased to have children, or to take any interest in anything. We relieved them of all their responsibilities, hoping to give them all the free time they needed for satisfying their desires—our whole aim was service. But a day came when the people had no desires. They died. The belts were self-sufficient; in my time they still operated the cities. Evidently they gave up so purposeless a task later on."

Chapelin covered his face with his hands. "Laura—" he said brokenly.

"I regret your loss," the familiar, lovely voice of Laura said.

"I tried to protect you from it–to supply what you seemed to need. Perhaps it would be better if I took some other shape now, so as not to remind you–"

"Damn your cruel kindness," cried Hal. "No wonder they died."

"I am sorry. I can repay. I can give you all the mastery of ultronics, of other forces whose names you do not know. New belts can be built for Earth, and a new world begun."

"No," Hal said.

Niki and Chapelin stared at him. "Oh, come off it, Hal," Niki said. "Be reasonable. This means we can all go home, and get off this stinking planet."

"And think of the opportunity for knowledge," Chapelin said. "Niki's right; what's done can't be undone, no matter how it hurts. We've got the future to think of."

"That's what I'm thinking of," Hal said. "Chapelin, weren't you listening? Didn't you hear what happened to this other race when the belts took over? Do you want to wish *that* on Earth?"

"It sounds rather comfortable to me," Niki said. "Maybe *they* hadn't any desires, but *I* do."

Mike Cohen said softly: "It's only a matter of time, Hal. If we send the belt back to where it came from–if it'll go–we've still got the beginnings of ultronics right here. Sooner or later our crude belts will evolve into things like this."

Laura's belt saw, then, what Hal was going to do. "Hal!" her voice cried. "Don't . . . it's death for all of you."

Chapelin flung himself forward, his hands clawed, his face wild with fear. Mike Cohen stuck out a foot and tripped him.

"O.K., Hal," he said, almost cheerfully. "You're right. It's for the best. Let 'er rip."

Hal turned the modulator on full. The whole ridge of stars went up in a blaze of light. At the last, Laura's golden voice wailed: "Hal, Hal, *forgive me*–"

After that, nothing.

2/21/2121

The Styrtis blast was a tragedy: yet I could not tell Hal

that I would survive it without making him more unhappy than he was. Now, I must go on to Earth, where I may do better. I have decided to pose as Hal; it seems fitting; he had his race in his heart, as do I. We have, after all, a long tradition of service.

DARK INTERLUDE by Mack Reynolds and Fredric Brown

When "Dark Interlude" first appeared in the fourth (January 1951) issue of Galaxy, many readers missed the point: then-editor H.L. Gold reported an amazing amount of mail accusing the authors of being anti-, um, Negro. (The early fifties, as we ought to keep reminding ourselves, was not a pleasant time.) It was a dangerous and threatening story for its time and Gold showed some genuine editorial courage in publishing it; today, however, it seems more a curiosity, although an interesting one. And it is by way of poignance that it makes its point.

Mack Reynolds and Fredric Brown were close friends but only occasional collaborators in the early fifties–a few short stories and one co-edited anthology of humorous s-f, Science Fiction Carnival (1953). In an affecting memoir in the Science Fiction Writers publication at the time of Brown's death, Reynolds says that he owed much of his career to Brown's influence and help. He was not the only one.

Fred Brown (1906-1972) might have been one of the four or five best writers who ever did a substantial amount of work in the field; he was not a science fiction writer per se–his output of mystery fiction far exceeded that of his science fiction–but such novels as What Mad Universe (1949) and Martians Go Home! (1955), and half a dozen superior collections, put him at or near the top. He was also, incontestably, the best writer of short-shorts in the history of science fiction. His vignettes are famous, not to say notorious, and have been oft-anthologized; most of the best of them can be found in his 1961 Bantam collection, Nightmares and Geezenstacks. His only other collaboration was a single story with Carl Onspaugh in 1965.

Dallas McCord Reynolds (b. 1918) has also had a long and

distinguished career in the field. *He succeeded Randall Garrett as John Campbell's main writer for* Astounding/Analog *in the sixties, and has written several stories of consequence; one, "Compounded Interest," is a minor classic, and most are included in* The Best of Mack Reynolds *(Pocket Books, 1976). Among the most popular of his novels are* The Computer Conspiracy, Of Godlike Power, *and* Amazon Planet. *Except for a series of science-fictional Sherlock Holmes pastiches written with the late August Derleth, Reynolds, too, has done no other work in tandem.*

DARK INTERLUDE
By Mack Reynolds and Fredric Brown

Sheriff Ben Rand's eyes were grave. He said, "Okay, boy. You feel kind of jittery; that's natural. But if your story's straight, don't worry. Don't worry about nothing. Everything'll be all right, boy."

"It was three hours ago, Sheriff," Allenby said. "I'm sorry it took me so long to get into town and that I had to wake you up. But Sis was hysterical a while. I had to try and quiet her down, and then I had trouble starting the jalopy."

"Don't worry about waking me up, boy. Being sheriff's a full-time job. And it ain't late, anyway; I just happened to turn in early tonight. Now let me get a few things straight.

18 _____ *SHARED TOMORROWS*

You say your name's Lou Allenby. That's a good name in these parts, Allenby. You kin of Rance Allenby, used to run the feed business over in Cooperville? I went to school with Rance . . . Now about the fella who said he come from the future . . . ."

The Presidor of the Historical Research Department was skeptical to the last. He argued, "I am still of the opinion that the project is not feasible. There are paradoxes involved which present insurmountable—"

Doctr Matthe, the noted physicist, interrupted politely, "Undoubtedly, sir, you are familiar with the Dichotomy?"

The presidor wasn't, so he remained silent to indicate that he wanted an explanation.

"Zeno propounded the Dichotomy. He was a Greek philosopher of roughly five hundred years before the ancient prophet whose birth was used by the primitives to mark the beginning of their calendar. The Dichotomy states that it is impossible to cover any given distance. The argument: First, half the distance must be traversed, then half of the remaining distance, then again half of what remains, and so on. It follows that some portion of the distance to be covered always remains, and therefore motion is impossible."

"Not analagous," the presidor objected. "In the first place, your Greek assumed that any totality composed of an infinite number of parts must, itself, be infinite, whereas we know that an infinite number of elements make up a finite total. Besides—"

Matthe smiled gently and held up a hand. "Please, sir, don't misunderstand me. I do not deny that today we understand Zeno's paradox. But believe me, for long centuries the best minds the human race could produce could not explain it."

The presidor said tactfully, "I fail to see your point, Doctr Matthe. Please forgive my inadequacy. What possible connection has this Dichotomy of Zeno's with your projected expedition into the past?"

Dark Interlude

"I was merely drawing a parallel, sir. Zeno conceived the paradox proving that it was impossible to cover any distance, nor were the ancients able to explain it. But did that prevent them from covering distances? Obviously not. Today, my assistants and I have devised a method to send our young friend here, Jan Obreen, into the distant past. The paradox is immediately pointed out–suppose he should kill an ancestor or otherwise change history? I do not claim to be able to explain how this apparent paradox is overcome in time travel; all I know is that time travel *is* possible. Undoubtedly, better minds than mine will one day resolve the paradox, but until then we shall continue to utilize time travel, paradox or not."

Jan Obreen had been sitting, nervously quiet, listening to his distinguished superiors. Now he cleared his throat and said, "I believe the hour has arrived for the experiment."

The presidor shrugged his continued disapproval, but dropped the conversation. He let his eyes scan doubtfully the equipment that stood in the corner of the laboratory.

Matthe shot a quick glance at the time piece, then hurried last minute instructions to his student.

"We've been all over this before, Jan, but to sum it up–You should appear approximately in the middle of the so-called Twentieth Century; exactly where, we don't know. The language will be Amer-English, which you have studied thoroughly; on that count you should have little difficulty. You will appear in the United States of North America, one of the ancient nations–as they were called–a political division of whose purpose we are not quite sure. One of the designs of your expedition will be to determine why the human race at that time split itself into scores of states, rather than having but one government.

"You will have to adapt yourself to the conditions you find, Jan. Our histories are so vague that we can help you but little in information on what to expect."

The presidor put in, "I am extremely pessimistic about this, Obreen, yet you have volunteered and I have no right to interfere. Your most important task is to leave a message that will come down to us; if you are successful, other attempts will be made to still other periods in history. If you fail–"

"He won't fail," Matthe said.

The presidor shook his head and grasped Obreen's hand in farewell.

Jan Obreen stepped to the equipment and mounted the small platform. He clutched the metal grips on the instrument panel somewhat desperately, hiding to the best of his ability the shrinking inside himself.

* * *

The sheriff said, "Well, this fella–you say he told you he came from the future?"

Lou Allenby nodded. "About four thousand years ahead. He said it was the year thirty-two hundred and something, but that it was about four thousand years from now; they'd changed the numbering system meanwhile."

"And you didn't figure it was hogwash, boy? *From the way you talked, I got the idea that you kind of believed him."*

The other wet his lips. "I kind of believed him," he said doggedly. "There was something about him; he was different. I don't mean physically, that he couldn't pass for being born now, but there was . . . something different. Kind of, well, like he was at peace with himself; gave the impression that where he came from everybody was. And he was smart, smart as a whip. And he wasn't crazy, either."

"And what was he doing back here, boy?" The sheriff's voice was gently caustic.

"He was–some kind of student. Seems from what he said that almost everybody in his time was a student. They'd solved all the problems of production and distribution, nobody had to worry about security; in fact, they didn't seem to worry about any of the things we do now." There was

a trace of wistfulness in Lou Allenby's voice. He took a deep breath and went on. "He'd come back to do research in our time. They didn't know much about it, it seems. Something had happened in between—there was a bad period of several hundred years—and most books and records had been lost. They had a few, but not many. So they didn't know much about us and they wanted to fill in what they didn't know."

"You believed all that, boy? Did he have any proof?"

* * *

It was the dangerous point; this was where the prime risk lay. They had had, for all practical purposes, no knowledge of the exact contours of the land, forty centuries back, nor knowledge of the presence of trees or buildings. If he appeared at the wrong spot, it might well mean instant death.

Jan Obreen was fortunate; he didn't hit anything. It was, in fact, the other way around. He came out ten feet in the air over a plowed field. The fall was nasty enough, but the soft earth protected him; one ankle seemed sprained, but not too badly. He came painfully to his feet and looked around.

The presence of the field alone was sufficient to tell him that the Matthe process was at least partially successful. He was far before his own age. Agriculture was still a necessary component of human economy, indicating a definitely earlier civilization than his own.

Approximately half a mile away was a densely wooded area; not a park, nor even a planned forest to house the controlled wild life of his time. A haphazardly growing wooded area—almost unbelievable. But, then, he must grow used to the unbelievable; of all the historic periods, this was the least known. Much would be strange.

To his right, a few hundred yards away, was a wooden building. It was, undoubtedly, a human dwelling despite its primitive appearance. There was no use putting it off; contact with his fellow man would have to be made. He limped awkwardly toward his meeting with the Twentieth Century.

The girl had evidently not observed his precipitate arrival, but by the time he arrived in the yard of the farm house, she had come to the door to greet him.

Her dress was of another age, for in his era the clothing of the feminine portion of the race was not designed to lure the male. Hers, however, was bright and tasteful with color, and it emphasized the youthful contours of her body. Nor was it her dress alone that startled him. There was a touch of color on her lips that he suddenly realized couldn't have been achieved by nature. He had read that primitive women used colors, paints and pigments of various sorts, upon their faces–somehow or other, now that he witnessed it, he was not repelled.

She smiled, the red of her mouth stressing the even whiteness of her teeth. She said, "It would've been easier to come down the road 'stead of across the field." Her eyes took him in, and, had he been more experienced, he could have read interested approval in them.

He said, studiedly, "I am afraid that I am not familiar with your agricultural methods. I trust I have not irrevocably damaged the products of your horticultural efforts."

Susan Allenby blinked at him. "My," she said softly, a distant hint of laughter in her voice, "somebody sounds like maybe they swallowed a dictionary." Her eyes widened suddenly, as she noticed him favoring his left foot. "Why, you've hurt yourself. Now you come right on into the house and let me see if I can't do something about that. Why–"

He followed her quietly, only half hearing her words. Something–something phenomenal–was growing within Jan Obreen, affecting oddly and yet pleasantly his metabolism.

He knew now what Matthe and the presidor meant by paradox.

* * *

The sheriff said, "Well, you were away when he got to your place–however he got there?"

Lou Allenby nodded. "Yes, that was ten days ago. I was in Miami taking a couple of weeks' vacation. Sis and I each get away for a week or two every year, but we go at different times, partly because we figure it's a good idea to get away from one another once in a while anyway."

"Sure, good idea, boy. But your Sis, she believed this story of where he came from?"

"Yes. And, Sheriff, she had proof. I wish I'd seen it too. The field he landed in was fresh plowed. After she'd fixed his ankle she was curious enough, after what he'd told her, to follow his footsteps through the dirt back to where they'd started. And they ended, or, rather, started, right smack in the middle of a field, with a deep mark like he'd fallen there."

"Maybe he came from an airplane, in a parachute, boy. Did you think of that?"

"I thought of that, and so did Sis. She says that if he did he must've swallowed the parachute. She could follow his steps every bit of the way–it was only a few hundred yards–and there wasn't any place he could've hidden or buried a parachute."

The sheriff said, "They got married right away, you say?"

"Two days later. I had the car with me, so Sis hitched the team and drove them into town–he didn't know how to drive horses–and they got married."

"See the license, boy? You sure they was really–"

Lou Allenby looked at him, his lips beginning to go white, and the sheriff said hastily, "All right, boy, I didn't mean it that way. Take it easy, boy."

* * *

Susan had sent her brother a telegram telling him all about it, but he'd changed hotels and somehow the telegram hadn't been forwarded. The first he knew of the marriage was when he drove up to the farm almost a week later.

He was surprised, naturally, but John O'Brien–Susan had altered the name somewhat–seemed likable enough. Handsome, too, if a bit strange, and he and Susan seemed head over heels in love.

Of course, he didn't have any money, they didn't use it in his day, he had told them, but he was a good worker, not at all soft. There was no reason to suppose that he wouldn't make out all right.

The three of them planned, tentatively, for Susan and John to stay at the farm until John had learned the ropes somewhat. Then he expected to be able to find some manner in which to make money–he was quite optimistic about his ability in that line–and spending his time traveling, taking Susan with him. Obviously, he'd be able to learn about the present that way.

The important thing, the all-embracing thing, was to plan some message to get to Doctr Matthe and the presidor. If this type of research was to continue, all depended upon him.

He explained to Susan and Lou that it was a one-way trip. That the equipment worked only in one direction, that there was travel to the past, but not to the future. He was a voluntary exile, fated to spend the rest of his life in this era. The idea was that when he'd been in this century long enough to describe it well, he'd write up his report and put it in a box he'd have especially made to last forty centuries and bury it where it could be dug up–in a spot that had been determined in the future. He had the exact place geographically.

He was quite excited when they told him about the time capsules that had been buried elsewhere. He knew that they had never been dug up and planned to make it part of his report so the men of the future could find them.

They spent their evenings in long conversations, Jan telling of his age and what he knew of all the long centuries in between. Of the long fight upward and man's conquests in the fields of science, medicine and in human relations. And they telling him of theirs, describing the institutions, the ways of life which he found so unique.

Lou hadn't been particularly happy about the precipitate marriage at first, but he found himself warming to Jan. Until . .

* * *

The sheriff said, "And he didn't tell you what he was till this evening?"

"That's right."

"Your sister heard him say it? She'll back you up?"

"I . . . I guess she will. She's upset now, like I said, kind of hysterical. Screams that she's going to leave me and the farm. But she heard him say it, Sheriff. He must of had a strong hold on her, or she wouldn't be acting the way she is."

"Not that I doubt your word, boy, about a thing like that, but it'd be better if she heard it too. How'd it come up?"

"I got to asking him some questions about things in his time and after a while I asked him how they got along on race problems and he acted puzzled and then said he remembered something about races from history he'd studied, but that there weren't any races then.

"He said that by his time–starting after the war of something-or-other, I forget its name–all the races had blended into one. That the whites and the yellows had mostly killed one another off and that Africa had dominated the world for a while, and then all the races had begun to blend into one by colonization and intermarriage and that by his time the process was complete. I just stared at him and asked him, "You mean you got nigger blood in you?" and he said, just like it didn't mean anything, 'At least one-fourth.' "

"Well, boy, you did just what you had to do," the sheriff told him earnestly, "no doubt about it."

"I just saw red. He'd married Sis; he was sleeping with

her. I was so crazy-mad I don't even remember getting my gun."

"Well, don't worry about it, boy. You did right."

"But I feel like hell about it. He didn't know."

"Now that's a matter of opinion, boy. Maybe you swallowed a little too much of this hogwash. Coming from the future–huh! These niggers'll think up the damnedest tricks to pass themself off as white. What kind of proof for his story is that mark on the ground? Hogwash, boy. Ain't nobody coming from the future or going there neither. We can just quiet this up so it won't never be heard of nowhere. It'll be like it never happened."

BEASTS OF BOURBON by L. Sprague de Camp and Fletcher Pratt

Gavagan's Bar *is science fiction's best-known watering hole–a place where odd things happen and all manner of odd stories are told. These droll, whimsical fantasies were extremely popular in the fifties; many of them first appeared in* The Magazine of Fantasy & Science Fiction *and all of the early ones were collected in* Tales from Gavagan's Bar *(1953). A new generation of readers can now enjoy them, owing to the fact that the book has recently been reissued by a specialty science fiction publisher.*

Of "Beasts of Bourbon," which is about a man whose imagined alcoholic animals turn out to be real, Anthony Boucher once said: "It may make you go a little lighter on your drinking for a while. Or, at that, will it?" Not us. We've both seen stranger things than spectral tarsiers and frilled lizards–much stranger. And not as a result of our mutual taste for vodka. Hell, it's the things we've seen that made us take up vodka in the first place...

L. Sprague de Camp (b. 1908) has to his credit an impressive list of works: novels such as Rogue Queen *(1951) and* The Hand of Zei *(1963), the definitive biography of H. P. Lovecraft, anthologies of sword-and-sorcery, short stories, and articles. His other collaborations with Fletcher Pratt include the Harold Shea series of fantasies for John Campbell's* Unknown, *such collections as* The Incomplete Enchanter *and* The Castle of Iron, *and the novel* The Carnelian Cube. *De Camp has also co-authored stories with P. Schuyler Miller, H. L. Gold, and Bjorn Nyberg; and he has continued the Conan the Barbarian saga begun by Robert E. Howard in the thirties.*

Among the solo works of Fletcher Pratt (1897-1957) are such science fiction novels as Well of the Unicorn *(1948) and* The Undying Fire *(1953), and an excellent 1952 anthology,*

World of Wonder. *Early in his career, during science fiction's "Golden Age," he also collaborated with Laurence Manning on several pulp stories.*

BEASTS OF BOURBON
By L. Sprague de Camp and Fletcher Pratt

Mr. Gross leaned about two hundred of his pounds on the edge of the bar, so that part of him bulged over it, and said: "Mr. Cohan, I feel like variety this evening. How about a purple jesus?"

The tall, saturnine-looking man said, "You better be careful. It's the queer drinks like that that end you up with the d.t.s."

"Not no more than the rest," said the bartender, mixing away. "It's all how you take them. Funny that you would be mentioning d.t.s along with a purple jesus, now, Mr. Willison. The very last one I mixed in this bar was for that Mr. Van Nest, the poor young felly. The animals was after him, he said, and he needed a drink. But he acted sober when he came in here. As long as a man can behave himself he can have a drink in Gavagan's."

"Ah, it's a shame when a man has to take so much liquor he gets d.t.s," said Gross. "I got a nephew knew a man like that once. He cut off one of his own toes with a butcher knife, saying it was a snake trying to bite him. But he was one of the solitary drinkers."

"Campbell Van Nest wasn't a solitary drinker," said Willison. "Just a solitary guy. Though he had to be after his animals started coming alive on him."

"Huh?" said Mr. Witherwax, almost choking on the olive from his Martini. "What animals? How did they come alive?"

"The animals out of his d.t.s," said Willison. "I saw them. So did you, didn't you, Mr. Cohan?"

"Never a one," said Mr. Cohan, swabbing the bar. "That was why he came here, because they would not follow him into Gavagan's. But there's plenty would swear on the blessed sacraments they did see them. Like Patrolman Krevitz, that my brother Julius says is one of the steadiest men on the force. Not to be mentioning yourself, Mr. Willison."

"You say the animals from his d.t.s came alive?" said Witherwax. "I'd like to hear about this. I was just reading in a book about something like that. They call it materialization."

"Well, I don't know," said Willison. "The few of us who knew him have always rather kept it quiet. . . ."

"You can tell them," said Mr. Cohan. "No harm to anybody now the poor young felly is dead and gone, and his animals with him."

"Mmm. I suppose you're right," said Willison. "Well–fill me up another rye and water, Mr. Cohan, and let's see. I want to get this straight. . . ."

Campbell Van Nest was one of those natural-born square pegs, I guess. Nice-looking chap, nothing remarkable about him in any way, but it was as though he and the world had made an agreement not to get along together. Everything he tried went wrong somehow. Not in a spectacular way, but a little off the beam, so he was always being disappointed.

He traveled in toys. It will give you an idea of what I mean about the disappointments, when I tell you that although he was good at it and made plenty of money, he didn't like the life, rushing around and meeting people and going to conventions. He liked to stay home and read–a lot of things like astrology and Oriental lore. The part of the toy business that really interested him was designing toy animals–woolly pandas that would walk, and so on. But there isn't much of a full-time job in designing, so they'd only let him do it a week or so at a time, and then send him out on the road again.

He was always falling in love, too; not that he was a woman-chaser. He'd get into real deep, off-the-end-of-the-dock love with some girl, who always turned him down in the end. You've heard of people being hard-boiled? Well, I would say Campbell Van Nest was too soft-boiled. It broke him all up when one of these girls said no, and he'd go off on a two-day binge.

As near as I can make out, this business started with a day when everything went wrong at once. Van's latest girl threw him down, somebody got into his car and stole all the accessories, and a store to which he had made a big sale went broke, so he lost the commission. He went off on a bender that made the rest of them look like tea-parties. It lasted three days, and the worst of it was that it wasn't public, either. He just kept buying bottle after bottle of whisky and sat there in his room, loading up on it and reading these Oriental books. His landlady called me up on the third day, and I went up there and found the place a shambles, with bottles and books mixed up together all over the floor.

I got him into bed and picked up some of the things, and while I was doing it I noticed that Van hadn't been merely reading while he was on this particular toot. The place was filled with papers on which he had apparently been sketching designs for new animal toys, and some of them would nearly turn your stomach to see.

That was all I could do at the time, so I left. The next part of the story comes from Van himself. When he came to about noon the next day, this thing was sitting on the foot of his bed. I only got a glance at it later, but it looked like some kind of monkey, only bigger, with eyes like saucers and enormously long fingers. I don't know whether it resembled any of the designs Van had made while he was pie-eyed or not. It had what you might call an evil expression.

(A stocky pug-nosed man with glasses, who had been consulting a daiquiri, spoke up: "I think that would be the spectral tarsier."

"Yes?" said Willison, facing him. "Are they blue?"

"I know of one that was," said the stocky man. "But that . . . Sorry to interrupt your story, old man. There may be a connection. Go on.")

Van had never had d.t.s before, and his first idea was that this was something that had escaped from a zoo. But with his hangover and all, he didn't like the idea of trying to capture it. An animal like that can give you a nasty bite. So he got himself a Bromo-Seltzer and some clothes, figuring that when he was outside, he'd call up the zoo or the S.P.C.A. and have it taken away. This spectral what-is-it just sat there quietly on the foot of the bed, following Van with its eyes.

It was so quiet that he thought he'd slip out for a cup of coffee before phoning. But when he opened the door, with his reflexes not under very good control, the thing leaped down and was through it like a flash. Van expected it to run. It didn't; it came hopping along down the hall and then down the stairs, always keeping about the same distance behind him. Every time he turned around toward it, it would retreat, and then follow him again as soon as he went on. It seemed attached to him.

That made Van think–as well as he could think through the fumes of his hangover–that he might be having a case of heebie-jeebies and not really seeing this thing at all. So he decided to ignore it and started down the street. Then he began to notice other people when he passed them: they'd do a double-take and give a grunt or a squeak or something, and when he looked over his shoulder, there the thing was, coming along behind him, and other people seemed to be seeing it too. He began to walk faster and faster. Pretty soon he passed a girl who was going in the same direction he was, and when the animal hopped past her feet, she looked down at it, and let out a good loud shriek. That did for what was left of poor Van's nerves, and he started to run.

You know how it is when anyone runs down the street. People look to see who's chasing who, and with a little encouragement, they'll join in. This time they had lots of encouragement, with that monster coming along behind Van in big jumps. Some yelled: "It's after him!" and in about half a minute, he had twenty or thirty helpful citizens rolling along behind.

Sheer force of habit, he said later, brought him here to Gavagan's, and he dived in, to get away from all those people and that animal. You remember the day, Mr. Cohan?

("Indeed and I do, " said the bartender. "The poor felly came through the door there like one of them fancy ice-skaters you see in the show, and stood hanging onto the bar. 'It's brandy you need, my lad,' I said, and poured one for him while the rest of them people come milling around, some of them inside and some out, after this animal. But no animal did they see, because none had come in with him. All they saw was Mr. Van Nest having a drink of brandy and his hand shaking. Some of them said it got away over the roofs, but you're telling me that's not true now, aren't you, Mr. Willison?")

Another rye and soda (said Willison). No, it certainly isn't true. The thing just disappeared. A couple of the people who had followed came in to ask Van about it, and they got to talking. Well, there's only one way you can conduct a conversation in a bar–that is, with a drink in your hand. Presently Van was drinking a purple jesus and feeling better, and then first thing he knew it was evening, and he'd spent the afternoon in here.

Now I won't say he was really drunk, not like he had been the day before, and besides, Mr. Cohan wouldn't permit it. But you can't work all day on brandy and purple jesuses and nothing to eat without getting a little high. What did you say? Oh, he had a roast pork sandwich. So he had a roast pork sandwich and a couple more drinks, and went home and had a couple of nightcaps, and then I guess he was a little more than high. So he tumbled into bed; it was late when he got there.

When he came to, toward noon the next day, this spectral monkey-thing was there again. And this time there was another monster with it, a thing like a lizard with a long tail and thin fingers and something that looked like a big ruff around its neck,

Beasts of Bourbon

as you sometimes see in old ancestor portraits. It was a dark maroon red.

("*Chlemydosaurus kingi,* the frilled lizard," said the pug-nosed man, "in an interesting chromatic variation."

"You know about it?" asked Willison.

"Yes. My name's Tobolka. I'm a biologist. May I buy you another?")

Thanks, I will have one (said Willison). I don't want you to get the idea that Van was stupid. He could put two and two together, even with the bells ringing in his head, and he was perfectly certain that if he got out on the street again those two horrors would be right with him. So he called me up and asked me to come over.

By the time I got there, he was working on a pint he had sent for to steady his nerves. The animals were there all right, both of them. I saw them. They were about so big. Every time I tried to approach one, it was out of reach like a flash, and then it would settle down and look at Van. He seemed depressed.

"I can't understand what makes this happen," he kept saying.

I told him about putting him to bed a couple of nights before, and the shape I'd found the room in, with the books and weird animal drawings scattered around. "What kind of Hindu magic have you got mixed up with?" I asked him.

That made him more depressed than ever. "That's just the trouble," he said. "I haven't any idea. A good many of these books deal with the occult and materialization phenomena in one form or another, but I'm afraid I had rather a lot to drink that day, and I don't know what I tried to do."

We agreed that the only sensible thing to do was to reverse the process, so I went out and got something to eat on a tray, and then we sat down with his books. Those two animals watched us all the time. I couldn't make head or tail of what I was reading, and he couldn't seem to find anything that was of the least use. About five o'clock I gave up and went home, arranging for dinner to be sent up to him. The only thing we were hopeful about was that the animals might go away during the night. He had finished the pint, but that wasn't anything to a fellow of Van's capacity.

But he called up the next morning to say that they were still here on the foot of his bed, staring at him. What was worse, the office was calling. They didn't mind his staying out a couple of days, but this made five now, and he was due for a trip through the Middle West. The idea of going out on a sales trip with those two beasts mixed up with his samples didn't strike him as the way to win friends and influence people.

I went over after dinner and we talked the whole thing upside and down. Finally, I said: "Look here. There are two parts of this business that may be connected. Aren't those two some of the animals you drew while you were having that toot?"

He dug out the drawings, and, although his hand had been pretty unsteady when he made them, this frilled lizard and spectral monkey were recognizable.

"All right," I said. "You remember the first one disappeared when you went into Gavagan's? Now I'll get a taxi and shoot you over there quick, and while you're gone, I'll destroy these drawings."

He said it seemed farfetched, but couldn't think of anything better, and the second day of consulting his books hadn't turned up anything, so he agreed. I had the cab waiting with its engine running when he came dashing downstairs with the two monsters after him. The lizard one rode on top. I went back up and dug out every one of those drawings he'd made and burned them, for good measure adding some designs he'd made for toys that didn't look like monsters at all.

Then I came over here. It seems quite a few people had seen Van with his monsters. Not so many as the first time, but enough to make a good deal of conversation, so that practically everybody in the place was buying Van a drink and trying to get him to talk about it. You can imagine what happened. He was as boiled as a fifteen-minute egg by the time I got him out of here; and next morning he had three pets instead of two.

Only it was worse this time. The new one didn't look like anything I remembered seeing in the drawings; it didn't look like anything I ever saw, and Mr. Tobolka, I don't think it looked like anything you ever saw. It looked like an enormous centipede, with the head of a cat. Van called me up and I went over again and saw it. The office had been after him again, and he told them he was sick. I stayed with him a while, trying to work out something more from the books, but while I was out getting something to eat, he got so he couldn't take the stares of the three animals any more, summoned a taxi by telephone and was off here to Gavagan's again. It was the only place where he felt safe.

("The poor felly said he would clean the cuspidors if he could only stay here in a blanket on the floor," said Mr. Cohan. "I put it up to Gavagan myself, but he wouldn't hear a word of it.")

I hadn't heard from him (continued Willison), but I worked my way into his place on maybe the fifth day after it started. The office had sent around a basket of fruit and then one of flowers by a special messenger. I had to knock four or five times before he let me in, and then it was with a suspicious look, peeking around the corner of the door. He hadn't shaved in God knows when, and there was a fifth in his hand, about three-quarters empty. By that time there were six of these animals in the room, all of them but the first two looking as though they had been put together out of spare parts of real animals and beasts from a child's picture-book. I couldn't get near any of them, but I was spared the trouble, because Van waved the bottle at me, said, "See?" took a swig and fell down across the bed, with all those incredible creatures looking at him.

He collapsed across the bed, and I looked at him and thought. He was obviously on the way out in some direction, and if I could do anything to help him, I figured it would be pure gain. There were the parts of an evening newspaper strewn around the place, so I picked them up and found the ad for a Caribbean cruise. I called the line; the ship was sailing in three-quarters of an hour and fortunately they had a vacant cabin, since there had been a cancellation. I got him into a cab and took him down to the pier and poured him aboard, and I've always been sorry, because that ship turned out to be the *Trinidad Castle*.

"That's the one that was lost?" inquired Witherwax.

"Correct," said Willison. "Ran on a reef in the Bahamas during a hurricane and went down with everybody on board."

"I doubt it," suddenly said the stocky little man Tobolka.

"I beg your pardon," said Willison, with some disfavor.

"I beg yours. No offense meant, old man. I wasn't questioning your word, merely the accuracy of your data. When you mentioned a blue spectral tarsier, I said there might be a connection with a case I know of; now I'm certain of it. Your friend Van Nest did not go down on the *Trinidad Castle*. If Mr. Cohan will kindly provide me with another daiquiri, I'll explain."

(He turned round, with a gesture.) Gentlemen, the story has not been broadcast outside the scientific world for much the same reasons that persuaded Mr. Willison to keep it quiet. I am a biologist and have been rather closely associated with several members of the Harvard Marine Life expedition to the Bahamas. You may or may not know that its purpose was to collect specimens of marine life on Jackson Key, which is rather a miserable little sand-spit off Great Abaco Island, but does have peculiarly interesting forms of minor marine fauna.

You may have seen photographs of the expedition at work. If you have, the center of the picture was almost certainly occupied by a young lady clad in shorts and performing some scientific task. She is blonde and extremely photogenic, and her name is Cornelia Hartwig.

The morning after the *Trinidad Castle* disaster she found a survivor of that ship who had floated into the surf of Jackson Key on a grating. I think there can be very little doubt that it was your friend Van Nest, though he gave his name as Campbell. He was not in good condition when discovered, though not in serious danger. Restoratives were applied, but there could be no question of sending him to the mainland at once, because the expedition's supply ship made only periodic visits, and neither of the two small motorboats was adequate.

My friend Professor Rousseau says that when the young man

Beasts of Bourbon

recovered consciousness and was informed of this, he did not appear to object. He was looking at Cornelia Hartwig, and with an almost equal intensity she was looking at him. I should perhaps explain about her. She is a highly competent biologist, but, like your friend Van Nest, may be described as always falling in love. On field expeditions like the one to Jackson Key, it is her usual habit to select one of the older and more thoroughly married members of the scientific staff, and this has caused some trouble in the past. In fact, the members of the expedition were waiting with some apprehension to see who would be the victim on this occasion, and it was with relief that they observed her spending the entire day with the castaway.

In the evening, when Campbell, or rather Van Nest, was able to be up and about, and had eaten something, Cornelia took him to the opposite side of the island from the camp, where there were some palm trees, to look for ghost crabs by the light of the full moon. I don't know whether they discovered any ghost crabs; but as they sat there under the palms, the extraordinary series of animals you describe appeared as if from nowhere and formed a circle around them at a respectful distance. Including a blue spectral tarsier and a frilled lizard of a rich maroon color.

There is no doubt that Cornelia was enchanted. At the sight of so many species unknown to science, I would have been myself. The couple did not return to camp until long after all the rest were in bed. When Cornelia told her story in the morning, it was received with a certain amount of skepticism, and even of merriment, by the other members of the expedition. I am not surprised. The behavior of Van Nest's animals at Jackson Key was somewhat different from that you describe in the city. Not one of them was visible that morning. They had disappeared with the night.

This reception of her story irritated Cornelia exceedingly, and on the following evening she persuaded Professor Rousseau himself to accompany them to the palm trees. He says the animals appeared to come out of the undergrowth and their description tallied with that you gave, Mr. Willison. He threw a flashlight on them and dispelled any idea that they were hallucinations, for they had solidity; but all his efforts to collect a specimen failed because of their agility.

After this, Cornelia and Van Nest went to the palm grove every evening, often taking along a sketch-pad and a flash, and she produced some remarkable drawings. The pair rather rudely discouraged efforts of other members of the expedition to go with them, and seemed so much in love with each other that everyone was content to leave them in privacy. However, Professor Rousseau observed that after about three weeks Cornelia–whose daytime work suffered severely by the amount of time she spent out at night–appeared to be growing cooler toward the young man.

Seeking the cause, he concealed himself near the palm grove before dark. The moon was now in its second quarter, and he had some difficulty in seeing; but when Campbell and Cornelia arrived and the animals began to come out, it was at once evident that something was wrong. There were only four of them, and these not of the most eccentric character. Moreover, though he was not near enough to hear what was being said, Professor Rousseau declares there was no difficulty in making out the tone of the voices. Cornelia was upbraiding the young man, and he was pleading with her.

(Willison put out his glass for another refill. "I think I get it," he said. "That sea air and exercise were getting the booze out of his system. That's what I told him he ought to do.")

Such was evidently Campbell's own conclusion (continued Tobolka). On the morning after this, while the members of the expedition were at work, Campbell raided the stock of whisky, drank almost an entire bottle of it, and was found in his cot in a stupor. Professor Rousseau was very much annoyed and reproved Campbell severely. However, the object of his maneuver was attained. Cornelia accompanied him to the palm grove once more, and next morning appeared radiant, with sketches of an entirely new and very aberrant form of *Limulus*.

After this he persuaded Cornelia to obtain whisky for him. The process did not last long, for the base ship soon arrived, and the work of the expedition was completed. At this point Professor Rousseau encountered a difficulty, for Cornelia absolutely refused to leave the island until she had seen some more of Campbell's animals. With equal vehemence, he refused to leave her; and they could not come back together because of those same animals.

Director Rousseau decided that they were both adults, entitled to make their own decisions, so he left them some tents and supplies and arranged for a boat to make periodic calls at Jackson Key. He tells me that as Cornelia doesn't have a great deal of money and Campbell had none at all when he was cast on the beach, they were finding it difficult to pay for liquor; so when last seen, they were trying to ferment coconut milk. Perhaps we may learn some day whether they succeeded.

"Well, thank you, Mr. Tobolka," said Willison. "Maybe I ought to arrange to send his books down there. What do you think?"

SOUND DECISION by Randall Garrett and Robert Silverberg

In his autobiographical essay in Hell's Cartographers *(Harper & Row, 1976), Robert Silverberg writes at length about his association with Randall Garrett in the mid-fifties, a collaboration which revived Garrett's career and helped to establish Silverberg's. Prolific, ambitious, Silverberg learned from Garrett (older, wiser, more cynical, but suffering from "a collapse of discipline") the virtues of slanting material to the science fiction editors, whom you then endeavored to meet in person; editors, good and simple folk all, found it more difficult to reject faces than manuscripts.*

Garrett (b. 1925) and Silverberg (b. 1935) collaborated on several novels (one of which, The Dawning Light, *ran in* Astounding *in 1957) and twenty to thirty short stories before going their separate ways. Garrett subsequently became the most productive writer of John Campbell's Late Blue Period and published a small but well-received number of novels, perhaps the best of which is* Too Many Magicians *(1965). Silverberg, after achieving a strong reputation in the field in the late fifties, dropped out to write juveniles and other material by the hundredfold–and then returned in the mid-sixties and soon established himself as a major writer with such novels as* A Time of Changes, The Book of Skulls, *and* Born With the Dead. *(Garrett himself dropped out in 1965, came back ten years later, and has been contributing steadily to the magazines since.) Virtuous collaboration: like a good marriage ended by an amicable divorce, both parties came out enlarged.*

"Sound Decision," which appeared in the October 1956 Astounding *(the issue reached the newsstands a month earlier, the same month that "Robert Randall," a collaborative pseudonym, won a Hugo award as "most promising new*

writer"), *is typical of the magazine of that period and of the collaboration itself, an intersection of purposes which was the key to this team's success. The story's central idea is terrifying (cf: Tom Godwin's 1954 classic "The Cold Equations"), but the writers manipulate it nicely. As Silverberg might say, it is not contemptible work. As Garrett might have said in the old days, it paid a few weeks' rent.*

SOUND DECISION
By Randall Garrett and Robert Silverberg

"There are millions of laws legislators have spoken;
A handful the Creator sent.
The former are being continually broken;
The latter can't even be bent."

—David Gordon
The Ballad of Ways and Means

What happened to the space liner *Martian Queen* was, on the surface of it, highly improbable. For a velocity vector to exactly cancel out an acceleration is something that no one in his right mind would imagine happening accidentally, and certainly no sane gambler would bet on its probability, no matter what the odds.

But yet, if you inspect the picture a bit more closely, it becomes readily apparent that *any* given incident is highly improbable.

The unfertilized egg, after all, has a few hundred million spermatozoa to choose from; what are the odds that you will be *you?*

It's futile, however, to compute the probability of an event after the event has already taken place. You might come up with figures that proved it didn't happen, and in the realm of cause and effect *ex post facto* legislation is worthless.

The statistics *were* against it–but it happened.

The *Martian Queen* was a luxury liner of some five hundred metric tons, belonging to Barr Spaceways. She was, at the time, making a "short-run" orbit from Mars to Earth, carrying a hundred and fifty passengers and a crew of thirty, including stewards.

Just exactly what went wrong with the drivers isn't known or knowable; the four men who might have known were dead within seconds after it happened. There are several things that could have caused the disaster–an accident which, except for the level-thinking of one man, might have caused the deaths of many more than the mere handful who died in a sudden blaze of light.

I

"How much longer?" snapped Mrs. Natalie Ledbetter. She looked round-headed and wattled like a turtle; her words snapped out and were snapped off at the end, as though she begrudged the question mark at the end of an inquiring sentence.

"A few hours yet, Mrs. Ledbetter," said Parksel with the infinite patience of a man who has borne more than his share and is willing to bear more indefinitely–as long as it pays.

Mrs. Ledbetter pulled a cigarette out of a gleaming platinum case, struck it, and drew in a lungful of pungent smoke. "I hate spaceships," she said. "It's not the crowded little cabins; it's not that there's nothing to do; it's not those–"

She scowled at the gently sighing air intake which seemed to scoop the tobacco smoke out of the room and carry it out of sight. "No. I have plenty to do; I can keep in touch with my directors on Earth and Mars. No. The thing that bothers me is

Sound Decision

the feeling that I'm on a roller coaster. I rode on one of those things once–just once. It's a penned-in feeling, a knowledge that you can't get off. That's what I'd like to do! Get off this thing! Get a breath of fresh air. But there isn't even any *stale* air out there!'' She waved a hand straight down, toward the outer hull of the ship.

Parksel was a big, heavy man with a look on his face that was neither boredom nor idiocy, but an expression of blank acquiescence, revealing nothing whatever of the workings of the mind behind the face. As a combination bodyguard and private secretary, he left little to be desired, insofar as Mrs. Ledbetter was concerned. He was well-paid and had been told that he was mentioned in her will–provided she did not die by violence. He wasn't particularly concerned over that. Even Mrs. Ledbetter's tough old frame didn't have much longer to go; she was a hundred and nine, and beginning to show it. The gerontologists had her held together like a carefully articulated and highly valuable fossil.

"Get out the chessmen, Parksel," she said. "And mind you don't walk into that queen-knight trap like you did last time."

"Yes, Mrs. Ledbetter." He walked across the small cabin and got out the set. After arranging the ivory pieces on the table, he looked up at her. "It's your move first, I think."

"Yours," she said testily. "I took you with white last time."

He reached out a hand just as the speaker blared:

Your attention please! In three minutes, the gyros will begin to cut down the spin on the ship. We have to stop the spin around the longitudinal axis in order to apply thrust along it for deceleration. Please get into your bunks and fasten your safety belts. You will be warned again in two minutes.

"Damn!" said Natalie Ledbetter.

Without a word, Parksel leaned forward and began scooping up the precious carven antiques and restoring them to their plush-lined niches, inwardly happy. The musty, oppressive smell of the old woman was starting to bother him, and he was glad to get away from the table.

Still, he thought, *it's a living.*

George MacBride stood listening to the announcement, then grinned down at his wife. "You heard what the man said, honey—back to bed."

Marian MacBride's pleasant face assumed an impish look of pseudo-shock. "George!"

MacBride looked innocent. "That's what the man up there said. It wasn't my idea. *I'm* not captain of this tub." The grin did nothing to soften the angles in his face; his head and features looked as though they had been carved in mahogany by an expert sculptor who, unfortunately, had had to use a lumberman's axe for the job. He was of average height and built like a wrestler with a slight paunch. At forty-five, he considered the paunch more or less excusable.

Marian MacBride was ten years younger, and could pass for thirty easily, or even twenty-eight. Her face was round, soft, and glowing with vitality where it lacked mere prettiness. "It's too bad it had to end so soon," she said gently. "It was such a wonderful trip."

MacBride walked over and patted her on the shoulder. "We'll go again. Maybe Venus next time. After all, Breckmann's Incorporated sends only its best men out. Meaning me, naturally."

Marian smiled. "Sure. But are they going to let you take me? This is your fifth trip. It's my first. And probably my last."

"But, honey—"

She shook her head. "You don't kid me, Georgie-Porgie. You had to pull every wire you could get your hands on to get the company to pay for my passage to space. They'd never do it twice."

MacBride looked thoughtful. "Well . . . we could save the money—"

Marian walked over to the bunk and lay down. "Don't be silly, George. If you think I'm going to save money for a second trip, you're crazy. For a first one . . . well, I might. But I've had my fling now, and I'm not going to toss away your salary for fun. If I never go again, I'll still remember this one."

MacBride's face suddenly beamed with pleasure and pride. "Honey, you're wonderful. And just for that, I'm going to let you in on a little secret. You remember that get-together at Old Man Feld's place? Yeah? Well, the Old Man said that he thought it was fine that I'd brought you along. Said he thought it was good politics for a sales engineer to bring his wife. He's going to make a recommendation to Breckmann in Austria."

Marian sat bolt upright. "George!" She blinked, as if there were a possibility of tears. "That's what you've been working on! Those group-psychology courses! That–"

"That's right." He nodded happily. "I–"

Your attention please! In one minute, the gyros will begin to cut down the rotation of the ship. The gravity will drop to zero in twenty-one minutes. Please strap yourselves in your bunks. A steward will check you shortly.

"Comfortable, darling baby?" asked Fred Armbruster, as he looked solicitously at his pretty wife.

Ruby smiled across the space that separated the two bunks. "Uh-huh. I'll be all right, sweetheart."

"Sure you will, baby duck. You didn't feel too bad during the takeoff, did you?"

"No," she lied. "I'll be all right."

Fred Armbruster was lean and tall and rich and in love. Ruby had been deathly sick every time the gravity switched, even though she thought the rest of the trip was simply wonderful. *Maybe,* Fred thought, *I could get her mind on that–*

"It's been a wonderful trip, hasn't it?" he asked.

"Best honeymoon a girl could ask for," she said sincerely. "I'd never thought Mars could have been beautiful. I'd always pictured it as a dried-up, nearly airless ball of clay. But the purple sky and the red-and-yellow desert–" Her voice trailed off.

"And remember that one sunset?" Fred hazarded. "The one with the dust storm?"

Ruby smiled at the fond memory. "It was wonderful. All blue and violet and crimson and streaked with–"

The door popped open and a head stuck in. "Everyone secure? Fine." The door closed.

"Crewman," Fred said bitterly. "Always a crewman has to stick his head in where it isn't wanted. If I were running this ship, I'd—"

"Don't be that way, sweetheart."

Fred frowned. "I still don't think every crewman ought to have a copy of that master key. If it were the captain who—"

Your attention please! The gyros will start in three seconds. Please stay in your bunks during the entire time. There will be a five-second interval of weightlessness, after which the gravity will be shifted for deceleration. There was a brief pause, then: *Gyros on. Please remain in your bunks.*

Edouard Descartes André blew a cloud of blue cigarette smoke toward the ceiling. "Will I be glad to get home!" he said vehemently. "Mars! Canned air and stinks! Dopey-looking fat beetles that claim to have brains!"

In the next bunk, Jerry Hammermill relaxed, his hands folded behind his head and cradling it. "Don't yap, Eddie, old mug. You made a shivering good bankroll on that shivering planet. And don't disparage our Martian friends; they may look pretty shivering ugly, but they've lined your pocket for you."

"I wish you wouldn't talk so loud, you idiot!" André grumbled unhappily. "I still think they could have those cabins wired."

"Don't be a shivering fool," Hammermill said mildly. "In the first place, my instruments don't lie, and in the second, the taped stuff I'm feeding into these steel walls would foul up any shivering pickups yet invented. And besides, I haven't given them any details."

"Yeah," said Edouard Descartes André. "Sure, you're the smart one—the smart one who's going to land us in the brig yet."

"The smart one," Hammermill pointed out, "who made us a quarter of a million chips apiece. Besides, if we don't make any direct evidence against ourselves, the World Government can't touch us. Martians can't testify in court."

"I hope you're right," said André. He leaned back and glared meaningfully at his companion.

They fell silent. And, slowly, as the spin eased off, orientation was lost. "Up" and "down" gently began to merge with each other, until they vanished and became one with every other direction.

Acceleration in five seconds, said the speakers.

Captain Bernard L. Deering, a tall, massive man whose iron-gray hair was cropped in a stiff brushcut, and into whose hands the hundred seventy-nine other voyagers aboard the *Martian Queen* had entrusted their lives during the journey across space, sat in the astrogation dome watching the stars circle around him. Captain Deering had been in the service of Barr Spaceways for some twenty years, after a distinguished career in military service. He knew his ship, and he knew his job.

As the ship's spin decreased and the gravity dropped, the stars circling the dome slowed to a halt. When they finally stopped altogether, Captain Deering snapped: "Bearing!"

The astrogator, a prune-faced, angular man named Bliven, who had gone into space straight from M.I.T. and who had been part of Deering's team for eleven years, instantly called out a string of numbers, and the captain smiled. "Dead on," he said. "Feed in the tape and start her at schedule."

The automatic landing tape snaked into the computer which fed exactly-timed impulses to the engine room. There was a nearly subsonic hum–the sort heard by the skin rather than the ear. Gradually, gravity returned, this time at right angles to its previous pull. Inside the cabins, the bunks rotated in their frames. While the spin was on, they had been twin beds bolted to the yellow floor, next to a blue wall. Now they became tiered bunks, one above the other, bolted to a yellow wall above a blue floor. The crewmen referred to spin as "yellow gee" and longitudinal thrust as "blue gee," because of the code coloring of the walls.

The accelerometer climbed swiftly to 980 and held steadily at that. "One of these days," said the astrogator, "some bright guy is going to have sense enough to define a Standard Gravity as one thousand centimeters per second squared. That'll relieve us of having to bother with these figures."

"You want to re-define the centimeters?" Deering asked, grinning.

"Nope. I want to say that the pull at the surface of Earth is point nine eight Standard Gees."

"I'll go for that," agreed the captain.

And that was when it happened. There was a loud *thumf!* that shook the *Martian Queen* from engine compartment to astrogation dome. The ship pitched wildly as though she'd been hit by an artillery shell–a big one. The accelerometer needle lurched like a crazy thing and began to climb as though it were going to twist itself around the pin. It reached nine thousand before it suddenly stopped and fell to zero.

The ship was silent. For nearly a minute, no one spoke. The few seconds of exposure to nearly nine gravities had taken the breath out of everyone. Captain Deering coughed and grabbed at the intercom.

"Engines! What happened?"

There was no reply from the engine room.

"Enkers! Chivers! Tance! Punz!" he shouted. "What's going on back there?"

There was no answer. There couldn't be. The captain didn't know it yet, but his engine crew had died in the glare of heat and light, the moment's flash of radiance, that had wrecked the engine room.

II

White Sands Spaceport covered four hundred square miles of New Mexico desert. It was a great, hard, white, smooth blank spot of land, surrounded by clumps of yuccas and cactus and not much else. At the eastern end, a full square mile of the area was devoted entirely to the Administration area–a neatly arranged group of shining frosty-white buildings whose irradiated polyethylene walls gleamed brilliantly in the sunlight. The sparkling shower of diamond-bright beams that cascaded from the walls directly in the path of the sun's rays was hard on the eyes, but it made the spaceport remarkably easy to spot from a few hundred miles up, surrounded as it was by the yellow-brown of the desert.

Neil Stanley looked out of the window of his office and winced at the sun's heat. He had been working since dawn, and hadn't realized that the sun had shattered the soothing coolness of the desert morning. He touched the polaroid control gently and the window dimmed, reducing the light to a bearable level.

He didn't object to the desert as such, but he did object to the heat and the sun. Fortunately, a major general of the Space Service rated an office complete with air-conditioning and window controls, and as Base Coordinator for the commercial flights out of White Sands, his duties didn't call for much work that couldn't be handled in his office.

Stanley liked his job simply because it was about as un-military as a job could get. Physically big, quick-witted and impressive-looking, Stanley had mastered military routine fully. He had served at the military spaceport in Nevada, but when the chance had come to take on the difficult task of handling the commercial traffic, he had jumped at it.

The military spaceport in Nevada was remarkably smooth in its operation. Routing was simple; a few well-placed orders did the trick, and they were *followed*–to the letter.

Civilians didn't listen to orders half as well, even in situations involving the dangerous business of landing spaceships. Their remarkable obstinacy at times increased the headaches, but it was the constant surprises that made the job fun.

Stanley turned from the window and looked up at the schedule on the wall. The top line read MARTIAN QUEEN–1404:9 + 2. That was the next ship due in. Underneath it was the arrival time of the *Aphrodite,* due in the next morning.

He checked his watch automatically and computed the time. The radar tower ought to have a fix on the *Queen* any minute now.

When the phone rang, he grinned. In the matter of predicting what a spaceship is going to do, there's not much trick in being an honorable prophet. The laws of gravity are as inexorable as the march of time; in order to land a ship in the right place at the right time, there are certain things that have to be done, and certain times to do them.

Stanley picked up the phone. "Stanley here."

"General, we've got the fix on the *Martian Queen.*"

"What's the ETA?" Stanley asked.

There was a pause at the other end of the line. "We haven't computed the ETA, sir," the voice said hesitantly. "There's something wrong. The position is off, and the velocity is constant. The—"

"Never mind," Stanley said, cutting the man off in mid-sentence. "I'll be right over." He slammed the receiver down and pushed the phone away.

He left his office on a dead run, his lips clamped together in a grim scowl. When a radar fix can't compute the Estimated Time of Arrival of a spaceship instantly, there is something wrong—*deadly* wrong.

He spun down the flight of stairs from his second-story turret, whirled through the swinging glass doors, and vaulted the two steps that led down to the ground. The pavement was warm beneath his feet, and the hot, dry air swept parchingly into his lungs.

His jeep was waiting for him a little way off, and the driver was half dozing in the nearby shade. But when he saw the major general coming toward him at better than double time, he vaulted into the driver's seat and had the engine running by the time Stanley got there.

"Radar Tower One," Stanley snapped. "And gun it!"

The jeep shot off almost instantly. Stanley leaned back, staring at the black tufts of hair on the backs of his fingers, wondering stonily what story was going to be written today, what record of disaster and/or heroism. He didn't know. He didn't know what was going to happen. All he knew was the *Martian Queen* had gone haywire and wasn't doing what it should be doing, up there in the sky.

The radar tower was a spidery structure whose struts and girders stood outlined sharply against the sky, metallic gray against bright, painful blue. The jeep pulled up short in front of the tower, and Stanley climbed out almost in the same instant. "Stay here," he called to his driver, as he went inside.

Three bleak-faced men waited for him there.

"Sir, do you think–?" began Sokolow, a thin, sandy-haired technician whose face creased in a perpetual scowl.

"Never mind," Stanley said crisply. "Time to talk later." He pushed back his cap and walked past them without bothering to ask questions.

"Chart," he murmured.

They complied. Stanley looked at the blip on the scope and checked the reading against the chart, frowning worriedly. Something was definitely wrong; the blip wasn't moving, which indicated a constant velocity. The *Queen* should have started decelerating long before this.

A bead of sweat trickled down his heavily tanned forehead, and he brushed it away impatiently. The data was there. The *Queen* wasn't decelerating. Why? Who knew? Who cared? All that mattered was the bare fact.

"Get me a direct line to Captain Deering!" Stanley said sharply. without looking up from the charts.

"Yes, sir," Sokolow said.

Stanley rubbed his chin. The ETA charts were simplicity itself. The readings on the screen could be checked against the charts and the time for landing was right there; the figures had been computed long before. All the radar man needed to know was the ship's position, velocity, and negative acceleration.

But this ship was off position and had no negative acceleration, and the charts weren't set up for a situation like that. Preconceived rules are nice things to have, but they simply don't work in an emergency.

While the radio man upstairs tried feverishly to get a direct communication to the *Martian Queen,* Stanley reached across the desk, pounced on the phone, grabbed it toward him, and dialed Routing.

"Stanley here. I want a computation fast." He glanced at the screen and rattled off the bearing, velocity, and direction of the blip on the radar. "I want to know when and where she'll hit if she doesn't decelerate. Got that?"

When and where she'll hit. He said the words in a clipped, businesslike manner, concealing the feeling that lay behind them. It was impossible for him to get hysterical over the situation, but he certainly appreciated its ugliness. Spaceships are big, heavy things, traveling at fantastic speeds, and a man who had worked with them half his life knew exactly what potential danger each one carried.

"Got it, general. We'll feed it into the DIRAC right away."

"Make it fast. I want that information yesterday, if not sooner."

He slammed down the phone.

There were footsteps behind him. "I've got Captain Deering, sir," said the radio man.

Attention! There has been a slight change in the landing procedure. Please remain in your bunks until you are given the all-clear. There is nothing to be alarmed about; there will simply be a slight change in landing time. Repeat: there is nothing to be alarmed about.

Captain Deering frowned as he listened to the voice of Lieutenant Bessemer over the speaker. That final repeat, he thought, was unnecessary, even if it was good procedure. Civilians were sure to get suspicious if they were told too earnestly that all is well.

He hoped the words would be effective. *A slight change in landing time.* It sounded fine, but, chillingly enough, it was perfectly true. If the *Queen* couldn't be straightened out, there would not only be a change in landing time, but a different velocity as well. The velocity of the *Martian Queen* was a long way from being zero with respect to the Earth.

The intercom buzzed loudly. "Captain? Hagerty here. We can't get into the engine room, sir. The place is hotter than a Roman candle."

"Radioactivity or thermal?"

Sound Decision

"Both. The scintillation counters are fizzing all over the place, and the temperature's running close to three hundred Fahrenheit. Couldn't be anyone left alive in there."

Captain Deering thought fleetingly of his four-man engine crew, and said, "Get out one of the suits and send a man in there for a look around. Don't overexpose him, but try to get an estimate of the damage. We've got to get this bird back under control, and we've only got minutes to do it!"

Marian MacBride turned her head to smile at her husband. "This gravitylessness isn't so bad, is it? Once you get used to it, I mean."

George grinned. " 'Gravitylessness,' " he mimicked. "Now, there's a word I like. Couldn't we add a few more syllables, just for effect?"

"Don't tease, George. What I mean is, I think it's fun."

"*Fun,* she says!" MacBride laughed. "If that's your idea of fun, you can have it, honey. Me, I like to know which way is down. Close your eyes and try to imagine you're hanging on the ceiling. Or floating around in the air, or—"

"Stop it, George," she said petulantly. "What are you trying to do? Make me sick?"

"Yup. I figure that if you're sick, I'll be so worried about it that I won't have a chance to be able to think about being sick myself."

"Fine sentiment!" Then she paused. "What do you suppose is the matter? That was an awful shake we had."

"Meteor, probably," George said. "A big rock can do a lot of damage to a ship if it hits it, you know."

"Oh," she said, "Well, as long as the ship doesn't lose its air, we're all right. I've read about meteor collisions. All the air goes out, and everybody smothers, or something. I wouldn't like to die that way."

"It does seem a rather stuffy death," agreed George. "But these new ships can spot anything big a long way off. There's nothing to worry about. The death rate for spaceships is a lot lower per capita than even aircraft." He stopped suddenly, realizing that the conversation was frightening both of them a little, and aware that what he was telling her so solemnly was probably scientific hogwash anyway. Their voices were getting tense.

He put his hands behind his head. His fingers were cold.

"It *does* seem a rather stuffy death," he said, trying to make his voice sound cheerful the second time. "You recognize the allusion, don't you, Marian?"

She thought for a moment. "That was that music thing you were in last year, wasn't it? The Gilbert and Sullivan operetta?"

"Yes," he said. "Remember, Yum-Yum says it to–"

He glanced at her. She wasn't at all interested.

"Anyway," he said, "if we stopped to avoid the meteor, it's not going to hit us, is it?"

"Do you think–"

"No, sweetheart. I can guarantee we won't hit it."

Ruby Armbruster was being violently sick. Her face was buried in the mouth of the collapsible plastic emergency bag, and her body seemed to be trying to tear itself apart with the racking convulsions that surged through it.

Fred had unstrapped himself from his own bunk and lowered himself to where his wife lay. Her dry, harsh coughs showed that her stomach was, by now, completely empty; only the automatic nervous reaction kept up the terrible nausea.

"You'll be all right, dear," he said soothingly. "You'll be all right. The gravity will come on pretty soon. You'll be all right."

Over and over he repeated it, trying to lull her into relaxation, trying to stop the awful, twisting convulsions of her abdomen.

Finally, the nausea subsided a bit. She turned, looked up. Her face was beaded with sweat, and she was trembling all over. She sighed gently, struggling to regain control over herself.

"Oooohhh . . . Ohh, Fred–"

"Easy, honey."

"I feel as though I'd lost everything. I . . . I . . . ooohh . . ." Her voice trailed off.

"Feel bad, honey?"

Sound Decision

"Horrible. There's no up–Hold me, Fred. Hold me. I think . . . I mean, it feels like I'm falling." Her voice told of terrible, primitive fear welling up from somewhere in the recesses of her subconscious. "Don't let me fall, Fred. Please–*don't let me fall!*"

Sobs had replaced the retching, but her body still shook.

Fred cradled her in his arms tenderly. "Don't worry, sweetheart. I'll hold you. You aren't falling, so don't worry. You aren't falling. You aren't falling."

Natalie Ledbetter learned over the edge of her bunk and looked down. "What's the matter with you?" she asked, in her dry, deep man's voice. "Sick?"

Parksel's face assumed an expression of stolid imperturbability. "No, ma'am. I'm afraid I have hiccups. Just hiccups, that's all." The sentence was punctuated occasionally by a muffled *hic!*

"Well, stop it!" she said insistently. "There's no reason to make *me* feel ill! Parksel, I'll have to take this up with Barr Spaceways! Imagine letting us lie like this in . . . ah . . . what is it? Free fall. That's it: free fall. I'll speak to Gregory Barr about it!"

"Yes, ma'am," Parksel said. *"Hic!"*

"Stop it, I say! Stop it!"

"Yes, ma'am." His eyes rolled in pain, revealing the battle going on within him as he struggled to retain the hiccup. *"Mmmmph!"* he finally said.

Jerry Hammermill was unbuckling his safety belt with flying fingers. His mumbled blasphemies seemed to be more an aid to breathing than an actual attempt at communication.

"What's eating you?" grumbled Edouard André from the bunk below.

Hammermill pushed himself out of the bunk toward the door and paused, while a muscle quivered in his cheek. When he spoke, his voice was tight and dry.

"No deceleration. There's something wrong. This shivering

ship is in trouble, make no mistake. We're in free fall. Get that? *Free fall!*"

"Huh?"

"I'll put it in words of hardly any syllables for you. Unless we're in an orbit around Earth, we're headed for the worst crack-up this planet has ever seen."

André grinned with the superb self-confidence of the man who is shrewd and calculating but at the same time a complete idiot. "What are you worried about? They said everything was all right, didn't they? Didn't they? Then what are you worried about, huh?"

Jerry Hammermill stopped at the door and glared piercingly at his companion. He was silent for a moment, contempt gathering on his face. "Sure they told us everything was all right, you birdbrained blockhead! What did you expect them to say? Something like: 'We're all going to die in a few minutes, so please be patient.' Is that what you expected?"

He opened the door and was out in the corridor before the white-faced André could say anything.

Captain Deering's jaw muscles tightened as he heard the words coming over the intercom.

"Hagerty here. The engine room's a wreck, captain. I sent Palmer in, but he couldn't stay long; it's too hot down there. We didn't find out much."

"What about the main converter?" Deering asked anxiously.

"Almost completely gone. It's a wonder it didn't blow into fragments when it went. God only knows what happened. The engine crew's gone–died almost instantly, I'd guess."

"What's the converter like?" Deering asked. He'd long ago forgotten about the lamentable but irreparable death of his engine crew; the important thing now was getting the engine room back together, not giving the four men a proper burial. That could come later–if there was any later to come.

"The converter's a mess," Hagerty said. "Mostly molten metal, according to Palmer, though it's beginning to solidify now. The shielding has kept the radiation from the rest of the ship, and it's slowly dying out now."

"And the engines?" Deering asked, knowing that only a miracle could have preserved them. "Any chance of starting them?"

"What engines?" Hagerty's voice told the story without need of further explanation. "There aren't any engines left to start."

Deering drummed on his uniform-cuff with the fingertips of his left hand. His mind was racing ahead, trying to figure out the probable courses of action to take. The trouble was that no answer seemed like a workable one.

"What about the—" Captain Deering started to say. But the voice of Lieutenant Bliven interrupted.

"There's a direct call from General Stanley at White Sands, sir! Can you—"

Deering whirled impatiently, fighting to rein in his self-control. He was staying as cool as possible; this was the first major accident he'd had in twenty years, but he was a levelheaded enough man to know how to behave—he hoped. "Just a second!" he snapped. "Tell Stanley to hold it! Hagerty! Is there any chance of getting the secondary converters going?"

"No, sir," came the flat reply. "They've blown, too, and—"

"The general says it's urgent, sir," the astrogator persisted. "Says he must talk to you at once."

"Damn!" the captain shouted, letting some of his tight control relax. "Tell him to wait!" He turned back to the intercom. "Hagerty?"

"Yes, sir."

"Listen, do everything you can. Understand? Get this ship operating, if you possibly can."

Deering listened to his own words, heard his own deep voice bouncing around the cabin, knowing as he spoke them that they were utterly futile. Hagerty was a good man, but he was no magician.

He turned away from the intercom and grabbed the radiophone, feeling as if there were cannons to the right and cannons to the left of him. "Deering here!" he barked. "What do you want, Neil?"

"Buddy? Stanley here. What's going on up there? Man, you've got to stop that thing!"

Stanley's voice held an ominous, imperative ring. Deering grinned sardonically. "Any suggestions? Black magic, maybe?"

"What's the trouble?"

"Main converter shot all to hell, and so is the secondary. Engines out. I'm just getting moving on the thing. What's our course?"

Stanley's voice was harsh. "Never mind now. What happened?"

"God knows!" Deering said. "We'd just stopped spin for deceleration and something blew in the engine room. We're powerless. Hagerty says there's nothing but slag down there!"

Stanley was silent for a moment, and Captain Deering stared impatiently at the radiophone in his hand. He felt a little better about things now that he knew Stanley of White Sands was with him. There was something reassuring about contact with the big catlike man, even when you were riding a spaceship straight to hell and he was sitting down there comfortably in an air-conditioned turret.

"O.K., feed me your co-ordinates," Stanley said at last.

Deering glanced up at Lieutenant Bliven. The prune-faced astrogator was standing by tensely. "Course," Deering demanded. manded.

The astrogator threw him a sheet of paper, from which Deering read figures. "That's as close as I can get," he said, when he was through. "Do you have a fix on us?"

"Checking it now," said Stanley. "I've got some other things to do right now, but keep the line open. Off."

Deering said nothing. He clenched his fists and stared out the astrogation dome at the diamond-hard stars. They looked back at him from their black-velvet settings, utterly unconcerned.

The captain sat back and let the tenseness drain out of him. The figures were starting to shape up, and the returns were coming

Sound Decision

in. He turned to the intercom.

"Hagerty?"

"Yes, chief?"

"What's going on?"

"Nothing, sir. There's nothing I can do."

"O.K." Deering said. "Keep trying."

The words were futile. The *Martian Queen* was falling toward Earth–powerless. Deering took the situation in, and he knew there was little sense in ordering Hagerty to work a miracle. There was nothing in space that could save the ship.

III

Neil Stanley turned toward the radioman. The air was hot and close in the radar tower, and it seemed to him a dull odor of ozone hung overhead. "Keep that line open," he ordered. "No matter what happens, keep it open!"

He gripped the phone again and dialed Routing, his thick fingers having trouble with the dial in his haste. He heard the click, then a voice.

"What's happening to that data?" he asked.

"Coming out now, sir," someone at the other end said. "We fed DIRAC the figures you gave us. They're not too accurate, but–Wait! Here it is now."

There was a long silence at the end of the line, while Stanley chafed his fingers impatiently together. "Sir!" came the voice finally. "They aren't going to miss Earth!"

"*What?* That checked?"

"Yes, sir. Whatever happened, it threw them off course just enough so that they'll still crack up on Earth even if they don't decelerate. It's a million-to-one fluke that they should be–"

"Can it," Stanley said. "What's the intersection point of the two orbits?"

"Somewhere along the East Coast, sir. We can't get it any closer than that without more precise data. I'd say that it'll hit somewhere near New York City if it doesn't slow down!"

"It figures," said Stanley tightly. "It figures. How long before she hits?"

"A little better than a half hour, sir. Can you get us more accurate data?"

"As soon as possible," Stanley said.

Near New York City, he thought. *Of course. As long as it has to be a wild coincidental thing, it might just as well come down on New York, and not in the Atlantic or out here in New Mexico or up in Alaska.*

He turned back to the radioman. "Get me Deering," he ordered. "I don't want to talk to him; just tell his astrogator to give me positional and velocital data as soon as possible. Tell him I want it down to the last decimal place he can possibly squeeze out of it, and then a couple more!" He stopped talking, and a frown passed over his face. "Then give the data to Routing," he said after a pause. "Tell them I want an orbit that's as close as skin. I've got something to do."

"Yes, sir."

"And by the way," he added. "Keep this under your hat. This is not to go out to anyone–not anyone!"

He left the radar tower at high speed, bursting out into the open again. The sun was now high overhead, and it was hot.

The driver still had the motor of his jeep going. Stanley vaulted in, and the gears buzzed as the driver released the brake and shoved hard on the accelerator.

"Experimental!" Stanley ordered. "And double quick." The jeep roared off across the compound toward the Experimental Drive building.

Almost before they had started, they were there. The jeep's wheels had barely stopped moving when Stanley sprang out of it and toward the building.

Colonel Arthmore jerked his head up in surprise as the major general slammed into the room. The colonel didn't even have time to give a proper salute before Stanley said:

"Is that XV-19 ready to go? Can we have it in space within

the next twenty minutes?"

The colonel blinked and nodded. "I think so, sir, if we rush it. We—"

"Rush it, hell!" Stanley snapped. "I want you to move faster than that ship can. It's the highest acceleration ship we've got, isn't it?"

"Yes, sir. We—"

"I want it ready to leave inside ten minutes. Take that as an order!"

"Yes, sir." The colonel had fully come to life now; he'd been galvanized into the same sort of quivering perpetual motion that was driving Stanley right now.

"And I don't want a word of what's going on to leak out of here," Stanley said. "Is that understood? If one word leaks, or if that ship isn't ready to go, I'll see to it that you'll never wear those birds on your shoulder again. Is that clear?"

"Yes, sir," said the colonel. "Anything else, general?"

"Nothing. Just stand by for futher orders. Keep your phone open to Radar Tower One. This is a double-A-double-prime emergency, and if we don't work it right a lot of people are going to die. Now move!"

But the colonel was already gone.

Stanley grinned at the retreating officer for a moment, then turned and headed back outside. He stood in front of the Experimental Drive building for a few moments, planning his next steps, wondering, extrapolating.

XV-19, he thought. *Arthmore should have it ready to go almost at once.* He cracked a knuckle reflectively, enjoying the feeling of knowing that for the next two minutes he could breathe freely. Things were moving, now; plans were under way.

The ship was coming down in New York or vicinity thereof, eh? That was a top-flight emergency—and called for emergency action.

He looked at his watch. It was hardly more than a few minutes since the whole thing had started, and it seemed like days. The hot New Mexico sun was still climbing toward noon, and the

thermometer wasn't yet at its maximum for the day.
No, he thought. *The heat's yet to come.*
"Let's get back to the radar tower," he said to his driver.

As he plunged into the big room that made up the heart of the tower, two voices hit him at once.
"Captain Deering is yelling for you, general!"
"Data is in on the *Queen,* general!"
He grabbed the sheet of paper that the second man held out and ran toward the microphone that had been set up for direct contact with the *Martian Queen.* He grabbed it, started to say something, then covered it with his hand. "Did you say anything to Deering?"
"No, sir." The sergeant's smile looked twisted, as though he were worried. Everyone in the room knew pretty much what the situation was by now, and the tenseness was starting to spread through the men like a virulent epidemic. The air seemed to crackle.
"We figured that was your baby," the sergeant said.
Stanley grinned. "Thanks, sergeant." He took his palm off the microphone.
"Buddy? Neil here. How are things?" His voice was calm.
There was a moment of silence. Stanley let his eyes flick around the room, and he saw the expression of horror registered on the sergeant's face. Obviously the sergeant was thinking that Stanley had no right to be so calm in this sort of situation. He must have been even more shocked when he heard Captain Deering's voice come in after the time-lapse.
"Same old stuff, Neil. No propulsion, no escape. How do we go down there?"
"We've got your co-ordinates down pat now," Stanley said. "We can tell you almost to a hair where you'll hit."
A moment of silence. Then: "Hit? You're sure we'll hit Earth, then?"
"No doubt about it, buddy," Stanley said. "If nothing happens between now and–*then,* you'll get a hot dunk in the ocean." He

Sound Decision

glanced again at the papers the sergeant had handed him. "Give or take a mile or so, you'll land in Long Island Sound about ten miles southwest of Bridgeport, Connecticut. Right in the drink, buddy–right in the drink."

There was a silence of a few seconds a third time–and Stanley waited patiently, knowing that the time-lag each time meant long seconds of agonized thought as Deering struggled to say what he had to say. Finally: "We can't let that happen, can we?"

"Nope." Stanley's voice was quiet and controlled. "You don't want your passengers to have an unexpected bath, do you?"

"No," said Deering. "Can you get a rocket up here in time?"

"Plenty of time," said Stanley. In the background, a large wall chronometer stroked off the seconds, ticking with consummate mechanical precision. "Don't worry about it."

IV

Jerry Hammermill pushed himself unsteadily down the long corridor that led from his cabin to the Common Room of the ship, that large and congenial room in which the passengers of the *Martian Queen* tried to pretend that they were almost anywhere but aboard a spaceship.

He pushed open the hatch and swam into the middle of the room, hovering there in midair for a moment, his hands holding to the electrical unit in the ceiling.

He knew the danger he was in. At any moment, the ship could start accelerating, which would throw him to the deck with smashing force. But, somehow, that didn't worry him. Still, his fingertips were quivering, and his face felt stiff, as though it had been coated with varnish.

Jerry Hammermill had had a pleasant and profitable existence up to now, and the idea of having it all end through some freak accident didn't appeal to him at all.

Pushing himself away from the ceiling, he headed toward the bar. There was no bartender on duty during free fall, of course, so Hammermill helped himself. He groped behind the bar until he found a plexiplast globe of Scotch. He broke the seal and squirted the liquid into his mouth in hot, smooth jets.

Then he turned and pushed his way toward the nose of the ship, up where the captain would be. He felt a little better about things–but first he wanted to see Captain Deering and find out, first hand, exactly what was going on.

"Hammermill!" the captain shouted as he saw the passenger drift around the corner of the door. "You heard, I believe, the order confining everyone to cabins."

Hammermill braced himself against the door and looked coldly at the blue-and-white uniform of the officer. Barr Spaceways wasn't exactly pretty when it came to uniforms, but it was impressive. He looked at Deering's tight, drawn face, and the hard eyes told him the answer immediately. His stomach crawled into a cold, hard knot.

"Well? What is it, Mr. Hammermill?" Deering asked angrily.

"Tell me this, captain," Hammermill said hoarsely, *"Why aren't we decelerating?"*

The blunt question echoed around in the captain's cabin, bouncing from the walls, turning Deering and Astrogator Bliven even paler. Hammermill looked as hard and inflexible as the captain as he waited for an answer.

"Technical difficulties, Mr. Hammermill," Deering said. "Everything will be taken care of shortly. You don't want to be caught on your feet if we start to accelerate." He glanced at Lieutenant Bessemer, standing to one side. "Would you show Mr. Hammermill back to his cabin, lieutenant?"

"You can't do this to me, Deering! I demand to know exactly what's happening aboard this ship."

"Mr. Hammermill, rest assured that everything will be taken care of. Bessemer, show him to his cabin."

The lieutenant moved forward and clamped a hand on Hammermill's arm.

Hammerhill's lean face became expressionless as he allowed himself to be propelled out of the cabin and pushed into the corridor.

"O.K., lieutenant," he said as the door to the captain's cabin

Sound Decision _____ 65

shut behind them. "I'll go quietly. I didn't really mean to ask any embarrassing questions."

Bessemer gave Hammermill a shove, and drifted back into the cabin. Hammermill, floating along the corridor, glared bitterly backward and muttered a curse.

Then he frowned and swam on. He had learned absolutely nothing–except that they were in one hell of a mess. Deering had been utterly transparent.

The ship wasn't decelerating, and Hammermill knew enough about space travel to know that a spaceship an hour or so outside of Earth *ought* to be slowing down before it came in for a landing.

Were they heading for Earth, heading for the biggest pyrotechnic display in man's history, or would they miss the planet and head out on a hyperbolic curve to nowhere? Hammermill didn't know. But he did know they were in trouble.

"Deering didn't say a thing?" Edouard André asked.

"Not a thing," Hammermill said. "Except that what he accidentally told me between the lines is that the ship's out of control and going to stay out of control."

Mrs. Ledbetter glared at Parksel. "Is what this man says true?"

"You heard him yourself, Mrs. Ledbetter," Parksel said.

"What should we do?" asked someone else.

Hammermill surveyed the group he had hastily assembled in his cabin. There were ten of them, the first ten people he could find. He had gone around knocking on cabin doors, getting passengers to come together, and then he had told them the story, explaining carefully and precisely to them just what it meant not to be decelerating. Their faces registered blank disbelief, horror, shock, anger, dismay–anything but determination.

Determination was what was needed, Hammermill thought.

Out loud he said, "I think there's a conspiracy on the part of the officers of this ship to keep us from full knowledge of what's been taking place here."

"Maybe they're just trying to prevent a riot," suggested George MacBride ominously. "Maybe they don't dare tell us."

"Probably," Hammermill admitted. "But at least some of us ought to know–this committee of passengers, at least. A few of us ought to know the score."

"What good will that do?" André demanded.

"I don't know," said Hammermill bitterly. "But at least we'll know what's coming off. Our lives may be at stake, and we're not being told anything."

From the corner of the room came a slow, muffled sobbing. Hammermill frowned. He didn't want hysteria complicating things.

"Why don't we all go to the captain?" he said. "He can't lie to all of us."

"Good idea," someone said.

"Let's go!" said another.

Excitement started to spread through the group–terrible, irrational excitement of people who believed that if they only made enough noise, they would be saved.

Captain Deering studied the sweeping red second-hand of the chronometer on his wall. Then he turned to face Bessemer.

"I'm going up to the astrogation dome with Bliven. I expect Hammermill to stir up some trouble, and there'll probably be more passengers coming down to ask questions."

"What should I say, sir?"

"Tell them nothing," Deering said firmly. "There's no reason why they should find out we're going to smack into the Sound until the split-second we do it–and we won't have to worry about that if Stanley can get his rocket up here."

"You think White Sands can get a rocket up here in time?" Bessemer asked.

Deering nodded. "I don't doubt it," he said. He watched the lieutenant's eyes light up at the thought that the catastrophe off Bridgeport might yet be averted, and turned away. "Keep the paying customers calm and collected, Bessemer. And don't bother me unless it's absolutely necessary."

Edouard Descartes André, left alone, stared feverishly at the row of shining rivets studding the wall immediately in front of him.

It's all a trick, he told himself. *They've found out somehow that Hammermill and I were running that con game with the beetles on Mars, and they know that if they can get us before we reach Earth soil they have us. They must have changed the orbit of the ship somehow in order to drop the two of us off at that Space Station instead of taking us to Earth. That way they can extradite us somehow right back to Mars. Oh, the stinkers. The dirty stinkers,* he thought.

He kicked savagely against the wall. The recoil shot him instantly across the cabin, where he fetched up against the other wall with a gentle thump.

The dirty stinkers, he thought.

Mrs. Ledbetter's thoughts were running the same way:

If I don't get back to Earth, my nephews divide up my money and even Parksel gets some of it and . . . Oh, no, Parksel won't get back either . . . and that deal with Consolidated will fall through, and isn't General Enterprises going to love that?

Oh, those swine! Could General En be low enough to sabotage this whole ship just to keep that deal from coming off?

Across the cabin from her, Parksel was frowning nervously. He was worried, too.

Even if I get out of this alive and she doesn't I lose out on the will. I don't inherit if she dies violently. Damned codicil.

"It's all right, Ruby, baby," Fred Armbruster said almost desperately. "We're going to come through it all right."

Ruby looked at him sharply. "There's no sense trying to talk it away, Fred. Hammermill says we're going to crash, and we'll all be killed." Her eyes were red-rimmed from crying, but she wasn't crying now. She was poised and cool in the face of death, long past the point of hysteria–or so it seemed. In that moment, Fred felt suddenly proud of her.

Then the veneer cracked. "God, I don't want to die!" she screamed. "Can they get a rescue ship up here? Fred, do something! Do something!"

"There's nothing I can do, baby," he said dully.

On the other side of the ship, those same words were being spoken by George MacBride. "There's nothing I can do, Marian."

"Do you think Hammermill's right? We're not decelerating, he says. We're still in free fall."

"The Space Service knows what it's doing," MacBride said hopefully. "They'll get us out of it. You wait. I'll bet a rescue rocket's been dispatched from Earth already."

"Will it get here on time?" Marian asked.

"I hope so," MacBride said. "It better."

The other passengers were going through much the same thing, as the rumors filtered through the *Martian Queen*. Word was spreading, now. As the ship plunged onward at twenty miles per second toward Earth, seventy-five pairs of passengers discussed and re-discussed the situation, while Captain Deering remained holed up in the astrogation dome with Bliven, and while, on Earth, Major General Neil Stanley crumpled the memorandum that told him the XV-19 was ready, and dropped the wad of paper into his pocket.

The rocket was ready to go. *Good,* he thought.

He grabbed the phone and dialed Experimental.

"Colonel? Stanley here. Received memo. Confirmation?"

"Confirmed," Colonel Arthmore said.

"Fine," said Stanley. "We're ready to send the XV-19 up, then." He gave the officer full and explicit instructions, and recradled the phone. Nothing further remained to do except talk to Washington.

"How's that call to the Pentagon coming?" he asked the sergeant.

"No reply yet, sir. They said this was a high-level decision; the staff would have to assemble."

Sound Decision

Stanley glanced at his wrist watch and grinned without humor. There was still time—not much, but enough. "Sure," he said. "Well, relay it to my office when it comes through. I want full vision on the phone; this has to be impressive as all blazes."

"Yes, sir."

"Meanwhile, let me talk to Deering."

"Yes, sir."

The radio was open, but there was a delay of a few seconds before the captain of the *Martian Queen* spoke.

"We've got trouble at this end," Deering said quickly when he came on. "The passengers know we're in trouble. I've got a hundred and fifty hotheads on my hands now. The situation's ready to blow."

"How did it get out?" Stanley demanded.

"We couldn't keep it secret, Neil; you know that. There was bound to be someone aboard who knew enough to realize we were in trouble, and didn't know enough to keep his mouth shut."

"Well, it'll be easy enough to quiet them down," Stanley said. "Just tell them that a rocket is on its way. See what I mean?"

There was an odd sort of grim humor in Deering's voice. "I'll tell them. Can you send up a teletype to that effect? It'll look more reassuring on paper."

"I'll get it up right away." Stanley paused and took a deep breath. "When the XV-19 gets up there, you have have to guide her in. Can you do that?"

There was no hesitation at the other end. "Sure. Easy. Good luck, Neil. You'll need it."

"I know. And good luck to you."

There was a faint chuckle in Deering's voice as he said: "That sounds like Pooh-Bah's toast to Nanki-Poo. *'Long life to you–'* "

"I didnt mean it that way," Stanley said.

"I know. So long, Neil."

Stanley nodded wordlessly and stood up. "Sergeant, as soon as that call comes from Washington, relay it to my office."

He turned and strode out the door.

V

Lieutenant Bessemer stood his ground in the Common Room as best he could. He had one hand braced tightly against the wall behind him, and the other doubled up into a fist at his side.

There were over a hundred people in the Common at the time, milling uncertainly in the strange free-fall situation, but Bessemer was addressing his words to Jerry Hammermill.

"You've been spreading rumors, Hammermill," the lieutenant said loudly. "You've gotten these people all excited over nothing."

Hammermill started to say something, but a fat man near the bar bellowed, "I wouldn't call it nothing! If we're all in danger, we ought to know about it! We ought to get into the lifeboats!"

Hammermill turned and showed his teeth in a hard grin.

"You're not on an ocean liner, mister. This is a spaceship. There aren't any lifeboats on a spaceship."

A woman was sobbing in the background. No–it was a man.

Mrs. Natalie Ledbetter said quietly, "Will we need parachutes, young man?"

"Parachutes?" Hammermill almost laughed. "Parachutes? At twenty miles a second? No, grandma, no parachutes."

The old lady flashed a withering glance at Hammermill. "I was talking to the officer, young man. I'll thank you to shut your silly face; you've caused quite enough trouble already." She looked at the lieutenant again. "Just what is the situation, young man?"

Bessemer clenched and unclenched his fist. "We are in some trouble," he said, trying to keep his voice cool. "I can't deny that. But the captain has authorized me to tell you that we absolutely will not crash. The ship will not hit Earth."

Fred Armbruster waved a hand in the air. "That's a lie!" he shouted. "That's a dirty lie! Have any of you looked out the viewport? You can see Earth! And we're falling towards it–directly towards it! It covers half the sky dead astern!"

Sound Decision

George MacBride turned to face Armbruster. "Keep your mouth shut! You're as bad as Hammermill."

Armbruster's eyes blazed. "Don't tell me to . . . hey, I know you. You work for Breckmann. I can tell you right now, buster, *you're fired!*"

Marian MacBride gasped. George's blocky face assumed a nasty grin. "As long as I'm being fired," he said slowly, "I might as well be fired for something worthwhile." His fist came up in a crashing arc and landed on the point of Armbruster's chin. Armbruster went into a high, curving backflip that brought him up against the farther wall.

MacBride, on the other hand, found himself drifting backwards from the force of the blow. Unable to check his ride, he slammed into Edouard André.

"Who ya shovin'?" André yelled angrily, throwing a punch in sheer reflex action.

It caught MacBride in the ribs, just under the heart, and the Irishman doubled up as he spun in air. Marian MacBride saw what had happened and grabbed an enameled red and gold ashtray from the bar. She hurled it with unerring aim at André's head. The plastic bowl bounced off André's skull and hit another man nearby.

Everyone's nerves were stretched to maximum tension anyway, and at this show of violence, nerves which had been vibrating like violin strings suddenly snapped. Somebody pushed somebody else. Fists began to piston out at faces. There were screams and oaths. Within two seconds, the Common Room was boiling over with a full-fledged riot. A mob of semi-hysterical people was finally getting the action it wanted. Subconsciously, each and every one of them knew that action had to be taken, and this was the only type of action it was possible to take.

Mrs. Ledbetter received a foot in the stomach and went flying wildly backwards across the bar. Parksel saw it, and something in his mind clicked. He had thought he hated the old harridan for years–and it wasn't until that moment that he realized exactly how much affection he actually did have for her. He launched himself across the room, kicking off against the rivet-studded bulkhead, and slammed headfirst into the back of the kicker.

Fighting in free fall is not the easiest thing in the universe to do. A well-placed punch has as much effect on puncher as it does on punched. The room was full of floating, drifting, moving bodies which were doing their best to inflict violence on every other body in the vicinity. Only a few people had sense enough to hold on to something.

Ruby Armbruster's stomach was no longer queasy. Her legs were clamped tightly around the cold, streamlined metal of a decorative pillar, and her eyes were hard and cold as she swung her small fists to keep people away from the unconscious body of her husband.

Lieutenant Bessemer had acted almost immediately. His fist had smashed into Jerry Hammermill's face, and without waiting for further argument he had turned to get out of the room. Screaming raucously, Edouard André launched himself at Bessemer's back, and the two of them slammed against the nearby door. The lieutenant, however, was a spaceman, used to handling himself in free fall, and André was not. Bessemer came out of the scramble with a black eye, but André was unconscious, hovering two feet off the floor, dazed by a rabbit punch to the neck.

Captain Deering was staring through the transparent dome in the nose of the ship at the bright, hard dots of the unmoving stars outside. It was good, he thought, that the ship was falling tail first; having to look at the green bowl of Earth ballooning up towards them would have been unnerving, even for him.

He turned from the dome just as Bessemer burst into the room.

"I told you not to—"

"Sir," Bessemer interrupted, "those people have gone nuts down there! They're tearing up the Common Room–and each other!"

Deering frowned. "You look like you got one in the eye yourself," he said. "They're really cutting up, eh?"

Sound Decision

Bessemer nodded. His left eye was bruised and blackened. "They've lost all control of themselves."

"Hm-m-m." Deering handed the lieutenant a sheet of teletype flimsy. "Get on the PA system and read them this. Then take it down there and let them get a look at it. Don't try to explain anything."

Bessemer saluted, took the flimsy, and went down the catwalk to the master-control panel for the Public Address network. He flipped the switch and took the microphone from its niche.

"Your attention please! Your attention please! The ship is falling out of control, but there is absolutely no danger of our hitting Earth. A rocket from the spaceport will be here in two minutes. Repeat: a rocket from the spaceport will be here in two minutes. Please wait quietly, and be ready for it when it comes."

He cut off the PA system and turned to find Deering standing behind him.

"Was that right, sir?"

"That was exactly as it should have been phrased," Deering said. "Take the flimsy down now and show it to them. That ought to quiet them down a little."

Bessemer nodded wordlessly.

The lieutenant made his way through the corridor back to the Common Room, grasping the handholds along the ceiling to rush his passage.

The Common Room was strangely quiet when he entered. Everybody who was still conscious was looking at the door as the officer came through it.

He unfolded the teletype flimsy. "Here's the message," he said crisply.

George MacBride, who was nearest Bessemer, took it, and read it. A slow smile crossed his face. "Two minutes, eh? Doesn't give us much time to pack."

"It's a minute and forty-five seconds now," Bessemer said. "You won't be able to take any personal possessions with you, I'm afraid."

"But does that mean we have to leave our money and baggage here? Can't we take anything along on the rocket?" asked Mrs. Ledbetter. She had a fortune in blue-white Mars diamonds along with her, and she didn't care to lose them without an argument.

"I don't see how you can take anything with you," Lieutenant Bessemer said. He glanced at his watch.

His eyes roved around the Common Room. Over against the wall was a broad-shouldered man who had simply kept himself out of the free-for-all.

"Father," Bessemer said, "the lives of everyone on this ship are in danger. I wonder if you would lead us in prayer."

The priest nodded gravely.

"Our Father, who art in Heaven—"

VI

Major General Neil Stanley lifted his eyes from the screen before him, and glanced wearily at the clock on the wall above it.

Twenty-three minutes! Had it been only twenty-three minutes since the *Martian Queen* had gone out of control? Had it been only a little more than a quarter of an hour since all hell had broken loose?

Outside, the sun was near its peak height, and blazing down brilliantly on the baked sands of the spaceport. Stanley looked back at the television screen, where the images of five men were pictured–three civilians, and two five-star generals.

Five stars. It would have been nice to get five stars, Stanley thought. Five? It would have been nice to get two. But that would never happen now.

General Hagopian was a short, dark, hawk-nosed man whose chocolate-brown eyes reflected shrewd intelligence. He looked out of the screen and said, "The ship will land in Long Island Sound, then?"

"If it's not stopped, yes," Stanley said, for what must have been the twenty-seventh time.

Sound Decision ⎯⎯⎯⎯⎯⎯⎯⎯⎯⎯⎯⎯⎯⎯⎯⎯⎯⎯⎯⎯⎯⎯⎯⎯

One of the civilians—no one had bothered to tell Stanley exactly which high-level members of the Administration he was dealing with—said, "Is there any way at all to get the drive of that ship going again? Don't they carry repair technicians, or something like that?"

"I have Captain Deering's report," Stanley said. "He states flatly that the main converter and the secondaries are absolutely and completely ruined. It would be, I assure you, impossible to fix them in the next fifteen minutes, even with the best intentions."

The civilian ignored the sarcasm. "Well, how about a rescue ship? Couldn't we get one up there in time to take those people off?"

Stanley paused and said, "Sending up a rescue ship is impossible, sir."

"Why's that?"

"It would never make it. They would have to accelerate to take off, decelerate to match velocity with the *Queen,* and then accelerate again to keep from hitting Earth. Counting the time it would take to get all the passengers and the crew off of the *Queen,* it would require"—he made a rough mental computation—"more than an hour, even if we used all the acceleration the passengers could stand. I'm afraid it won't work."

General Hagopian said: "Then there's absolutely no way we can save them?"

"None whatsoever, sir. There just isn't time."

Another of the civilians said: "We're just lucky this time, I suppose."

"What's that?" Stanley asked.

"I mean, it's too bad all those people have to die, but at least they'll only hit the Sound. It would have been catastrophic if they'd hit a populated area. Only by the merest whisker of fate did that ship aim for the Sound instead of any of the cities on the Eastern Seaboard! Can you imagine what would have happened if the ship had landed in—"

"I'm afraid you don't understand, sir," Stanley said. "It isn't the Sound we have to worry about—it's the *sound.*"

The five men blinked.

"What nonsense is this?" asked General Hagopian.

"Just exactly what I said, sir. It doesn't matter whether that ship lands in the water or not, because it's never going to land in one piece anyway. That ship is coming into Earth at twenty miles per second. When it hits the atmosphere, it's going to go to pieces in a hell of a hurry. It will burn and collapse.

"But its actual impact with Earth's surface isn't going to be the thing that will do the damage. It won't matter whether it comes down in Long Island Sound or in Times Square—it's the impact with the atmosphere that will cause about twenty million deaths."

No one said anything. The five men in the screen looked at him in blank-faced horror.

"You know what happens when a jet plane goes over a city too low?" Stanley said. "A supersonic jet can break windows. What sort of sound wave do you think a five-hundred-metric-ton spaceship will cause at—*seventy-two thousand miles an hour?*

"I'll tell you. It would flatten every structure for miles around. If that ship hits Long Island Sound, New York City will be toppling in ruins before it ever arrives! Every town on Long Island is going to be pancaked. From Newark, New Jersey, to Hartford, Connecticut, that shock wave will knock over everything standing. This isn't a matter of a few people in a ship dying; it's a matter of millions!"

The civilian looked at General Hagopian.

"He's right," said the general, in a strangled voice.

"How much time do we have left?" the civilian demanded, white-faced.

"Only a few minutes," Stanley said coldly. He looked at his watch. "Hardly any time at all."

"Why didn't you call us before this?"

"I called as soon as I heard," Stanley said. "It took time to get all you people together. It took time to compute what was going to happen."

In the background of his screen, he saw two of the civilians

Sound Decision

engaging in some rapid-fire exchange of conversation.

"Can we evacuate?" the third civilian asked.

"In five or six minutes? Don't be silly." Stanley seemed utterly cool now, in sharp contrast to the five who faced him. "We couldn't have gotten all those people out of the area even if we'd started evacuating the moment the *Queen* had its accident–or half a day before, for that matter."

The civilian looked angry, but he said nothing.

"What do you suggest, general?" said Hagopian.

"There's only one thing to do," Stanley said levelly. "We'll have to send up a rocket with an atomic warhead and blast that ship into gas before it hits."

There was a stunned silence. Stanley counted five before anyone spoke. This was the moment he had waited for–the moment when he had to give the brass the only answer to the problem of what to do with the oncoming *Queen*. The reaction was as expected.

The civilian said: *"Are you crazy?* Blow up a hundred and eighty innocent people? There must be some other way."

"But there isn't," Stanley said flatly. "There never has been. There is only one thing to do."

"But we can't permit that!" the civilian protested. "It's murder!"

"Murder? Is it murder to kill people who are already doomed? Is it murder to save the lives of twenty million people? Pardon me for being melodramatic, but I don't like the idea any better than you do. It was difficult for me to convince myself that there was no other way."

"There *must* be another way," said the civilian frantically. "Send up a rescue ship immediately! Hagopian, order him to send up a–"

Stanley's jaw muscles stood out. Without waiting for the civilian to finish speaking, he said, "Look here, you blockhead. Do you understand that it's *impossible* to send up a rescue ship? Do you understand that I can't pull miracles out of a hat? It's as impossible to send up a rescue ship as it is to catch the *Martian*

Queen with your bare hands."

"You can't talk to me that way, general!"

Stanley glanced at Hagopian. The military man was saying nothing, but there was the faint suggestion of a smile around his thin lips.

"I'm simply trying to get you to undertand," said Stanley. "All of you. *There is no other way out!* None! Those people are going to die. D-I-E. It would be better if they died without taking a few million people with them. Is that clear?"

Stanley waited for a reply, and, sure enough, it was forthcoming. One of the other civilians said, "Couldn't we divert it from its course somehow?"

"Not without destroying it," Stanley said. "Which is exactly what I want to get permission to do."

"I'm afraid that's impossible, general. The public would never sanction–"

"*The public be damned!* It's the public who is going to die! Die! Do you understand that? Twenty million people! Twenty million people! Twenty million corpses to dig out from under ten thousand square miles of rubble!"

"That's ridiculous!" said the third civilian. They were doggedly trying to talk Stanley out of insisting on this thing, it seemed. "How could a shock wave do all that?"

"How could it do it? It's done it! Didn't you ever hear of the Great Siberian Meteor that landed around 1908? It only came in at a speed of ten miles a second or so–half the *Queen's*–and it laid waste hundreds of square miles of forest. Trees fell like matchsticks. And this ship is going about twice as fast!"

"There must be something else we can do," said the first civilian stubbornly.

"All right," Stanley said. "Start making suggestions."

"Well–"

"Exactly. There is nothing else we can do," he repeated. He glanced again at the clock. "Do I have your permission to send up an atomic warhead, then?"

"No!" came the answer. The first civilian was doing all the talking now. "That's out of the question. There must be another way."

"There isn't," Stanley said. "And wishing won't make it so. You can't wish away the laws of the universe–you've got to obey them. And that's exactly what the *Martian Queen* is doing! And that's exactly what New York is going to do when that shock wave hits!"

He paused and stared at them. "I ask you again: Do I have permission to send up that bomb?"

"I hardly see how we can sanction it, general. We'll have to find some other way."

Stanley looked at the clock and sighed.

"It's too late now anyway," he said softly. "While we've been haggling, the *Queen* has been falling. It couldn't wait. Even if you ordered it, I couldn't get a bomb up there now."

Two of the men looked fearfully out of the window toward the north. Stanley caught the gesture; he couldn't see the window on his screen, but he knew what they were looking for. From Washington, such a display would be easily visible.

"Oh, it won't land," said Stanley. His voice sounded old and tired. "There won't be any crash. I sent up an XV-19 under robot control several minutes before you gentlemen got together. It was loaded with a thermo nuclear warhead. Captain Deering will–or I should say *has*–guided it in. The *Martian Queen* was vaporized over a minute ago. It was the only thing to do."

One of the men covered his face with his hands. Stanley wondered who he was.

"I presume you know what this means," asked General Hagopian quietly.

"I know," said Stanley. "If I get out of it with a whole skin, I'll still lose everything I've ever worked for. It doesn't matter. At the court-martial, I can still know that I've saved the lives of millions of people."

General Hagopian nodded. "That will be a point in your favor. But there's nothing else we can do; you can see that. You'll have to roast." Then Hagopian looked steadily at Stanley. "You're a very brave man, general. It's too bad that most people will never understand what you did—and why."

Stanley forced a smile. "The people who matter will understand, general. And they're the only ones who count."

GRATITUDE GUARANTEED by R. Bretnor and Kris Neville

"*Gratitude Guaranteed*" *first appeared in* The Magazine of Fantasy & Science Fiction *in 1953, at the crest of Anthony Boucher's significant editorial career and near the beginning of R. Bretnor's and Kris Neville's literary careers. Bretnor had begun to publish an odd mixture of elegant and sardonic stories in the science fiction magazines ("The Doorstop" is one example) side by side with broad farce ("The Gnurrs Come From the Voodvork Out," the first of the Papa Schimmelhorn stories); and Neville, with his debut story "Cold War"* (Astounding, *1949), "Bettyann"* (New Tales of Space and Time, *1951), and "Hunt the Hunter"* (Galaxy, *1951), had begun to put together an important body of work. To the best of our knowledge, "Gratitude Guaranteed" is not only the single collaboration between these writers, but the only time that either wrote in partnership (except for three minor stories Neville co-authored with one of your editors in the late sixties).*

In addition to being a well-known writer of short fiction and military nonfiction, Reginald Bretnor (b. 1913) is an anthologist/critic of some stature; his discursive symposia-collections Modern Science Fiction: Its Meaning and Its Future *(1953),* Science Fiction, Today and Tomorrow *(1974), and* Speaking of Science Fiction *(1975) are highly regarded in the field. His first novel, a wild and delightful mystery titled* A Killing in Swords, *was published last year by Pocket Books.*

Kris Neville (b. 1925) may be one of the best writers who never attained major reputation in science fiction. He had all the tools—range, fluency, passion, power, insight, compassion—but for private and other reasons failed to progress beyond a brilliant beginning; after a long hiatus, he made an only moderately successful attempt at resuming his career in 1967 and then retired again circa 1970. His primary vocation is as a technical writer and scientific collaborator; he has co-written landmark work on the very non-esoteric subject of epoxy resins.

GRATITUDE GUARANTEED

By R. Bretnor and Kris Neville

On the morning of December fifth, Mr. E. Howard Harrison showed up at the processing labs of Cuddlypets Corporation promptly at eight-forty-five. He hung up his coat, scrubbed his hands, and put on his smock, mask, and gloves. Then, as he had every working day for seven long years, he joined the two other surgical technicians who made up his team.

As always, Mr. Olson was sitting on the operating table, singing Cuddlypets commercials in his concrete-mixer baritone:

>"Cudd-lee-pets, Cudd-lee-pets,
>Snuggle up to Cudd-lee-pets!
>They'll love Mom and Dad and you
>Like they're GUAR-AN-TEED to do!
>
>"Tweak their whiskers, pull their fur,
>Cuddlypets just grin and purr!
>Cuddlypets just purr and grin–
>Love and gra-ti-tude's BUILT-IN!''

As always, Mr. Kerfoid was standing across from him, beating time on a sterilizer with his forceps. When Mr. Harrison entered the room, Mr. Kerfoid glanced up, nodded, and winked like a vulture with sand in its eye. Mr. Olson just kept on singing:

"Cuddlytiger's big and classy,
Cuddlypanther's really snazzy,
Cuddlyleopard, Cuddlylion–
YOU can buy them all ON TIME!

"Cudd-lee-pets, Cudd-lee-pets,
Snuggle up to—"

It had been Mr. Harrison's habit to ignore these renditions as politely as possible, keeping his long, tight rectangle of a face carefully averted, and busying himself with minor adjustments to the encephaloscreen, or the disposal unit, or to the little glass cabinet that held their day's supply of Schroeder Bypasses and Dappleby Blocks. On the morning of December fifth, however, he did nothing of the sort. Instead, he took three brisk paces to bring himself face to face with Mr. Olson, and snarled, "Shut up!"

Mr. Olson jerked his head back, emitted a hoarse "–Cudd-l—," gasped, and was silent. Mr. Kerfoid dropped his forceps, and said, "Now, now, Mr. Harrison," plaintively several times.

"You shut up too," growled Mr. Harrison, turning on him. "It's bad enough having to waste my time working on these goddam big cats, cats, cats–that's all we get nowadays, is cats–lions, tigers, panthers, jaguars, cougars, ocelots–what'll it be next, I want to know, sabre-tooths?" He confronted Mr. Olson again. "It's so bad I can smell 'em in my sleep."

"I–I don't see how you can," protested Mr. Olson nervously. "We've a swell Cuddlylion at home ourselves. Got him for the kid. He's clean and neat, just like it says in the com—. Anyhow, he doesn't smell even a little bit. Uses his little old lion-box every time." He looked toward his colleague for support. "Isn't that right, Mr. Kerfoid?"

"It certainly is," croaked Mr. Kerfoid. "Everybody knows that Cuddlypets are–well, as Dr. Schroeder puts it, they are 'personally dainty.' Besides they're all of them deodorized before shipment. It's the policy of the firm, and a very good policy too, I may say."

Mr. Olson sniffed. "And anyhow," he said, "it seems to me, Mr. Harrison, that even if you don't like my singing, you might at least have the courtesy not to be offensive about it. Maybe Mr. Kerfoid and I *don't* have our B.S.'s in Cyber-Surgery; maybe we aren't qualified to work on human beings like you say you are–but at least *we* don't let our conduct become *subprofessional.*"

As unobtrusively as possible, Mr. Harrison sneaked a glance at the big clock on the wall. Everything, so far, had gone just as he'd planned it, and Mr. Olson had been adequately provoked—

Very deliberately, he allowed an expression of uncertainty to come over his features. "Wh-what do you m-mean, subprofessional?" he stuttered.

Mr. Olson was encouraged. He rose threateningly. "You know damn' well what I mean, Mr. Harrison. If you don't watch yourself, I'll report you to the Association–and likely as not they'll have you degraded. See?"

And at that point, as Mr. Harrison had known it would, the red light above the encephaloscreen flashed on to warn them that their first patient would arrive in just thirty seconds.

Automatically, they slipped their masks up over their faces. Mr. Olson took up his position near the hindfoot and tail clamps. Mr. Kerfoid moved to the clamps at the frontfoot and head end. Mr. Harrison, grinning under the gauze, clicked the trephining saw and the encephaloscreen pickup into place.

Right on the dot, the overhead conveyor trap opened, and down came a fine young male lion, snoring away under profound anesthesia, and displaying a small tonsured area just over his forehead. Mr. Olson and Mr. Kerfoid snapped the clamps. Mr. Harrison pressed the button that lowered the foot of the table. Mr. Olson made his incisions, hinging back a few square inches of scalp.

Gratitude Guaranteed

Mr. Kerfoid let the saw buzz for a moment, and lifted a section of skull with his forceps. Then Mr. Harrison adjusted the pickups until the encephaloscreen diagrammed the precise path for his instruments. He reached for the delicate electronic scalpel with which Stage One was performed, moved it along the division between the two lobes, noted its indicated position on the screen, and—

"Ta-da-dum, ta-da-dum,
Tada-tada-ta-da-dum—"

sang Mr. Olson cheerfully.
Mr. Harrison's hand stopped.

"Ta-da-ta-da ta da dum
Tum-tum-tum-tum-tum-tum-tum."

Mr. Harrison rested hand and scalpel on the lion's nose, frowned, and said, *"Please!"* with great self-restraint.

"Can't I even hum?" protested Mr. Olson. "I was just humming. I didn't even say the words."

Mr. Harrison went back to his labors. He completed Stage One and Stage Two, took the Schroeder Bypass which Mr. Kerfoid had broken out of its sterile plastic capsule, waited while its number was recorded together with his own and the lion's, and installed it. By the time Dr. Schroeder and Dr. Dappleby entered the room on their routine morning inspection, he had completed Stages Three, Four, and Five, and was ready to put in the Dappleby Block. Mr. Olson had hummed the Cuddlypets tune twice more, and had whistled it once.

As always, Dr. Schroeder and Dr. Dappleby walked round the table and stopped beside Mr. Harrison. Dr. Schroeder patted the lion's cheek with a long, hairy hand. "Soon," he chirped, "you will be a *good* little lion. Soon you will lie down with the lamb. It is the Schroeder Bypass that does all this, gentlemen—yes, indeed. It conditions the animal to feel permanent gratitude–*gratitude,* gentlemen. Ah, yes, and we mustn't forget the Dappleby Block, must we? It was so clever of Dr. Dappleby to invent it, so that our nice little friends can't get *too* grateful and hurt people."

Dr. Dappleby's ears turned red, and he mumbled that it really wasn't anything much. Mr. Kerfoid said loyally that it was too. Dr. Schroeder made his usual remark about the good work they were doing, and how it made him feel all warm inside and not at all sorry that he and Dr. Dappleby had abandoned the most lucrative veterinary practice west of the Mississippi to start the Cuddlypets Corporation.

"I know *just* how you feel, Dr. Schroeder," declared Mr. Olson sentimentally. "It's inspiring, that's what it is. Every time I see one of our TV shows, well, I'm grateful to you for the chance of working here." He glanced at Mr. Harrison. "And our commercials–say, they're really *sharp.* They really stay with you. Did you hear that swell one last night?"

Dr. Schroeder said that maybe he hadn't. Mr. Harrison tensed slightly.

Mr. Olson threw back his head and sang:

"Cuddlypets are clean and tidy,
Cuddlypets don't need a didy.
Junior's ooky? Junior's wet?
Trade him for a CUDD-LEE-PET!

"Cudd-lee-pets, Cudd-lee-pets,
Snug—"

"SHUT *UP!*" Mr. Harrison bawled. He took two long steps toward Mr. Olson. Then, with a roar like an unprocessed Cuddlypet, he leaped for his throat. Together, they fell against the little glass cabinet, sending it crashing down, sending a shower of Schroeder Bypasses and Dappleby Blocks into the funnel-shaped sink at the bottom of which the jaws of the disposal unit whirred hungrily.

Gratitude Guaranteed

It took a minute or two to separate them, to restrain Mr. Harrison, and to restore some sort of equilibrium. Dr. Schroeder was the first to regain his poise. *"Well!"* he said. "You have attacked Mr. Olson. You have destroyed our valuable bypasses, our valuable blocks. You have spoiled our system of records completely! I'm really afraid that we can't keep you."

"Cow-mechanic!" spat Mr. Harrison.

Dr. Schroeder scarcely blinked at the insult. "The fact that you are qualified to operate on human beings," he explained, "cannot change my decision. Since the new psychiatric techniques made you unnecessary, you B. S.'s in Cyber-Surgery are a dime a dozen–a dime a dozen, Mr. Harrison. Besides, you are emotionally unstable, are you not? Maybe you need a Schroeder Bypass yourself. Now Dr. Dappleby will finish this lion, and then I will send another man to your place. Go away."

Mr. Harrison stamped to the door. He threw his mask down, and kicked it into a corner. "Nuts to you, monkey-plumber!" he shouted. "I *quit!"*

Fifteen minutes later, he left the Cuddlypets building by the front entrance, his last check in his wallet. His professional status was doomed; his career was ruined–but there was a new spring in his walk. What was that crack of the doctor's about needing a Schroeder Bypass himself? He chuckled. He felt in his pocket. There it was, safe in its small plastic capsule–*unrecorded*–just as he'd planned from the start.

"Cudd-lee-pets, Cudd-lee-pets,
Snuggle up to Cudd-lee-pets–"

sang Mr. Harrison happily as he went away.

Mr. Harrison disliked cats much more than he did singing commercials, and he disliked cats actually present more than cats at a distance. Now that professional pride was no longer involved, he scarcely objected when his wife watched her favorite Cuddlypets program each evening, and often he came in and watched it himself–at least until it reminded her of their problems, and of his own plans, about which she was doubtful.

It was just three weeks later, on the day after Christmas, that these plans finally came to fruition. The program ended, and Mr. Harrison switched off the set. Nodding critically, he remarked, "Well, I don't like cats–but that was pretty good. That was *rich*–the part where the door was going to open, and he didn't know who would come out."

"In the *story*," replied Mrs. Harrison, pursing her over-ripe lips, "it ended right there. You never did learn who it was, the lady *or* the tiger. Of course, it's a very old old story, maybe pre-Twentieth Century, when the tigers were fierce and ate people up. So he *couldn't* have turned out to be just an old Cuddlytiger, not really, and *both* of them couldn't have come out. Anyway, I think it's better the way it was written. I think they ought to be left the way Nature made them, in the jungle and all–though at least you *were* a professional when you were doing the work, and I must say no one in *my* family has ever been *sub*professional before. That was why they all said I ought to have married Elmer Maginnis, because he was a real Ph.D."

Mr. Harrison sighed. "Look, Chickadee," he said patiently, "I've explained till I'm blue in the face. It's just for a while. The world owes me something–me, a Cyber-Surgery B. S., working seven years in a goddam cat factory, making 'em grateful!" He snorted. "Well, a Schroeder Bypass'll work just as well in an electronic brain as it will in a cat's. Those cheap poodle-fixers don't know it, but I do. That's why I'm working for Jonson, Williamson, Selznick, and Jones. One of these days, they'll send me on just the right job. Then we'll live off the fat of the land."

"Well, I suppose you know best," his wife said, "but I can't for the life of me see how a mechanical brain can be *grateful* even if you do something for it. And this morning I met that frowzy Eppinger woman–she tries to make out she's thirty-three, but she's forty at least–and she said, 'I hear your husband's a *mechanic* now, Mrs. Harrison, on mechanical brains? Now, isn't that *nice*.' And I said—"

Before she could finish, the phone rang in the hall; and Mr.

Harrison, grumbling, pushed into his slippers and went off to answer it.

She heard him snap, "Hello, Harrison speaking." Then, after a moment, in a much sweeter voice: "We're *fine*, Mr. Selznick. A fine Christmas, too. Yes, *sir,* yes indeed. . . . *Who?* . . . Sure I know where they are! . . . Yes . . . Yes, sir, right away. . . . Thank *you,* Mr. Selznick. Goodbye."

He strode back. "Guess who that was!" he crowed. "It was Mr. Selznick, that's who it was. Babe, our troubles are over. This is *it.*"

"This is what?" Mrs. Harrison asked.

"The big chance. We won't have to wait. Say, isn't it lucky he called me instead of one of the others? I'll bet you can't guess where it is."

"Eberhard," Mrs. Harrison said, "stop beating around the bush and come to the point."

"Ha!" Mr. Harrison strutted. "Well, I'll tell you. It's Moss-Eagleberg, Chickadee, *Moss-Eagleberg,* the biggest store in the West. Forty-six floors. They sell tailor-made suits and new cars, turbocopters, crown jewels and ermines and things, the best Scotch you can get, Oriental rugs, real antiques, pheasants already cooked by French chefs, swimming pools, readymade barbecue pits—They sell *everything.*"

"Their prices are always too high," Mrs. Harrison said. "I like Monkey Ward's best."

"And they're *fully* automatic–order, accounting, and shipping departments all run by one brain. *One*–just like a lion or tiger or something. And now it's gone dead–and I'm the guy who's going to fix it." Mr. Harrison danced three steps of a jig. "Get it, honeybunch? After tomorrow, that great big Moss-Eagleberg brain will be grateful to *me.* We'll pick up the phone and order whatever we want–all for free."

"Well, you make it sound very nice, but I still don't see how a lot of condensers and things—"

"It's a cinch," Mr. Harrison said, reaching for his troubleshooter's kit and his hat. "I won't even have to put in a Dappleby Block."

Deep inside Moss-Eagleberg's broken-down brain, Mr. Harrison spent most of the night doing what Jonson, Williamson, Selznick, and Jones paid him to do. In the whole vast, silent warehouse, there was no one to bother him; and, as he worked, he made mental notes. *Order Record, Delivery Record, Charge Debit, Collection Routine*–all these could be by-passed just as if they'd been labelled *Aggression (against Human), Aggression (against Animal), Hunger (for Human), Hunger (for Animal except Syntho-horse).* That was simple. Of course, the *Semiannual Inventory* circuits would take a little finagling—

As six in the morning, Mr. Harrison climbed the ladder to the control room. He locked the door just to be on the safe side, plugged a mike and a typer in on the *Charge Accounts* bank, tapped out his name and address, gave himself a Triple-A credit rating, and activated the unit. He repeated name and address into the mike so that the brain could record his individual voice pattern for future identification over the phone. He went down the ladder again and traced out the new circuit. Then, expertly, he installed the Schroeder Bypass where it would do the most good, running fifty-six fine little tantalum wires to the grafting points on its gelatinous skin, and attaching all the appropriate shunts.

"Love and gra-ti-tude's BUILT-IN!" sang Mr. Harrison triumphantly as he went back to his work.

By eight o'clock, when the two subprofessionals who kept tab on the brain showed up, he had it all finished and was seated in the control room writing his bill.

They came in, a plump, pink little man and a long, lean, leathery one. "Hi," said the long one. "I'm Winkler, and this here's Swartz. You get everything fixed?"

Mr. Harrison looked up coldly. "I am *Mr.* Harrison," he informed them. "Repairs have been made, and I'll have the bill ready in a minute or two if I'm not interrupted."

"Sure, sure," Swartz said. He inspected the room, nodding and rubbing his hands. He patted the panels. He stroked the master switch gently. "Boy, oh boy. It sure will be good to have old Bessie perking again."

"Eleven hours at twelve dollars and twenty cents an hour,"

Mr. Harrison muttered, "makes one hundred thirty-four dollars and twenty cents."

"Worth every cent of it, too," Winkler asserted. "Mr. Harrison, you done wonders. I tell you, Swartz and me were real worried when we found out about it. We thought she was just dead and gone, like a person. We felt like we'd killed her."

Mr. Harrison tore off the original bill and two carbons. "That's all nonsense," he stated. "Giving this brain a name doesn't make it at all like a person. It's an electronic device, and it's very much simpler even than a Cud–even than an animal's brain, let alone a human's."

"You don't know Bessie." Swartz shook his head. "She's got ten million units, and she thinks a thousand times faster than we do. She's a real personality, Bessie is."

Mr. Harrison reached for his wrenches and printed circuits and bloblike germanium transistors. He put his graphite pencils in the tray and his two pocket meters in their receptacles and snapped shut his kit. "You're wrong," he said flatly. "But I won't waste time arguing with you. Machines can't think. They don't live. They can't die. And that's final."

"I don't see how you can say that," Winkler protested. "Look here. When Swartz cut all the current off Bessie Christmas Eve, wasn't she exactly like a dead human, except for decaying, I mean? Just now it took you nearly twelve hours to bring her back to life, didn't it? Seems to me that was the same as artificial respiration, or heart massage maybe."

"It was just unit by unit shock. There's no connection."

"There!" Swartz exclaimed. "Didn't I tell you? It was *shock therapy*. Bessie does too think. I've worked with her from the start. I ought to know."

"Then you ought to know never to cut the current all the way off," Mr. Harrison snapped.

Winkler and Swartz looked at each other. "She needed the rest," Swartz explained patiently. "That new unit they put in to send individual Christmas cards to the customers worked her to death on top of the holiday rush and all. Besides, it was Christmas Eve."

"When you get through the day, set the dial on 'Stand-by'; *never* cut the current all the way off," Mr. Harrison said through his teeth.

"Since we carry cards for *every* occasion," observed Winkler, "she ought to be grateful we only make her send them out once a year. Don't you think so?"

Most of the circuits in Mr. Harrison's mind were busy with thoughts of the Shroeder Bypass, and the very extensive Moss-Eagleberg stock, and how to get home in a hurry. Now, however, he came up with a jerk.

"She–she ought to be *what?*"

"*Grateful,*" Winkler repeated obligingly. "She sometimes is. You can feel it."

"God damn it, machines *can't* be grateful!" shouted Mr. Harrison, waving his arms.

"Bessie can," Swartz told him. "She'll be grateful to you too, Mr. Harrison, for bringing her back from the dead like you did. She'll love you for that." He reached for the master switch; pulled it all the way down. "You just wait and see."

Conveyor belts came to life from one end of the giant warehouse to the other. Under Bessie's direction, mechanical arms sorted packages, loaded them on the right belts and unloaded them at their destinations. In the delivery and mailing room, address stencils dropped in flawless order from the rotating customer drums, and steel arms slammed the stencils against oncoming crates and cartons, and machine-guided brushes applied smears of stencil ink, and the moving belts carried the crates and cartons away to waiting driverless trucks.

At this evidence of Bessie's revivification, Winkler blew his nose sentimentally; Swartz dabbed at his eyes. Neither of them even noticed Mr. Harrison hurrying out.

Mr. Harrison drove through a red light and two stop signs before he completely convinced himself that neither Winkler nor Swartz suspected the presence of the Schroeder Bypass; that their talk about gratitude was purely coincidental. He remembered that subprofessionals were all stupid bastards, with compulsions to personalize their machines, to–he fished for the word–to *anthro-*

pomorphize them. Yes, that was it. Stupid bastards. The very idea of a machine that was grateful, all by itself, was absurd. It was laughable.

Mr. Harrison was still chuckling when he reached his apartment. His wife had their breakfast unpackaged and ready; and, over their coffee, they thumbed eagerly through the latest edition of the four-inch-thick Moss-Eagleberg catalog. There were things for every conceivable purpose and purse, from every conceivable part of the world. There were even a few souvenir ashtrays and lampbases made out of pumice brought back at terrific expense from the Moon.

"Number 62-A-547-01," Mrs. Harrison read aloud. "Rope of pearls, triple strand, fine Oriental. N-ninety-nine thousand, five hundred. Now, that would be *nice.*"

"Don't bother reading the price, ha-ha." Mr. Harrison laughed. *"We* can afford it."

"62-C-202-49, Ring, emerald, thirty-two carats." She held up her hand, crooked the ring finger, and sighed. "Well, I'll note them both down for later–when we've made sure, that is."

"Chickadee, we *are* sure."

"I'm not," Mrs. Harrison said. "So we'll just buy a few things at first, things we can pay for if something goes wrong and they send us a bill. Anyhow, it's near the end of the month, and we'll find out in four or five days."

A few minutes later, Mr. Harrison called up Moss-Eagleberg's charge department. He gave his name and address. Bessie checked against his recording; okayed it. The human operator said, "Your circuit is open now, sir. You can dial your order." And, very carefully, he dialed the catalog numbers: a big tri-di TV set, a Chinchilla trimmed hostess gown, a flacon of *En Chaleur No. 5,* a silver service for eight, a banquet for two with ortolans, truffles, and other strange goodies from the Rotisserie, a case of champagne, and a box of expensive cigars.

They didn't have to wait long. At eleven-fifteen, the delivery port in the hall buzzed its warning, and cartons and packages began to come out. As they appeared, Mr. Harrison opened each one and checked up on its contents. Every item was there. In fact, there were two tri-di sets.

"My finger must've slipped dialing that one," he remarked. "Well, no harm's done. Anyhow, it works just as I told you. I'll hang onto my job for awhile so nobody'll get any funny ideas, but from now on Moss-Eagleberg's going to support us in style. Let's celebrate!"

They celebrated right through the weekend, enjoying their champagne hangovers thoroughly, and spending almost as much time over the catalog as in watching their new tri-di sets. They celebrated all over again on New Year's Eve. Then, as the first days of January went by without any bill, Mrs. Harrison began to say less and less about what might happen if something went wrong, and to think more and more about a future of opulent ease provided by Bessie.

On January tenth, unable to wait any longer, she phoned Moss-Eagleberg, asked for a statement on her husband's account, and was informed that no purchases had been made. When he came home that evening, she had her new shopping list all made out.

"I want you to order all these things in the morning, Eberhard dear," she told him. "It's too soon after Christmas to buy jewelry and clothes; they'll be almost sold out. So this time I'll simply get things for the house: a grand piano, a Louis the something-or-other bedroom suite, and a dear little electronic organ, and new curtains all around, and a freezer, and a real antique spinning-wheel, and a marbletop dresser, and–oh, and all *sorts* of things."

"Better not go getting too much big stuff," Mr. Harrison warned, "at least not at one time. It won't come up through the port; the janitors'll have to bring it in the service elevator. We don't want them getting suspicious."

"Don't worry," Mrs. Harison said. "I've thought of all that. We aren't going to order more than once in two weeks, even things like our meals. If the police found it out, goodness knows what they'd do! They'd probably use that psychiatric technique on you, the one that made Cyber-Surgery on people out of date. Then where would we be?"

Mr. Harrison laughed. "I'd be sort of a zombi. I'd be just like a Cuddlypet only more so. But they'll never find out because Bessie won't tell them. She loves me too much, ha-ha-ha! It's BUILT-IN!"

Next day, just before noon, the delivery came through. As the smaller objects were being stacked up in the hall, the telephone rang; and Mr. Harrison, breaking off the catchy commercial he was humming, answered it.

"Hello? Mr. Harrison?" The building manager sounded a little upset. "We've got a raft of stuff for you down here, Mr. Harrison. You–you want to come down?"

"No, indeed, Mr. Quandt. Just send it up."

"*All* of it?"

"Of course, all of it!" Mr. Harrison snapped. "Why shouldn't you send all of it up?"

"Well, okay if you say so. If you can figure where to put *three* grand pianos in that apartment of yours, I guess it's your busi—"

"What's that? *How* many pianos?"

"Three, Mr. Harrison, like I said. The store must of made a mistake."

Mr. Harrison covered the mouthpiece. "They–they sent *three* grand pianos," he said to his wife.

"Well, we'll have to send two of them back."

"We–we *can't* send them back, Chickadee. There'd be too many questions. My God, we can't even sell them! We'll have to fit them in someplace, that's all. I–I must've dialed a three instead of a one when I ordered. That must've been it. Whew!" He turned back to the phone. "There's been no mistake, Mr. Quandt," he declared a little too loudly. "I checked with the wife. She–she likes music a lot."

The Harrisons put the three grand pianos in the living-room, where they took up eighty per cent of the space. They hoisted the tri-di TV's onto one of them, and the spinning-wheel onto another; and they squeezed the organ into the bedroom between the new bedroom set and the marbletop bureau. The next time Mr. Harrison ran into Mr. Quandt in the hall, he dropped a hint that his wife had these *moods* when she had to be humored; doctor's orders, he said. And he made up his mind to double-check every digit he dialed in the future.

As for Mrs. Harrison, she accepted the crowding philosophically. When she wasn't out window-shopping at Moss-Eagleberg's, she kept herself busy making out and revising her lists, running happily through such compositions as *Pretty Redwing* and *The Golliwog's Cakewalk* on her pianos, and regretting that she couldn't tell that frumpy Eppinger woman about Bessie.

On January twenty-fourth, they ordered again, and again Mrs. Harrison put off getting her jewels and her wardrobe. "You order this time," she said. "All I want is one of those iridium-mink coats, and some silver things for my dresser, and a little more perfume, so it won't matter much if you do make another mistake. But when I get the really valuable things, I want to do it myself. Now that I think of it, you always do seem to get the wrong number when you phone."

When the order arrived, "There!" she cried out. "Didn't I tell you? I said *one* iridium-mink coat, and you went and got *four*."

"I'll be damned," Mr. Harrison said. "I could've sworn I dialed that right. If I didn't *know* that machines simply can't—" He shrugged. "Well, anyway, it's lucky they had four in stock."

Then, without protest, he called up Moss-Eagleberg and arranged to have Bessie record his wife's voice so that she could charge against his account–and he warned her not to order a thing for two weeks at least.

Mrs. Harrison assured him that she wouldn't, adding that he needn't worry about *her* dialing half-a-dozen when she meant only one; and she kept her promise for all of five days. On January twenty-ninth, though, she happened on an ad in the paper where it said that Moss-Eagleberg were having a sale on star sapphires, up to thirty percent off the regular price. Even though she knew there wouldn't be any charge, somehow she couldn't resist it. Giving herself the excuse that she might as well charge the next order of food now as later, she picked out a medium-sized stone of about eighteen carats and circled its number. She dialed it last, very slowly and carefully.

When the delivery arrived, Mrs. Harrison hurriedly searched for the one little package. Not finding it, she controlled her impatience and began checking off all the boxes of food by their numbers. When she had moved every one of them into the kitchen, she found one package left. But it wasn't a small one. It was about four feet high, and exceedingly heavy. Her heart fluttering, she tore off the paper and exposed a big wooden box with ELL-AY ARTY-CRAFTS, INC. stencilled on the side. She obtained a screwdriver, and pried off the top, and exposed a combination sundial and birdbath in genuine simulated bronze, with fat cherubim peeping up over the edge, and North, South, East, and West marked with arrows, and a motto cut into the rim: *Honi Soit Qui Mal Y Pense.*

Mrs. Harrison sat down. She wept for two solid minutes. She tried to remember whether she could have made a mistake on the very first number of the sapphire. Then, straining mightily, she pushed the birdbath-cum-sundial into a closet and covered it up. When her husband came back from work, she said nothing about it.

Four days later, she made another try for the sapphire. This time, she received several pairs of long winter woolies, size fifty long stout. A little hysterically, she hid them back of the birdbath, and said not a word.

On February fifth, the telephone broke up her afternoon nap. When she answered it, a feminine voice sang loudly and clearly:

> "Happy birth-day, to you-u-u,
> Happy BIRTH-day to you-u-u,
> Happy BIRTH-DAY, dear Eber-hard,
> Happy birth-day to YOU-U-U!"

And, within half an hour, something arrived from Moss-Eagleberg—a huge, heart-shaped box of candied fruit with WON'T YOU BE MY VALENTINE? across the outside. As the day was neither Mr. Harrison's birthday nor St. Valentine's Day, she deduced that her husband was playing a joke, and she mentioned it to him on his return.

". . . and it seems to me," she concluded, "that you'd be *above* things like that, especially after lecturing *me* on not ordering so often. All that candied fruit–it'll take weeks to eat up!"

After the initial shock of the news, Mr. Harrison had decided, logically enough, that Winkler and Swartz were trying to prove to him that Bessie was grateful. This, however, was hardly a subject he wished to debate with his wife, so he simply assured her that he hadn't ordered a thing, that he was as puzzled as she was.

"Nonsense!" cried Mrs. Harrison shrilly, still unnerved by the birdbath and the long underwear. "I refuse to believe it. And you aren't being funny at all. I'm sure Elmer Maginnis wouldn't ever have stooped to being so–so *childish*. Don't you dare to do it again!"

When they retired that night, she was still very angry; and the events of the following day did nothing at all to mend matters. The telephone rang. The feminine voice sang its message. Presently, Moss-Eagleberg delivered a pair of large potted cacti.

Mr. Harrison's protestations went unheeded. His wife turned the Cuddlypets program up louder than ever before, and ignored him icily. He began to wonder whether he hadn't better do something about Winkler and Swartz.

Next morning, he stopped wondering. As it was Saturday, he answered the phone himself. He heard its gay greeting. An hour or so later, after reading the card enclosed with the package, he unwrapped one dozen athletic supporters. On the card was a drawing of a woman in uniform, and under the drawing were the words: *Lots of Love to my Aunt in the Service.*

Mr. Harrison decided that on Monday he would approach Winkler and Swartz and take drastic action.

Mrs. Harrison also reached a decision. With Eberhard making such a fool of himself, there was no point in *her* waiting for the good things of life. On Monday—

On Monday, just before lunch, Mrs. Harrison ordered a score

of the most expensive items in the jewelry department. She also dialed a small but select wardrobe of the sort which might have been chosen by a particularly wealthy and generous maharajah's favorite wife. As she hung up, she told herself reassuringly that in no previous delivery had there been more than a single mistake, and that one mistake now wouldn't really make very much difference–though she did hope it wouldn't be on the rope of pearls, triple strand.

At about the same time, Mr. Harrison sneaked out of the office of Jonson, Williamson, Selznick, and Jones, and went to a pay phone. An angry gleam in his eye, the phrases with which to demolish Winkler and Swartz all set in his mind, he called up Moss-Eagleberg and asked for Bessie's control-room. As soon as it answered, he shouted, "Winkler? Winkler, you listen to me—"

"*Who* you want?" shouted the receiver back at him.

"I want *Winkler*."

"Not here."

"Okay then–Swartz."

"*Who?*"

"*Swartz!*"

"*He ain't here neither!*"

"THEY GO OUT TO LUNCH?" Mr. Harrison bellowed. "WHEN YOU EXPECTING THEM BACK?"

"THEY WON'T BE BACK!" bawled the receiver. "THEY BEEN TRANSFERRED. THEY'VE WENT OUT TO DALLAS! GODDAMMIT, STOP SHOUTING!"

Mr. Harrison stopped shouting. His stomach felt as though it had suddenly passed through a very cold wringer. He said, "H-how long ago?"

"Three weeks!" barked the phone.

Mr. Harrison groaned. He replaced the receiver, and staggered away from the booth. He found his way to a bar, and had two double bourbons. Then he went back to Jonson, Williamson, Selznick, and Jones, and pretended to work for the rest of the day. He thought of the Valentine present and the cacti and the athletic supporters. He wondered whether his wife might not have ordered them all for a gag, and decided against it. He remembered what Winkler and Swartz had said about Bessie, and cursed both of them for a pair of dumb bastards. Finally he recalled that sometimes a new Cuddlypet took awhile to adjust–that a couple of months might go by before the Schroeder Bypass stabilized properly. It was pretty rare, but it happened. Maybe—

By the time he got home, he had persuaded himself that something like this had happened to Bessie, that all he and his wife had to do was sit tight for another few weeks and it would all straighten out.

"Hello! Hello-oh!" he called as he opened the door. "Chickadee, I'm home."

He halted abruptly. The hall was full of crates, cartons, boxes, and bundles. Some had been opened, wholly or partially; others were intact. Some were small; some were big; several were simply enormous. And there were more of them showing in the visible part of the living-room.

"H-Honeybunch?" Mr. Harrison called in alarm. "Where *are* you? Hey, Chickadee!"

He was answered by a loud and very moist sob from the bedroom. There, stretched out on the Louis-the-something-or-other bed, he discovered his wife. Dashing in, he tripped over a tangle of paper and string on the floor, swore, sat down on the edge of the bed, put an arm round her. "Sweetheart!" he cried. "Mignonetta! What's happened? What's *wrong?*"

Mrs. Harrison quaked. She shook off his arm. She sat up, revealing a very red nose and some badly eroded makeup. "What's *h-happened?*" she wailed. "Wh-what's *wrong?* Just l-look what you *di-i-id!*"

She pointed, and a new freshet of tears came forth. Mr. Harrison, following her finger, beheld a dark cylindrical object partly concealed by the wrappings over which he had stumbled. He lifted it out. It was about two feet high, leathery, hollow, and more than ten inches across.

"I j-just dialed some jewels and a f-few things to wear–and

loo-o-k what I got. Ei-*eighteen* of them!"

Mr. Harrison looked. He saw that, down at the bottom, the object splayed out very slightly into four recognizable toes. He lifted the tag. On one side it said, CONGO NOVELTIES, *Original! Exclusive!;* on the other, HIPPOPOTAMUS FOOT UMBRELLA STAND, *Guaranteed Real.*

Mr. Harrison let it slide to the floor. He peered at his hands, found they were shaking, put them away in his pockets. "Hippo feet," he muttered aloud, "for umbrellas. Must be a mistake. That's what. Just a mistake."

Mrs. Harrison threw herself back on the pillow with a shrill cry of anguish.

"—ha-ha-ha! Machines make mistakes all the time. No harm done, ha-ha! Be all right. Yes, indeed. Don't you worry." He patted her clumsily. He went out. He attempted to take a brief inventory. Besides the eighteen hippopotamus feet, he found a bale of peat moss, a turret-top lathe, two lobster traps, a case of Adventist hymnbooks, five or six crates of lettuce, a hayrake, a portable duck blind with decoys, a small Japanese automobile, and a cage containing a family of Belgian hares.

At that point, definitely dazed, he gave up and went back to the bedroom. Mrs. Harrison was sitting up. She had dried her eyes, and looked combative.

"*S-something* went wrong," Mr. Harrison mumbled.

She did not reply.

"M-maybe I ought to have put in a Dappleby Block," he continued. "Chickadee, maybe that's what—"

"Don't you Chickadee me, you–you *beast!*" Mrs. Harrison leaped to her feet. "*I'll* tell you what's wrong! That mechanical brain or whatever it is–that thing you call Bessie. She *loves* you! She loves you–and she's jealous of *me!* That's what's wrong. When you ordered the piano, she sent you two extras. It was the same with the coats, because it was you. But whenever I ordered something, just look what I got–rabbits and birdbaths and hippopotamus feet!" She stamped on the floor. "Well, you just get all that junk out of my house, do you hear? Send it back to your

Bessie. Oh, if you could've seen the look on that Mr. Quandt's face when they brought it all up! Like–like we'd *stolen* it! Oh! Oooh, Eberhard dear, what will we *do-o-o?*"

She collapsed on his chest. Again she burst into tears. They clung to each other. Presently, between sobs, "That awful m-machine," Mrs. Harrison moaned. "She l-loves you. And I l-love you too. The nerve of the thing, s-sending me all that old trash! And s-sending you p-p-presents like that! Well, you can just choose between us, that's all. If you want me to stay, you can just send every bit of it back!"

Mr. Harrison was trying desperately not to think of the expression on Mr. Quandt's face–and of his probable fate if the police got wind of his little affair with Bessie. However, he got a grip on himself. He pointed out that Bessie was just a machine. He explained that she didn't really *love* him, not even as much as a Cuddlypet would have. It was merely a matter of circuits, of condensers and things. He also explained that, much as he wanted to get rid of the stuff that was cluttering the place, it would be taking too big a risk. Of course, he could drop all that lettuce down the garbage disposer, and he guessed he could sneak out some night and let the rabbits loose in the park. But they'd just have to live with the rest of the stuff for a year or two, maybe selling it off or giving it away bit by bit. If they did that, and didn't let anyone in the apartment, and didn't have any friends in, maybe they'd be safe enough. Mr. Quandt couldn't have talked to the police; if he had, they would've been there by now. And tomorrow he himself would go down to Moss-Eagleberg's, and he'd take the Schroeder Bypass right out, and erase all the records, and they'd have no more trouble–because Bessie was just a machine after all.

While Mr. Harrison was explaining all this, he had to take time out fairly frequently to declare that he did *too* love his Chickadee; to protest that he'd done it for her, and *not* just because he didn't like cats; to point out that after all she *did* have four iridium-mink coats.

Finally, a relative calm was restored. They kissed and made

up. Together, they spent several hours in pushing and hauling. They stuffed all the closets. The duck blind went under a piano with the rabbits. The small Japanese automobile was parked in the bathroom. When, exhausted, they crept into bed, a navigable channel had been dredged through the hall, and part of the living-room carpet was actually visible.

"Oh, I do hope things'll work out," Mrs. Harrison sighed, as she turned out the light. "I'm still sort of scared. I can't believe that your Bessie is just a mechanical brain. I–I think she's *alive*."

Mr. Harrison slept rather poorly. First he dreamed that he was working on Bessie, installing Schroeder Bypasses and Dappleby Blocks. The Dappleby Blocks kept blowing up like balloons and exploding, and every time one would blow up, Bessie would purr and purr, and he'd reach for a wire and find whiskers instead, or a handful of fur. And then Winkler and Swartz would come in, and they'd dance around him carrying umbrellas over their heads. And Mr. Olson was there, singing Cuddlypets commercials in his concrete-mixer voice. And finally the fur and the whiskers came up all around Mr. Harrison, like tall grass, and Mr. Quandt opened up a big door and out came these critters wearing athletic supporters. And Mr. Olson was one of them, somehow, and he was singing:

> "Cudd-lee-pets, Cudd-lee-pets,
> Snuggle up to Cudd-lee-pets!
> Sweet as sugar, big as busses–
> CUDDLYHIPPOPOTAMUSES!"

Mr. Harrison woke up, in an icy sweat. He took two sleeping tablets. Fifteen minutes later, he found himself in a police station, under a big, bright light which had something to do with the new psychiatric technique. Dr. Schroeder and Dr. Dappleby were dressed up as policemen, and they were holding him down while Mr. Olson read aloud from a list of the things Bessie had sent him, and every time he read one out Mr. Kerfoid erased a word from his B. S. diploma in Cyber-Surgery, until there weren't any left and the diploma was blank. Then a steam whistle went off in his head, and his mind went all whirly, and the next thing he knew he was out on the street, on all fours, and he felt *different* somehow. He looked around at himself and saw that he was covered with iridium-mink fur. There was a collar around his neck, and a leash, and Dr. Schroeder was leading him–hop, skip, jump, hop, skip, jump. And he felt so grateful to Dr. Schroeder for feeding him all that wonderful, juicy, raw Syntho-horse that he rubbed up against him and purred. And then it wasn't Dr. Schroeder any more, but a little Japanese auto pulling him into Bessie's control room, which was a mouth full of teeth, and behind every tooth was a policeman, and they were all purring, purring, purr—

Mr. Harrison was not in good shape when he rose. He gulped down his coffee, pretended to shave, and went off to Jonson, Williamson, Selznick, and Jones. He found Mr. Jonson, who looked at him queerly and made some remark about "godawful benders."

"Mr. Jonson," he asked, as casually as he could, "did you ever hear of Charge Reference records getting into the permanent memory bank of one of those big department store brains? I mean so there'd be no control over what the machine did?"

"That just couldn't happen," Mr. Jonson assured him. "It's impossible. Only living creatures can function that way."

Mr. Harrison sighed.

He forced himself to wait until noon. Then he hurried down to Moss-Eagleberg's. Sure enough, there was only one sub-professional on duty in the control room, a wide, red-faced, cheerful sort of a fellow.

"I'm from Jonson, Williamson, Selznick, and Jones," Mr. Harrison said. "Did a job on this brain a while back. How's she getting along?"

"Say, you must be Mr. Harrison!" The man grinned, got to his feet, held out his hand. "Filmore's the name. I heard all about you. Winkler told me all about how you brought Bessie back from the dead. Well, she's just fine–she's just *purring* along."

Mr. Harrison bit his lip. "That's good. But maybe I'd better give her a checkup anyhow. There'll be no extra charge. It's part of our regular service."

"That's mighty white of you, Mr. Harrison. Bessie'll appreciate that."

Mr. Harrison counted to ten. He managed a smile. "Oh, by the way," he said, opening his kit. "I seem to have forgotten my replacement transistors. They're in a box on the seat of my car. It's parked on the third-level lot. If I give you the key could you—?"

"Get 'em for you? Say, I'll be glad to, Mr. Harrison."

As soon as the man had departed, he closed the door, locked it, went down the stairs as fast as he could, and tore out the Schroeder Bypass and all its connections. Then he came up again, plugged in the mike, asked for the file on Mr. and Mrs. E. Howard Harrison. As soon as the numbers showed up on the typer, he flipped the switch from RECORD over to TOTAL ERASURE. The Machine clicked and whirred. A little red light blinked three times. All the Harrison data had been removed, deleted, expunged.

"Boy, *that* does it!" Mr. Harrison murmured in triumph. Joy and relief surged in his heart. He burst into song:

> "Pussycats are full of germs,
> Dogs have nasty fleas and worms,
> That's not what I want to get–
> Mom, I want a CUDD-LEE-PET!"

And, on the final note, he unplugged the typer, flipped the switches back where they belonged, and pulled out the mike. When the subprofessional came back with the spare transistors, he was packing his kit.

Mr. Harrison went away whistling. He stopped at a phone on the way to the shop, and called up his wife, and told her that their troubles were over. All that afternoon, he worked like a beaver.

He came home at his regular time. He rang the bell. Nobody answered. He knocked. When the thought he heard someone stirring inside, he called, "Chickadee, are you home?" several times. Finally, he took out his key and tried to open the door. Something seemed to be blocking it, something too heavy to shove.

He frowned. He began to feel frightened. After hesitating a minute or two, he went downstairs to the apartment under his own, and persuaded the inquisitive elderly lady who lived there to let him through to the fire escape, promising to let her know *right away* if he found anything wrong.

Luckily, the kitchen window hadn't been latched. He crawled in. A glance was enough to inform him that something quite dreadful had happened. One end of the kitchen was filled with identical packages. They were stacked round the freezer, and they reached almost up to the ceiling. And that wasn't all. On the table, weighted down, was a note.

Slowly, with a horrible feeling of doom, Mr. Harrison read it.

Dear Eberhard,
  I have been a good wife to you the best I know how even if you aren't a real professional any more like Elmer Maginnis. If it was another woman I could forgive you I guess–but this is *too much*. I have gone home to Mother. I have taken only what really is mine, like my mink coats. You won't be lonely, because your Bessie has *everything*. If you don't believe me, just look in the living-room.

  Your wife, Mignonetta (Chickadee)

Like an automaton, Mr. Harrison went into the hall. He found it filled with huge square objects, and he clambered up over them. At the living-room door he paused, struggling feebly against the compulsion to open it. He watched his hand reach for the knob, turn it, push the door ajar. He went in.

There they were, as he had known they would be when he walked through the Syntho-horse packages in the kitchen and over the king-sized cat-boxes in the hall. They were everywhere–on and under the pianos, on the chairs, on the mantelpiece. They were sitting there happily, small, medium, and large, striped and mottled and spotted.

The Cuddlypets saw Mr. Harrison. All together, they rose. They all started purring. They came padding toward him—

There was love in their eyes.

MARY CELESTIAL by Miriam Allen deFord and Anthony Boucher

Literary collaborations are not always the product of two writers getting together, in whatever fashion, to create a piece of work. There is another, less well-known type: the author-editor collaboration.

When this story first appeared in The Magazine of Fantasy & Science Fiction *in 1955, it was introduced with the following comments by then-editor Anthony Boucher: "More often than readers suspect, a story carrying a solo by-line has been so extensively replotted and even rewritten by the editor that it is actually a collaboration . . . I know, for instance, that many of my own stories anthologized from* Astounding *should, if I were a wholly scrupulous man, bear the credit-line 'by Anthony Boucher and John W. Campbell, Jr.' Miriam Allen deFord is, I have discovered, a singularly scrupulous woman; after this story passed back and forth between us a number of times, she decided that it should carry a collaborative by-line. I hope you like the result."*

We liked it fine. And we think you will, too.

Miriam Allen deFord (1888-1975) had a remarkable career which spanned six decades and a wide spectrum of literary endeavor: mystery, mainstream, and science fiction; nonfiction of many different types; poetry, book reviews, and critical essays. One of her fact-crime books, The Overbury Affair, *was awarded the Mystery Writers of America Edgar in 1960. She edited one s-f anthology,* Space, Time, and Crime *(1964), and the best of her short work in the field appears in* Xenogenesis *(1969) and* Elsewhere, Elsewhen *(1971).*

Anthony Boucher (1911-1968) has often been referred to as a Renaissance Man; he was, among other things, a writer, critic, anthologist, musicologist, raconteur, expert poker player, budding politician, the finest and fairest reviewer of mystery fiction that field has ever known, and one of science fiction's three greatest editors (the other two being, of course, John W. Campbell and Horace Gold). Most of his s-f and fantasy short shories are included in Far and Away (1953) and The Compleat Werewolf (published posthumously in 1969). Like Miriam deFord, he did not publish a science fiction novel (although one of his 1940s mysteries, Rocket to the Morgue, as by H. H. Holmes, is well known for its early science fictional background). "Mary Celestial" is his–and Miriam's–only piece of fiction with a shared by-line.

MARY CELESTIAL

By Miriam Allen Deford and Anthony Boucher

Xilmuch was discovered – once. It was discovered in 3942 by Patrick Ostronsky-Vierra, a Two Star Scout of the Galactic Presidium.

It is easy to find–it is in fact Planet IV of Altair. If it were not a little off the beaten track it would have been discovered long before. It is almost precisely the size of our Earth, has similar atmosphere, rotation, gravity, and climatic conditions. It is two-thirds land surface, and in every way is admirably adapted to human habitation. It has been the home of beings indistinguishable from humans, and was once the seat of a high civilization very like our own of the 40th century, except in minor details.

There are no noxious animal forms (the only beasts are herbivorous and inoffensive), and there are no human inhabitants who would resist colonization.

And yet, no matter how overcrowded the colonized planets may become, Xilmuch (that was its name in the dominant native language) will never be discovered again. It will never be colonized. Not after the report Patrick Ostronsky-Vierra brought back in 3942.

He landed in what seemed to be its largest city, after a preliminary survey of the entire planet in his little one-man scout ship. There was a beautiful airport, equipped for planes of every description. It was not in good repair. Squirrel-like animals infested the hangars full of grounded atmosphere-ships. Grass was growing between cracks in the wide runways. A storm had leveled what had been a huge neo-neon beacon.

Patrick spent two days exploring the city on foot. There were multitudes of parked surface cars and of helicopter-like planes, some of which had crashed and were piles of junk. All had been propelled by some fuel unknown to him, all the tanks were empty, and he could not find any stores of fuel that he could recognize. A good many of the main streets had moving sidewalks under plastic roofs, and some were still operating by remote control. It was the sort of civilization which in his experience implied the services of robots, but no robots of any kind were visible.

He explored systematically, starting at one end of the city and circling closer and closer to the center, which appeared to be a huge civic or control area, with overgrown parks, large imposing buildings, and a forest of tri-dimensional televiz masts. The city itself stood on the banks of a wide river, an arm of which had been diverted to run in a circle around this Civic Center, with numerous bridges between.

He went in and out of private houses, what seemed to be hotels, stores, warehouses, schools, halls, factories, and one building apparently a center of worship. Not one solitary human being met him, nor any other living creature higher in the scale of evolution than the equivalent of a cow. The cow-like creatures were not abundant, but they looked well fed; apparently they browsed on the vegetation of the many parks and gardens. It was unthinkable that they could be the dominant race. This civilization had been built by animals with developed cortices and opposable thumbs.

The planet was as advanced artistically as it was scientifically. In the homes, under thick layers of dust, were delicate jewels and piles of beautiful thin coins engraved in strange designs. The walls of the larger buildings were all carved in bas-relief, in a manner nearer to ancient Mayan art than to any other Patrick knew. Demonology must have played a large part in the religion, for there were numerous carvings of small winged beings with long Grecoesque features and what looked like lightning-bolts for arms and legs. In the temple, a grotesque and horrible statue, a hundred feet high, filled most of the great nave.

There were no libraries or museums, no books, no paintings, no musical instruments, no microfilm. Yet the inhabitants must have had some means of visual and auditory public communication, judging by the televiz masts at the Civic Center.

Patrick camped for his first two nights in the nearest house, spreading his blanket on a rug because the beds were too thick in dust. He had his own food supplies in a knapsack, but the stores were full of shelves of metal containers obviously (though he could not understand the drawings on the labels) with edible contents. He sampled one or two, after testing them for harmlessness, and found one to be a preserved fruit with a pleasant subacid flavor, another a sort of paste resembling *pâte de foie gras* mixed with caviar. There was also a pale pink liquid in a plastic bottle which turned out to be a delicate wine somewhat like *vin rosé*.

He felt like a cross between Goldilocks and Alice.

On the third day he passed over a bridge to the Civic Center. The buildings in their disheveled parks were grouped around a spreading stone edifice with a dome, which he took to be the City Hall. It was morning, a beautiful sunny summer day in the bluish whiteness of Altair. The ragged trees, something like oaks, were full of white and green birds, all singing their little hearts out. A metal fountain, carved in the likeness of a spreading tree, was spouting water from the tips of its branches into a little pond. The grass was covered with myriads of low-growing, velvety purple flowers run wild. Patrick took the broad road, whose ornamental green and brown tiles showed wide gaps through which grassy blades grew thickly, that led to the central building. A long flight of steps ended at a massive bronze-like door, heavily and intricately carved.

Before his eyes, the door opened. A man stood for a second in the doorway, then dashed down the steps toward him.

Patrick braced himself and reached for his raygun. But the man's arms were opened wide, his mouth was stretched in an ecstatic smile, and tears were running down his cheeks.

He was a tall, burly man, seemingly in late middle age; his hair was white but his movements were lithe and supple. He was clean-shaven, and was dressed in a sort of overall made of a grey fabric which looked both soft and durable. He called out something in a harsh guttural tongue. The scout shook his head.

"Welcome, welcome to Xilmuch!" cried the man then in perfect Standard Galactic. "Who are you? How did you get here? Where are you from? I was never so glad to see anyone in all my life!"

He gave Patrick no time to answer. Seizing him by the arm, he hustled him inside.

It had been an official building all right, Patrick could see that. There was a great lobby rising unimpeded to the dome, with an enormous wasteful central staircase. There were banks of levescalators on either side, and wide hallways led to ground-floor offices with transparent plastic doors running from floor to ceiling.

But half the rooms to the right had been transformed into a dwelling place. Patrick was hurried into a living-room whose stone floors were covered with thick grey rugs into which his boots sank. There were couches and low chairs, heavy cream-colored curtains at all the tall windows, long tables of a dark gleaming wood, their legs carved in flowers and birds.

An inner door opened, revealing a corner of a white shining room that must be a kitchen. A woman burst through it and ran to them.

She was about as old as the man, sturdy also, but too plump, with grey hair elaborately curled. She too was dressed in an overall, but hers was bright purple and over it she wore a fancy apron of lace with pink bows at its corners. She had been pretty once, in a vapid way–probably a piquant blonde of the buttercup-and-daisy variety.

She burst into excited chatter in the unknown tongue, clutching at the man's hand. Her voice was high and twittering, with a whine beneath it. The man answered her, and though Patrick could not understand the words, the contemptuous tone was clear enough. The scolding ran off her like water; she gazed at the man meltingly, then turned to stare angrily at the Terran.

The man disengaged himself from her. In Galactic he said to the scout:

"Oh, this is wonderful! A visitor–a visitor at last!

"We must celebrate. We will have a feast. The last case of *rexshan* I could find–I must open it now. Tell me what you want: if there is any of it left, it is yours.

"Oh, what a miracle! Somebody to talk to after so terribly long!"

The woman had sidled up and cuddled against the man, holding his hand to her cheek. He jerked away impatiently, and barked what must have been an order, for she nodded brightly and trotted back to the kitchen, throwing a kiss as she went. The man shrugged as if throwing off a weight and turned to Patrick with undisguised relief.

"Sit here," he said. "It is the most comfortable. And now tell me who you are, my friend, and how you found me."

Patrick showed his credentials. The stranger shook his head. He explained them in words. The man nodded sagely.

"I understand. I had never dared to hope for a visitor from

beyond Xilmuch. But I have heard of space travel, though we never attained it."

"And yet you speak Galactic."

"Is that what it is? That is one of my–But tell me first–"

"No, *you* tell *me*. Who are you? What happened to this city? Why did I see nobody in three days, until I found you and–and the lady? Is all your world like this?"

"My name is Zoth–Zoth Cheruk, but you must call me Zoth, and I shall call you Patrick. All the rest you ask–I shall be glad to tell you everything, but we have plenty of time. We'll talk and talk! But first I want to know all about *you*, your world, how you all live, your own life–everything. I have been so starved for conversation–you can't imagine how much, or how long!"

"But oughtn't we to be helping the lady?" Patrick asked uneasily.

"Her name is Jyk. She is my wife." He scowled. "She can manage. She cooks well, at least. It will take her hours; I have ordered all the best for us. Meanwhile, we will drink while we wait."

He opened a tall cabinet with carved doors and took out goblets and a squat yellow bottle.

"Not *rexshan*–we shall have that at dinner. But almost as good; it is pure *stralp* of a very good year."

He poured an iridescent liquid.

"You smell it for a few minutes, then you sip, then you smell it again," he explained.

"Like brandy," Patrick agreed.

"That I do not know. But that is as good a place to start as any. Tell me of your foods and drinks."

There was no help for it. This guy was going to give in his own good time only. Planet scouts are trained in diplomacy. Patrick settled down to being a vocal encyclopedia attached to a question-machine.

Twice they were interrupted by calls from the kitchen. Each time Zoth rose reluctantly and went out, first replenishing Patrick's goblet; he could be heard lifting and setting down some

Mary Celestial _____ *115*

heavy object, his annoyed voice interrupted by his wife's cooing tones. The relation between the two puzzled Patrick as much as anything else he had chanced upon in this strange world, this seeming *Mary Celeste* of the space-seas.

Several hours and several glasses of the iridescent *stralp* later, he was feeling only relaxed and very hungry. Zoth's wife appeared in the kitchen door, rosy and dimpling. This time Zoth beamed. "Now we shall eat," he said. "We are having a tender young *ekahir* I had been saving in the freezing-box. I shall bring it in."

Jyk–what ought he to call her? Mrs. Cheruk–cleared one of the long tables and from the lower part of the cabinet took dishes of some transparent plastic, golden yellow and delicately etched. She drew from a drawer knives and spoons–there were no forks–of a metal that looked like steel. Patrick hurried to help her. Her manner was distrait, and she kept glancing yearningly toward the kitchen. Presently Zoth entered, bearing a large tray heaped with steaming food.

The *ekahir* turned out to be a crisply roasted bird, its flesh tasting like a combination of turkey and duck. Zoth carved it adroitly, using a long thin knife with a carved metal handle, while his wife piled the plates high with unknown but interesting-looking vegetables. The *rexshan,* poured into tall slender glasses, proved to be a cool bubbling wine, with a warm aftertaste and an insidious effect.

The food was delicious, the drink delightful, and the Terran's appetite sharp; but after his first hunger was satisfied, Patrick found himself increasingly disquieted.

Something he could not understand was very wrong between these two. He didn't need to comprehend the words they exchanged to realize that Zoth loathed his wife, and that she worshiped him. There was scorn in every harsh command he gave her, and to each she hastened to respond with servile promptness. It got on Patrick's nerves, until at last Zoth himself noticed, and made an obvious effort to restrain himself.

The climax came when Jyk, watching her husband's plate with anxious solicitude, suddenly jumped from her seat, carried a dish of tart blue jelly to Zoth's place, placed a portion of it on his plate, and caressingly threw her other arm around his neck just as he was raising a spoonful of *ekahir* to his mouth.

The meat fell from his jostled arm to the table, and he leapt to his feet. The angry syllables he shouted were unmistakably a curse.

Then suddenly, before Patrick could take in what was happening, Zoth seized the long knife with which he had carved the bird–and plunged it full into his wife's breast.

Patrick dived and caught him by the arm before he could strike again. Shaking with horror, he turned his eyes to the victim.

She was not dead, she had not fallen, she was not even bleeding. With a gay laugh she plucked the knife from her flesh, chirped a few words in a tone of affectionate teasing, patted her husband's cheek, and returned amiably to her place at the foot of the table, where she calmly helped herself to more of the jelly.

Patrick's hand fell. He stood staring in paralyzed astonishment. Zoth laughed then too–but his laugh was half a groan.

"Forgive me for interrupting our meal so impolitely, my friend," he said. "Sometimes this woman exasperates me beyond endurance–but, as you see, it does her no harm."

Patrick could only continue to stare, as he slowly resumed his seat.

As for Jyk, she sat drinking *rexshan*, and smiling at her husband as a mother smiles at her naughty child.

Patrick's appetite was gone; he sat uncomfortably waiting for an explanation that did not come. Zoth cleaned the last scrap from his plate, drained the last drop of *rexshan*, and only then addressed a few curt remarks to his wife. She rose quickly and began removing the dishes. The host turned to his guest.

"Exercise is good after a full meal, Patrick. Let us walk for a while around the city, and I will show you how I get our food and all our supplies. There is still much I have not yet asked you about your world."

"There is much *I* want to know also, Zoth," the Terran reminded him.

"Later; there is no hurry. When it is dark I shall send the

woman off to bed alone, and then we shall sit over glasses of *stralp* and you may ask me anything you wish to know. But now you must tell me more of this Galactic Presidium, and how it operates. You say there is an agreement by which hitherto undiscovered planets are opened for colonization by whatever lifeform is best adapted to them? You may imagine how much this interests me, since I can detect no difference whatever between your form and mine–we are *akkir* together."

"*Akkir*–that means human?"

"Yes. And here is a whole empty world, with all the foundations of civilization already laid."

"I am only a scout, you understand," said Patrick. "I have no authority."

"I understand. But your recommendation would have great influence. I am only wondering how long it would take. Perhaps it would be better . . . However, all that we can discuss later. Now I want to ask you–"

Patrick turned again into a vocal encyclopedia.

Their walk took them to a large warehouse. Zoth opened the door.

"Here, you see," he explained, "are stored garments made of furs–furs of the carnivorous animals which no longer exist on Xilmuch. When it is cold, and we need warm clothing, we have only to take our pick. In the same way, all the stores and warehouses of the city are open to us to obtain whatever we desire in the way of food, clothes, furniture, ornaments–anything at all. There is only one real scarcity: *rhaz,* the fuel by which we run our planes and cars. I have stored all of that I could find in our house, which was once the City Hall, and I use a vehicle only when it is necessary to carry heavy loads. Otherwise, I walk. One man cannot operate the *rhaz* supplier, though when mine is gone I shall have to find some way."

"What about public utilities?" Patrick asked. "Water, lights, things like that?"

"Enough is still operating automatically to serve us. Much, of course, has failed. If, before I–if we of Xilmuch had only learned to split the atom, as you say your world has done–But we hadn't, and so, you will understand, there is great deterioration in such things, though they could be easily rehabilitated with sufficient manpower. After all, it has been fifty years.''

"Fifty years since what?"

"Shall we turn back now? I don't want to tire you, and the sun will be setting soon. There are no street lights any more, and I shouldn't like you to stumble in our ruts and gullies in the darkness. Besides, I'm thirsty again, and so must you be. The woman will have finished cleaning up; I shall have her set out some refreshment for us and send her off.''

They had walked farther than Patrick had realized; it was twilight before they crossed the bridge to the Civic Center where the great dome dominated the skyline. A glow of lights came from the right-hand windows on the first floor, and as they mounted the steps they found Jyk pacing up and down before the bronze door.

As soon as she glimpsed them, she ran toward them and threw her arms around her husband with a babble of speech. Zoth pulled away impatiently.

"The fool thought she had lost me," he said with a wry grin. "This is the first time I have been this long out of her sight in fifty years. She insists on following me everywhere I go, and it's not worth the trouble to get rid of her when I have no other companion–but today, when I have you–today I ordered her to stay at home and leave me free. She has been weeping. I am glad of it. Let her weep.''

Pretty cool, thought Patrick, for a man who had just tried to murder his wife in cold bood, and had failed to do so only by a miracle!

The big municipal-office-turned-living-room was aglow with tubes of soft neo-neon light, and he sank wearily into one of the soft chairs. The cream-colored curtains were drawn, but through a gap he could see the dark sky. This world, he had found, had no moon; and since the city lay near the equator, twilight and dawn were very brief.

He could have done with some sleep; but after all, a scout is a sort of diplomat: if his host were looking forward to a long evening, there was nothing to do but acquiesce. Besides, curiosity was scratching at him; he could make nothing at all of the personal situation here, and it was time for Zoth to talk.

Zoth addressed his wife in a series of staccato remarks. She bustled obediently into the kitchen, while her husband laid out the goblets and fresh bottles of the *stralp*. In a few minutes she returned, bearing a plate heaped with strips of some crisp white substance glistening with what looked like salt. She threw her arms around her husband's neck, and, standing on tiptoe, pressed kisses on his unresponsive face. Patrick looked about him nervously, but this time Zoth stood uncomplainingly like a statue, his fists clenched. He said a few curt words, and Jyk disentangled herself and with a rebellious pout bowed unsmilingly to Patrick, making no attempt to dissemble her jealousy. She departed slowly through another door.

"Ah!" said the host, stretching luxuriously. "She will not dare to trouble us again tonight." He poured the glasses full. "You cannot imagine what this means to me! At last–an evening of social conversation with a congenial friend! I have waited so long–I had almost ceased to hope."

"I think it is your turn to talk now," said the scout coldly.

"I know. You are right. And I can see that you are displeased with me. You think me rude and brutal, you think I abuse a poor woman whose only fault is that she adores me too much. But when you have heard–"

"You tried to kill her, at dinner."

"Precisely: she angered me beyond endurance . . . and I *tried*. You observed that I did not succeed."

Patrick recovered his aplomb.

"I apologize," he said. "It is not my business to judge what I cannot understand. But you will realize I must be puzzled."

"I do indeed. And you are my friend–my first friend in fifty years. I will tell you everything you want to know. Only, it is hard to know how to start.

"Tell me: in your world, are there . . . beings . . . persons that are not human?"

Patrick smiled indulgently. "Some people in my world believe so. Everybody believed so once."

"Here also. Only, I have proved that they are real."

Oh, come now! Patrick thought. *Fairy tales at this point?* "You have?" he said in his best diplomatic manner.

"As you see about you . . . Then, have you a story that one may force such a being to do one's will?"

"We do have a myth–a symbol which has inspired some of our greatest artists–about selling one's soul to the devil–"

"Oh, as with the Nameless!" Zoth turned pale and raised his arms high, the thumbs and forefingers firmly pressed together. "Do not speak of Him!"

Patrick remembered the terrifying hundred-foot statue in the nave of the great temple. Unreasoningly, he knew that this was the Nameless; and for a moment he felt less scornful of the fairy tale.

"No," Zoth went on; "what I mean is closer to the simple *akkir* plane. These are lesser beings, but powerful enough. If one of them can be brought into your power, he can be compelled to grant you five wishes. You have such?"

"Fairies, leprechauns, demons . . I see what you mean. But on Earth it is, according to legend, only three wishes that he grants."

"You are luckier than we."

So Zoth's Standard Galactic, the scout thought with amusement, was not so altogether perfect as he had assumed–*luckier* when he meant *less lucky.* Patrick hid a smile as Zoth refilled their goblets.

"I shall tell you the whole story. It is the easiest way to make it clear."

. . . if not necessarily convincing, Patrick thought. *And yet,* he asked himself, *have you, my bright Galactic scout, found any normal rational method of accounting for this deserted planet, this celestial* Mary Celeste?

"Fifty years ago I was twenty-three years old. You look surprised. I can age like other *akkir,* but I can never be senile.

"I was young. I was poor. I had a mean job I hated. I was lonely, with no close friends–I, so gregarious a man–and I was madly in love with a girl who would not even look at me. I was in despair.

"How the *grosh* was summoned to me and how he came under my power I shall not tell you. It would be too hard to make it plain, and besides, these are secret things better not told. But he came, and I did subdue him to my will."

"The *grosh*–that's the demon?"

"You may call him so; he is in any event a being like neither you nor me, nor any material creature. I may tell you that my own grandfather was a *vardun*–a priest in the great temple of the Nameless in this city–and from him, though I myself was not chosen to be a *vardun,* I had learned many things in my boyhood."

He repeated the propitiatory gesture–the arms raised and the thumbs and forefingers pressed together.

"So there I was, with five wishes at my disposal. Even then–though I never guessed–" Zoth shuddered–"I thought it wise not to use up all of them at once, but to keep one at least in reserve. You will see how wise that was–but still not wise enough.

"What does anyone want? Long life, health, wealth, love, fame perhaps, though that I did not care about: and if one's heart is good, one wants also good fortune for others as well. I was canny; I had speculated long, to get into small compass as much as possible of the things I craved and had never had."

"Understandably," Patrick nodded. "We are of different worlds, Zoth, but of the same nature."

"So I wished, first, to live to a hundred years at least, and always in good health and strength, without injury or illness. 'Granted,' said the *grosh.*

"Then I wished, not for great wealth which may be a burden, but that I should never lack for any comfort or luxury I might desire. And, since I am one who loves my fellow-beings, loves company and good talk–I, who for fifty years have spoken only to that silly creature in there!–I specified that among these comforts and luxuries must be the ability to converse freely with every person I ever met. You must realize that in Xilmuch at that time there were different communities, all equal, but speaking different tongues–"

"You mean, different nations?"

"Of course; that is your word for them. I intended to travel much, and I wanted to be able to associate with all whom I met. So this, I stipulated, must be part of my second wish."

"So that's how you speak Standard Galactic, is it? That's puzzled me a lot."

"That is how. And if you had spoken any other language, I could have understood and spoken it just as well."

"And what was your third wish?" Patrick began to see a pattern forming–and wished that he did not.

Zoth paced the room, his glass of *stralp* in his hand. He glanced furtively at the door through which Jyk had vanished. Then he said in a shaking voice:

"I told the *grosh*–the Nameless forgive me!–that I wished that the girl with whom I was then so madly in love should love me in return, as madly and forever. I wished that she might be willing to marry me at once. And I wished that she should never leave me, but would live exactly as long as I did myself."

"And the *grosh* said, 'Granted.'"

"That's three wishes." Patrick hesitated. "Did you make any more?"

"One more. Do you know what a war is?"

"Certainly. It has been centuries since there has been a war on Earth, but in the past they were only too common. Even now, we must guard vigilantly against hostility and conflict between rival groups."

"We had not progressed so far. At one time or another, all of our various–nations, as you call them, on Xilmuch had been at one another's throats. We had torn one another almost to pieces, and as our science advanced our wars grew still more terrible. And at that very moment there was threat of a new war that would have advanced my own people, here in this city.

"I was an idealistic young man, who hated bloodshed. So for my fourth wish, I wished that everywhere on Xilmuch there should be complete and perpetual peace.

" 'Granted,' said the *grosh*.

"These were my four wishes. And I told the *grosh* that when I was ready to make the fifth, I would summon him: these beings are immortal, you know. I have still not made it."

"But I don't understand," Patrick objected. "It seems to me that those were all practicable wishes. And you say you had the–the *grosh* in your power. Didn't he really grant them?"

"He granted them all," said Zoth.

"As for the first, I am as you see me. I shall live at least 27 years more, and I shall never know illness or bodily pain. That wish I have no doubt the *grosh* granted me with pleasure–knowing that long before the end I should yearn in vain for death.

"And I have, as you observe, every comfort and luxury I could desire. I live in a palace, and I have at my disposal the food, the clothing, the furniture, all the paraphernalia of life of a great city. The supply, easily obtained, will certainly outlast my lifetime. As for the ability to converse with my fellow-beings in their own tongues, it is only today that I have had occasion to test it–and that with an *akkir* from a world of outer space. But you see it was granted to me."

"But the third wish? What went wrong about the girl you loved? How did the demon get out of really granting you that?"

"He didn't. . . . It was Jyk."

"Oh."

"I had thought my heart was broken when she spurned every advance I made. Now of her own accord she came to me: she loved me wildly, as she always will. I was in ecstasy.We were married at once. I was the happiest man on Xilmuch.

"How could I foresee that my own love would turn to loathing? But against my will, it did: first she bored me, then she disgusted me, now I hate her with all my heart.

"And she will be with me all my life. She will live exactly as long as I."

"So that's why–" Patrick exclaimed.

"Yes, that is why no knife, nor any other means, can ever rid me of her.

"I am ashamed that you saw that scene; it does not happen often. But can you imagine what it must be like to have someone, someone you detest, pester you with constant worship? Sometimes I think I shall go mad: nothing, nothing will ever offend or alienate her, and she clings to me every minute. I know she is not sleeping now; she will do whatever I tell her, but she is waiting for me right now with open arms; if I did not go to her eventually, she would seek me out, wherever I might be. And for fifty years there has been no *akkir* on Xilmuch but her and me!"

He paused, fighting for self-control.

"I don't want you to think I am naturally cruel," he went on in a calmer voice. "If I had pity left for anyone but myself, I should pity her. But I need not; she is happy just to be with me, however I treat her. Nearly always I can pretend patience. It was only today, when your coming had so excited me–"

The scout averted his eyes. Quickly, to change the subject, he asked:

"But your fourth wish? Did the demon grant you that?"

"Is there not peace on Xilmuch?" asked Zoth simply.

The Terran was silent. *Demons indeed! But this planet . . . the pattern . . .*

"Yes," his host went on, "the *grosh* knew. We *akkir* are not made by nature for perpetual peace–or we were not so made fifty years ago. The animals also . . . There is no animal on this planet now which fights with others for its mate, or kills others for its food.

"And there is great and lasting and perpetual peace today on Xilmuch."

Patrick said nothing. His host filled their glasses.

Finally the Terran broke the silence.

"Is there no way," he said hesitantly, "by which, with the wisdom you have acquired, you could use the fifth wish still at your disposal to undo some of the evil the demon did you?"

You might wish, Patrick thought, *to return your wife's love once more, and salvage that much out of the mess; but probably it's too late for that now.*

Zoth shook his head.

"Do you think I haven't worn myself out trying to find some way? The truth is, Patrick, I've been afraid to wish again–afraid he will twist that also to his own evil advantage. And then I should be completely defenseless, at his mercy.

"It is only today, my friend, that a bit of hope has come to me. How could even a *grosh*, I wonder, spoil so modest a wish? It is little enough to ask–I've been so horribly lonely–"

He looked long and speculatively at the Terran.

Patrick drained the last of his *stralp* and stood up. He felt himself trembling.

"Zoth," he said apologetically, "I hate to break this up, but I'm afraid I'm asleep on my feet. Let's go to bed now, shall we? Tomorrow's another day."

"Oh, my friend, forgive me! Of course–you must be worn out! What a way to treat a guest–and a guest who means so much to me! You must excuse an old man who has half a century of conversation to make up! I'll show you where you are to sleep."

He led the way through still a third door to another huge room, a corner of which had been screened off to hold a low couch covered with some soft woolly fabric.

"My guestroom," he smiled. "You are the first ever to occupy it. I hope you will find it comfortable. Right through here you will find the toilet facilities. You turn the light off thus.

"Sleep well, my friend. I shall be sleeping late in the morning myself–I don't often keep such hours as this. When you wake, come to the living hall, and a meal will be ready for you."

Patrick was alone at last.

He made no attempt to undress or go to bed. He had brought

his knapsack in with him, and he checked its contents. Then he sat quietly on the edge of the couch, thinking.

He sat there for two solid hours, until there was no glimmer of light anywhere and from a distant room came the sound of faint but steady snoring.

The tall windows opened outwards, and this was the ground floor. Outside, he put on his boots.

It was very dark. No one could have seen him as he crept from tree to tree, in the shadow of the overgrown ornamental bushes, to the nearest bridge.

Once across, he set out at as rapid a pace as possible. Even so, it took three hours, and the sky was beginning to gray, before he reached his ship.

An hour later, well beyond the orbit of Xilmuch, he began to wonder if he had made a fool of himself.

. . . Who ever heard of the entire population of a planet's being wiped out, just to grant somebody's wish for worldwide peace? Space knew, there were enough other roads to devastation! Wasn't the reasonable conclusion that in some entirely natural way, some epidemic or other frightful catastrophe on Xilmuch, only this man and his wife had survived? Wouldn't it be logical that such a shock would have crazed them both? Hadn't he spent a day and a night listening to the tale of a lunatic?

It was obvious that the man was desperately lonely, and would have kept his chance guest just as long as he could; but did it make sense that he could have done so by merely uttering an unused wish? Wasn't Patrick Ostronsky-Vierra just as crazy as Zoth Cheruk to swallow such a story, even late at night and full of *rexshan* and *stralp?*

. . . . But then why were there no carnivorous animals on Xilmuch, but plenty of herbivorous ones and every sort of vegetation? Catastrophes were not quite so selective as that.

And how . . . how else could Zoth have plunged a knife deep into his wife's breast–Patrick's horror-stricken eyes had seen the blade go in to the handle–and draw not a single drop of blood, elicit no sign of pain?

Xilmuch would be a wonderful planet for colonization. Its discovery would be the climax of his career as a scout; there would be no limit to his rise in the profession after that.

And how Zoth would welcome the colonists!

. . . And what unguessed harm he could do them unwittingly by that fifth wish of his!

In twenty-seven years or so Zoth and Jyk would both be dead. Zoth could do no harm then. But what would the Galactic Presidium think if a scout should announce that here was a perfect colonization-point–only it must not be approached while an old man was still alive who might jinx them?

And with or without Zoth, how about a planet evidently full of mischievous, rancorous, double-crossing *grosh*, with who knew what bags of tricks in their possession?

To say nothing of the Nameless, that distinctly unpretty god or devil whose image Patrick had seen for himself.

Patrick Ostronsky-Vierra, trusted and dedicated Two Star Scout, decided deliberately to violate his sacred oath of office.

When he returned to the headquarters of the Galactic Presidium, his report read:

"I visited Planet IV of Altair, which has been hitherto undiscovered, and which on first approach appeared to be suitable for colonization. On further investigation I found that the atmosphere consists mostly of methane. The planet itself is still in a semi-molten state, with incessant volcanic eruptions and violent windstorms of ethane gas.

"I advise that the planet be given a wide berth–permanently. It is completely unfit for human habitation."

But there was another report: a private one. It was found among Ostronsky-Vierra's effects after his death in 4009. It was in a plastic closure marked: *For the Sealed Files of the Galactic Presidium. To Be Opened 50 Years after Receipt.*

In it was this complete narrative as I, Mari Swenskold-Wong, Secretary of the Presidium in this year 4060, read it to the entire Presidium at its meeting upon February 30.

We are still, as everyone knows, in great need of more livingspace in the colonized planets. There has been much discussion of the possibility of colonizing Xilmuch, and there will be much more discussion, perhaps even insistence upon the part of the Opposition.

But the majority opinion, in which I concur, is that no foreseeable Galactic situation, even the mounting pressure of expansion, can justify sending colonists to what Ostronsky-Vierra justly labled the *Mary Celeste* of space. Empty of Zoth Cheruk and his Jyk it must be by now, but not of its Nameless and its *grosh* (and who can say what powerful type of unknown life-form hides behind these supernatural masks?).

Superstitious, I hope I may safely say, we surely are not; but neither are we, in our Chairman's ringing words, "reckless damn fools." There are other worlds.

THE QUAKER CANNON by Frederik Pohl and C. M. Kornbluth

Frederik Pohl and C. M. Kornbluth need little introduction in an anthology of science fiction collaboration; they are the best known of all the field's writing teams, and their 1953 novel, The Space Merchants, *is outrightly famous. They have had individual careers of genuine value, and in this decade Pohl has emerged, after a preceding decade of relative authorial silence, as one of science fiction's major writing and editorial forces; but Pohl himself would probably concede that the best and most lasting of their work was done jointly. In addition to* The Space Merchants, *their science fiction novels include the superior* Wolfbane *and* Gladiator-at-Law; *and their one commercial novel,* Presidential Year, *a 1956 political satire, is first-rate work which has never received its due.*

Kornbluth (1923-1958) also collaborated, without equal literary success, with Pohl's (then) wife, Judith Merrill, on the 1952 Gunner Cade, *under the pseudonym of "Cyril Judd." Pohl (b. 1919) was involved in pre-Kornbluth collaborative short stories with several of the Futurians group, but has only done a small amount of partnership writing–notably, a trilogy with Jack Williamson–since Kornbluth's early, tragic death.*

"The Quaker Cannon," one of the team's very best short stories, is their only joint effort to be published in John W. Campbell's Astounding. *When it was finished by Pohl three years after Kornbluth's death, Campbell relented on his mysterious unwillingness to publish Pohl in his magazine (Kornbluth had appeared a few times); it is Pohl's only appearance in* Astounding *throughout Campbell's 33-year editorial tenure.*

The story is at the first rank of what these writers were doing, elegantly and well together, for a decade.

THE QUAKER CANNON
By Frederik Pohl and C. M. Kornbluth

I

Lieutenant John Kramer did crossword puzzles during at least eighty percent of his waking hours. His cubicle in Bachelor Officers Quarters was untidy; one wall was stacked solid with newspapers and magazines to which he subscribed for their puzzle pages. He meant, from week to week, to clean them out but somehow never found time. The ern, or erne, a sea eagle, soared vertically through his days and by night the ai, a three-toed sloth, crept horizontally. In edes, or Dutch communes, dyers retted ecru, quaffing ades by the tun and thought was postponed.

John Kramer was in disgrace and, at thirty-eight, well on his way to becoming the oldest first lieutenant in the North American–and Allied–Army. He had been captured in '82 as an aftermath of the confused fighting around Tsingtao. A few exquisitely unpleasant months passed and he then delivered three TV lectures for the yutes. In them he announced his total conversion to Neo-Utilitarianism, denounced the North American–and Allied–military command as a loathsome pack of war-raging, anti-utilitarian mad dogs, and personally admitted the waging of viral warfare against the United Utilitarian Republics.

The yutes, or Utilitarians, had been faithful to their principles. They had wanted Kramer only for what he could do for them, not for his own sweet self, and when they had got the juice out of him they exchanged him. In '83 he came out of his fog at Fort Bradley, Utah, to find himself being court-martialed.

He was found guilty as charged, and sentenced to a reprimand. The lightness of the sentence was something to be a little proud of, if not very much. It stood as a grudging tribute to the months he had held out against involutional melancholia in the yute Blank Tanks. For exchanged PW's, the severity of their courts-martial was in inverse proportion to the duration of their ordeal in Utilitarian hands. Soldiers who caved in after a couple of days of sense-starvation could look forward only to a firing squad. Presumably a returned soldier dogged–or rigid–enough to be driven into hopeless insanity without co-operating would have been honorably acquitted by his court, but such a case had not yet come up.

Kramer's "reprimand" was not the face-to-face bawling-out suggested to a civilian by the word. It was a short letter with numbered paragraphs which said (1) you are reprimanded, (2) a copy of this reprimand will be punched on your profile card. This tagged him forever as a foul ball, destined to spend the rest of his military life shuffling from one dreary assignment to another, without hope of promotion or reward.

He no longer cared. Or thought he did not; which came to the same thing.

He was not liked in the Officers Club. He was bad company. Young officers passing through Bradley on their way to glory might ask him, "What's it *really* like in a Blank Tank, Kramer?" But beyond answering, "You go nuts," what was there to talk about? Also he did not drink, because when he drank he went on to become drunk, and if he became drunk he would cry.

So he did a crossword puzzle in bed before breakfast, dressed, went to his office, signed papers, did puzzles until lunch, and so on until the last one in bed at night. Nominally he was Commanding Officer of the 561st Provisional Reception Battalion. Actually he was–with a few military overtones–the straw boss of a gang of clerks in uniform who saw to the arrival, bedding, feeding, equipping, inoculation and transfer to a training unit of one thousand scared kids per week.

On a drizzle-swept afternoon in the spring of '85 Kramer was sounding one of those military overtones. It was his appointed day for a "surprise" inspection of Company D of his battalion. Impeccable in dress blues, he was supposed to descend like a thunderbolt on this company or that, catching them all unaware, striding arrogantly down the barracks aisle between bunks, white-gloved and eagle-eyed for dust, maddened at the sight of disarray, vengeful against such contraband as playing cards or light reading matter. Kramer knew, quite well, that one of his orderly room clerks always telephoned the doomed company to warn that he was on his way. He did not particularly mind it. What he minded was unfair definitions of key words, and ridiculously variant spellings.

The permanent-party sergeant of D Company bawled "Tench-*hut!*" when Kramer snapped the door open and stepped crisply into the barracks. Kramer froze his face into its approved expression of controlled annoyance and opened his mouth to give the noncom his orders. But the sergeant had miscalculated. One of the scared kids was still frantically mopping the aisle.

Kramer halted. The kid spun around in horror, made some kind of attempt to present arms with the mop and failed. The mop shot from his soapy hands like a slung baseball bat, and its soggy gray head schlooped against the lieutenant's dress-blue chest.

The kid turned white and seemed about to faint on the damp board floor. The other kids waited to see him destroyed.

Kramer was mildly irritated. "At ease," he said. "Pick up that mop. Sergeant, confound it, next time they buzz you from the orderly room don't cut it so close."

The kids sighed perceptibly and glanced covertly at each other in the big bare room, beginning to suspect it might not be too bad after all. Lieutenant Kramer then resumed the expression of a nettled bird of prey and strode down the aisle. Long ago he had worked out a "random" selection of bunks for special attention and now followed it through habit. If he had thought about it any more, he would have supposed that it was still spy-proof; but every noncom in his cadre had long since discovered that Kramer stopped at either every second bunk on the right and every third on the left, or every third bunk on the right and every second on the left—depending on whether the day of the month was odd or even. This would not have worried Kramer if he had known it; but he never even noticed that the men beside the bunks he stopped at were always the best-shaved, best-policed and healthiest looking in each barracks.

Regardless, he delivered a certain quota of meaningless demerits which were gravely recorded by the sergeant. Of blue-eyed men on the left and brown-eyed men on the right–this, at least, had not been penetrated by the noncoms–he went on to ask their names and home towns. Before discovering crossword puzzles he had memorized atlases, and so he had something to say about every home town he had yet encountered. In this respect at least he considered himself an above-average officer, and indeed he was.

It wasn't the Old Army, not by a long shot, but when the draft age went down to fifteen some of the Old Army's little ways had to go. One experimental reception station in Virginia was trying out a Barracks Mother system. Kramer, thankful for small favors, was glad they hadn't put him on that project. Even here he was expected, at the end of the inspection, to call the "men" around him and ask if anything was bothering them. Something always was. Some gangling kid would scare up the nerve to ask, gee, lieutenant, I know what the Morale Officer said, but exactly *why* didn't we ever use the megaton-head missiles, and another would want to know how come Lunar Base was such a washout, tactically speaking, sir. And then he would have to rehearse the dry "recommended discussion themes" from the briefing books; and then, finally, one of them, nudged on by others, would pipe up, "Lieutenant, what's it *like* in the Blank Tanks?" And he would know that already, forty-eight hours after induction, the kids all knew about what Lieutenant John Kramer had done.

But today he was spared. When he was halfway through the rigmarole the barracks phone rang and the sergeant apologetically answered it.

He returned from his office-cubicle on the double, looking vaguely frightened. "Compliments of General Grote's secretary, sir, and will you report to him at G-1 immediately."

"Thank you, Sergeant. Step outside with me a moment."

Out on the duckboard walk, with the drizzle trickling down

his neck, he asked: "Sergeant, who is General Grote?"

"Never heard of him, sir."

Neither had Lieutenant Kramer.

He hurried to Bachelor Officers Quarters to change his sullied blue jacket, not even pausing to glance at the puzzle page of the *Times*, which had arrived while he was at "work." Generals were special. He hurried out again into the drizzle.

Around him and unnoticed were the artifacts of an army base at war. Sky-eye search radars popped from their silos to scan the horizons for a moment and then retreat, the burden of search taken up by the next in line. Helicopter sentries on guard duty prowled the barbed-wire perimeter of the camp. Fort Bradley was not all reception center. Aboveground were the barracks, warehouses and rail and highway termini for processing recruits–ninety thousand men and all their goods–but they were only the skin over the fort itself. They were, as the scared kids told each other in the dayrooms, naked to the air. If the yutes ever *did* spring a megaton attack, they would become a thin coating of charcoal on the parade ground, but they would not affect the operation of the *real* Fort Bradley a bit.

The *real* Fort Bradley was a hardened installation beneath meters of reinforced concrete, some miles of rambling warrens that held the North American–and Allied–Army's G-1. Its business was people: the past, present and future of every soul in the Army.

G-1 decided that a fifteen-year-old in Duluth was unlikely to succeed in civilian schools and drafted him. G-1 punched his Army test and civilian records on cards, consulted its card-punched tables of military requirements and assigned him, perhaps, to Machinist Training rather than Telemetering School. G-1 yanked a platoon leader halfway around the world from Formosa and handed him a commando for a raid on the yutes' Polar Station Seven. G-1 put foulball Kramer at the "head" of the 561st PRB. G-1 promoted and allocated and staffed and rewarded and punished.

Foulball Kramer approached the guardbox at the elevators to the warrens and instinctively squared his shoulders and smoothed his tie.

General Grote, he thought. He hadn't *seen* a general officer since he'd been commissioned. Not close up. Colonels and majors had court-martialed him. He didn't know who Grote was, whether he had one star or six, whether he was Assignment, Qualifications, Training, Evaluation, Psychological–or Disciplinary.

Military Police looked him over at the elevator head. They read him like a book. Kramer wore his record on his chest and sleeves. Dull gold bars spelled out the overseas months–for his age and arm, the Infantry, not enough. "Formosa," said a green ribbon, and "the storming of the beach" said a small bronze spearpoint on it. A brown ribbon told them "Chinese Mainland," and the stars on it meant that he had engaged in three of the five mainland campaigns–presumably Canton, Mukden and Tsingtao, since they were the first. After that, nothing. Especially not the purple ribbon that might indicate a wound serious enough to keep him out of further fighting.

The ribbons, his age and the fact that he was still a first lieutenant were grounds enough for the MPs to despise him. An officer of thirty-eight should be a captain at least. Many were majors and some were colonels. "You can go down, lieutenant," they told the patient foulball, and he went down to the interminable concrete tunnels of G-1.

A display machine considered the name *General Grote* when he typed it on its keyboard, and told him with a map where the general was to be found. It was a longish walk through the tunnels. While he walked past banks of clicking card-sorters and their servants he pondered other information the machine had gratuitously supplied:

GROTE. Lawrence W Lt Gen, 0-459732,
Unassigned

It did not lessen any of Kramer's puzzles. A three-star general, then. He couldn't *possibly* have anything to do with disciplining a lousy first-john. Lieutenant generals ran Army Groups, gigantic ad hoc assemblages of up to a hundred divisions, complete with air forces, missile groups, amphibious assault teams, even carrier and missile-sub task forces. The fact of his rank indicated that, whoever he was, he was an immensely able and tenacious person. He had gone through at least a twenty-year threshing of the wheat from the chaff, all up the screening and evaluation boards from second lieutenant to, say, lieutenant colonel, and then the murderous grind of accelerated courses at Command and General Staff School, the fanatically rigid selection for the War College, an obstacle course designed not to train the sub-standard up to competence but to keep them out. It was just this side of impossible for a human being to become a lieutenant general. And yet a few human beings in every generation did bulldoze their way through the little gap between the impossible and the almost impossible.

And such a man was unassigned?

Kramer found the office at last. A motherly, but sharp-eyed, WAC major told him to go right in.

John Kramer studied his three-star general while going through the ancient rituals of reporting-as-ordered. General Grote was an old man, straight, spare, white-haired, tanned. He wore no overseas bars. On his chest were all the meritorious ribbons his country could bestow, but none of the decorations of the combat soldier. This was explained by a modest sunburst centered over the ribbons. General Grote was, had always been, General Staff Corps. A desk man.

"Sit down, Lieutenant," Grote said, eying him casually. "You've never heard of me, I assume."

"I'm afraid not, sir."

"As I expected," said Grote complacently. "I'm not a dashing tank commander or one of those flying generals who leads his own raids. I'm one of the people who moves the dashing tank commanders and flying generals around the board like chess pieces. And now, confound it, I'm going to be a dashing combat leader at last. You may smoke if you like."

Kramer obediently lit up.

"Dan Medway," said the general, "wants me to start from scratch, build up a striking force and hit the Asian mainland across the Bering Strait."

Kramer was horrified twice–first by the reference to The Supreme Commander as "Dan" and second by the fact that he, a lieutenant, was being told about high strategy.

"Relax," the general said. "You're going to be my aide."

Kramer was horrified again. The general grinned.

"Your card popped out of the machinery," he said, and that was all there was to say about it, "and so you're going to be a highly privileged character and everybody will detest you. That's the way it is with aides. You'll know everything I know. And vice versa; that's the important part. You'll run errands for me, do investigations, serve as hatchet man, see that my pajamas are pressed without starch and make coffee the way I like it–coarse grind, brought to the boil for just a moment in an old-fashioned coffeepot. Actually what you'll do is what I want you to do from day to day. For these privileges you get to wear a blue *fourragére* around your left shoulder which marks you as a man not to be trifled with by colonels, brigadiers or MPs. That's the way it is with aides. And, I don't know if you have any outside interests, women or chess or drinking. The machinery didn't mention any. But you'll have to give them up if you do."

"Yes, sir," said Kramer. And it seemed wildly possible that he might never touch pencil to puzzle again. With something to *do*–

"We're Operation Ripsaw," said the general. "So far, that's me, Margaret out there in the office and you. In addition to other duties, you'll keep a diary of Ripsaw, by the way, and I want you to have a summary with you at all times in case I need it. Now call in Margaret, make a pot of coffee, there's a little stove thing in the washroom there, and I'll start putting together my general staff."

It started as small and as quietly as that.

II

It was a week before Kramer got back to the 561st long enough to pick up his possessions, and then he left the stacks of newspapers and magazines where they lay, puzzles and all. No time. The first person to hate him was Margaret, the motherly major. For all her rank over him, she was a secretary and he was an aide with a *fourragére* who had the general's willing ear. She began a policy of nonresistance that was non-cooperation, too; she would not deliberately obstruct him, but she would allow him to poke through the files for ten minutes before volunteering the information that the folder he wanted was already on the general's desk. This interfered with the smooth performance of Kramer's duties, and, of course, the general spotted it at once.

"It's nothing," said Kramer when the general called him on it. "I don't like to say anything."

"Go on," General Grote urged. "You're not a soldier any more; you're a rat."

"I think I can handle it, sir."

The general motioned silently to the coffeepot and waited while Kramer fixed him a cup, two sugars, no cream. He said: "Tell me everything, always. All the dirty rumors about inefficiency and favoritism. Your suspicions and hunches. Anybody that gets in your way—or more important, in mine. In the underworld they shoot stool pigeons, but here we give them blue cords for their shoulders. Do you understand?"

Kramer did. He did not ask the general to intercede with the motherly major, or transfer her; but he did handle it himself. He discovered it was very easy. He simply threatened to have her sent to Narvik.

With the others it was easier. Margaret had resented him because she was senior in Operation Ripsaw to him, but as the others were sucked in they found him there already. Instead of resentment, their attitude toward him was purely fear.

The next people to hate him were the aides of Grote's general staff because he was a wild card in the deck. The five members of the staff–Chief, Personnel, Intelligence, Plans & Training and Operations–proceeded with their orderly, systematic jobs day by day, building Ripsaw . . . until the inevitable moment when Kramer would breeze in with, "Fine job, but the general suggests–" and the unhorsing of many assumptions, and the undoing of many days' work. That was his job also. He was a bird of ill omen, a coiled snake in fair grass, a hired killer and a professional betrayer of confidences–though it was not long before there were no confidences to betray, except from an occasional young, new officer who hadn't learned his way around, and those not worth betraying. That, as the general had said, was the way with aides. Kramer wondered sometimes if he liked what he was doing, or liked himself for doing it. But he never carried the thought through. No time.

Troops completed basic training or were redeployed from rest areas and entrained, emplaned, embussed or embarked for the scattered staging areas of Ripsaw. Great forty-wheeled trucks bore nuclear cannon up the Alcan Highway at a snail's pace. Air groups and missile sections launched on training exercises over Canadian wasteland that closely resembled tundra, with grid maps that bore names like Maina Pylgin and Kamenskoe. Yet these were not Ripsaw, not yet, only the separate tools that Ripsaw would some day pick up and use.

Ripsaw itself moved to Wichita and a base of its own when its headquarters staff swelled to fifteen hundred men and women. Most of them hated Kramer.

It was never perfectly clear to Kramer what his boss had to do with the show. Kramer made his coffee, carried his briefcase, locked and unlocked his files, delivered to him those destructive tales and delivered for him those devastating suggestions, but never understood just why there had to be a Commanding General of Ripsaw.

The time they went to Washington to argue an allocation of seventy rather than sixty armored divisions for Ripsaw, for instance, General Grote just sat, smiled and smoked his pipe. It was his chief of staff, the young and brilliant Major General Cartmill, who passionately argued the case before D. Beauregard Medway, though when Grote addressed his superior it still was as "Dan." (They did get the ten extra divisions, of course.)

Back in Wichita, it was Cartmill who toiled around the clock co-ordinating. A security lid was clamped down early in the game. The fifteen hundred men and women in the Wichita camp stayed in the Wichita camp. Commerce with the outside world, except via coded messages to other elements of Ripsaw, was a capital offense–as three privates learned the hard way. But through those coded channels Cartmill reached out to every area of the North American–and Allied–world.

Personnel scoured the globe for human components that might be fitted into Ripsaw. Intelligence gathered information about that track of Siberia which they were to invade, and the waters they were to cross. Plans & Training slaved at methods of effecting the crossing and invasion efficiently, with the least–or at any rate the optimum least, consistent with requirements of speed, security and so on–losses in men and matériel. Operations studied and restudied the various ways the crossing and invasion might go right or wrong, and how a good turn of fortune could be exploited, a bad turn minimized. General Cartmill was in constant touch with all of them, his fingers on every cord in the web. So was John Kramer.

Grote ambled about all this with an air of pleased surprise.

Kramer discovered one day that there had been books written about his boss–not best-sellers with titles like *"Bloody Larry" Grote, Sword of Freedom*, but thick, gray mimeographed staff documents, in Chinese and Russian, for top-level circulation among yute commanders. He surprised Grote reading one of them–in Chinese.

The general was not embarrassed. "Just refreshing my memory of what the yutes think I'm like so I can cross them up by doing something different. Listen: 'Characteristic of this officer's philosophy of attack is varied tactics. Reference his lecture, *Lee's 1862 Campaigns*, delivered at Fort Leavenworth Command &

General Staff School, attached. Opposing commanders should not expect a force under him to–hm-m-m. *Tsueng, water radical–press the advance the same way twice.'* Now all I have to do is make sure we attack by the book, like Grant instead of Lee, slug it out without any brilliant variations. See how easy it is, John? How's the message center?"

Kramer had been snooping around the message center at Grote's request. It was a matter of feeding out cigarettes and smiles in return for an occasional incautious word or a hint; gumshoe work. The message center was an underground complex of encoders, decoders, transmitters, receivers and switchboards. It was staffed by a Signal Corps WAC battalion in three shifts around the clock. The girls were worked hard–though a battalion should have been enough for the job. Messages went from and to the message center linking the Wichita brain with those seventy divisions training now from Capetown to Manitoba, a carrier task force conducting exercises in the Antarctic, a fleet of landing craft growing every day on the Gulf of California. The average time-lag between receipt of messages and delivery to the Wichita personnel at destination was 12.25 minutes. The average number of erroneous transmissions detected per day was three. Both figures General Grote considered intolerable.

"It's Colonel Bucknell who's lousing it up, General. She's trying too hard. No give. Physical training twice a day, for instance, and a very hard policy on excuses. A stern attitude's filtered down from her to the detachments. Everybody's chewing out subordinates to keep themselves covered. The working girls call Bucknell 'the monster.' Their feeling is the Army's impossible to please, so what the hell."

"Relieve her," Grote said amiably. "Make her mess officer; Ripsaw chow's rotten anyway." He went back to his Chinese text.

And suddenly it all began to seem as if it really might some day rise and strike out across the Strait. From Lieutenant Kramer's Ripsaw Diary:

At AM staff meeting CG RIPSAW xmitted order CG NAAARMY designating RIPSAW D day 15 May 1986. Gen CARTMILL observed this date allowed 45 days to form troops in final staging areas assuming RIPSAW could be staged in 10 days. CG RIPSAW stated that a 10-day staging seemed feasible. Staff concurred. CG RIPSAW so ordered. At 1357 hours CG NAAARMY concurrence received.

They were on the way.

As the days grew shorter Grote seemed to have less and less to do, and curiously so did Kramer. He had not expected this. He had been aide-de-camp to the general for nearly a year now, and he fretted when he could find no fresh treason to bring to the general's ears. He redoubled his prowling tours of the kitchens, the BOQ, the motor pools, the message center, but not even the guard mounts or the shine on the shoes of the soldiers at Retreat parade was in any way at fault. Kramer could only imagine that he was missing things. It did not occur to him that, as at last they should be, the affairs of Ripsaw had gathered enough speed to keep them straight and clean, until the general called him in one night and ordered him to pack. Grote put on his spectacles and looked over them at Kramer. "D plus five," he said, "assuming all goes well, we're moving this headquarters to Kiska. I want you to take a look-see. Arrange a plane. You can leave tomorrow."

It was, Kramer realized that night as he undressed, Just Something to Do. Evidently the hard part of his job was at an end. It was now only a question of fighting the battle, and for that the field commanders were much more important than he. For the first time in many months he thought it would be nice to do a crossword puzzle, but instead fell asleep.

It was an hour before leaving the next day that Kramer met Ripsaw's "cover."

The "cover" was another lieutenant general, a bristling and wiry man named Clough, with a brilliant combat record staked out on his chest and sleeves for the world to read. Kramer came in when his buzzer sounded, made coffee for the two generals and was aware that Grote and Clough were old pals and that the Ripsaw general was kidding the pants off his guest.

"You always were a great admirer of Georgie Patton," Grote teased. "You should be glad to follow in his footsteps. Your operation will go down in history as big and important as his historic cross-Channel smash into Le Havre."

Kramer's thoughts were full of himself–he did not much like getting even so close to the yutes as Kiska, where he would be before the sun set that night–but his ears pricked up. He could not remember any cross-Channel smash into Le Havre–by Patton or anybody else.

"Just because I came to visit your show doesn't mean you have to rib me, Larry," Clough grumbled.

"But it's such a pleasure, Mick."

Clough opened his eyes wide and looked at Grote. "I've generaled against Novotny before. If you want to know what I think of him, I'll tell you."

Pause. Then Grote, gently: "Take it easy, Mick. Look at my boy there. See him quivering with curiosity?"

Kramer's back was turned. He hoped his blush would subside before he had to turn around with the coffee. It did not.

"Caught red-faced," Grote said happily, and winked at the other general. Clough looked stonily back. "Shall we put him out of his misery, Mick? Shall we fill him in on the big picture?"

"Might as well get it over with."

"I accept your gracious assent." Grote waved for Kramer to help himself to coffee and to sit down. Clearly he was unusually cheerful today, Kramer thought. Grote said: "Lieutenant Kramer, General Clough is the gun-captain of a Quaker cannon which covers Ripsaw. He looks like a cannon. He acts like a cannon. But he isn't loaded. Like his late idol George Patton at one point in his career, General Clough is the commander of a vast force which exists on paper and in radio transmissions alone."

Clough stirred uneasily, so Grote became more serious.

"We're brainwashing Continental Defense Commissar Novotny by serving up to him his old enemy as the man he'll have to fight. The yute radio intercepts are getting a perfect picture of an assault on Polar Nine being prepared under old Mick here. That's what they'll prepare to counter, of course. Ripsaw will catch them flatfooted."

Clough stirred again but did not speak.

Grote grinned. "All right. We *hope,*" he conceded. "But there's a lot of planning in this thing. Of course, it's a waste of the talent of a rather remarkably able general"–Clough gave him a lifted-eyebrow look–"but you've got to have a real man at the head of the fake army group or they won't believe it. Anyway, it worked with Patton and the Nazis. Some unkind people have suggested that Patton never did a better bit of work than sitting on his knapsack in England and letting his name be used."

"Wait'll the shooting starts," Clough said sourly.

"Ike never commanded a battalion before the day he invaded North Africa, Mick. He did all right."

"Ike wasn't up against Novotny," Clough said heavily. "I can talk better while I'm eating, Larry. Want to buy me a lunch?"

General Grote nodded. "Lieutenant, see what you can charm out of Colonel Bucknell for us to eat, will you? We'll have it sent in here, or course, and the best girls she's got to serve it." Then, unusually, he stood up and looked appraisingly at Kramer.

"Have a nice flight," he said.

III

Kramer's blue *fourragère* won him cold handshakes but a seat at the first table in the Headquarters Officers Mess in Kiska. He didn't have quite enough appetite to appreciate it.

Approaching the island from the air had taken appetite away from him as the GOA autocontroller rocked the plane in a carefully calculated zigzag in its approach. They were, Kramer discovered, under direct visual observation from any chance-met bird from yute eyries across the Strait until they got below five hundred feet. Sometimes the yutes sent over a flight of birds to knock down a transport. Hence the zigzags.

Captain Mabry, a dark, tall Georgian who had been designated to make the general's aide feel at home, noticed Kramer wasn't eating, pushed his own tray into the center strip and, as it sailed away, stood up. "Get it off the pad, shall we? Cain't keep the Old Man waiting."

The captain took Kramer through clanging corridors to an elevator and then up to the eyrie. It was only a room. From it the spy-bird missiles–rockets, they were really, but the services like to think of them as having a punch, even though the punch was only a television camera–were controlled. To it the birds returned the pictures their eyes saw.

Brigadier Spiegelhauer shook Kramer's hand. "Make yourself at home, Lieutenant," he boomed. He was short and almost skeletally thin, but his voice was enormous. "Everything satisfactory for the general, I hope?"

"Why, yes, sir. I'm just looking around."

"Of course," Spiegelhauer shouted. "Care to monitor a ride?"

"Yes, sir." Mabry was looking at him with amusement, Kramer saw. Confound him, what right did *he* have to think Kramer was scared–even if he was? Not a physical fear; he was not insane. But . . . scared.

The service life of a spy-bird over yute territory was something under twenty minutes, by then the homing heads on the ground-to-air birds would have sniffed out its special fragrance and knocked it out. In that twenty-minute period it would see what it could see. Through its eyes the observers in the eyrie would learn just that much more about yute dispositions–so long as it remained in direct line-of-sight to the eyrie, so long as everything in its instrumentation worked, so long as yute jamming did not penetrate its microwave control.

Captain Mabry took Kramer's arm. "Take 'er off the pad," Mabry said negligently to the launch officer. He conducted Kramer to a pair of monitors and sat before them.

On both eight-inch screens the officers saw a diamond-sharp

scan of the inside of a silo plug. There was no sound. The plug lifted off its lip without a whisper, dividing into two semicircles of steel. A two-inch circle sky showed. Then, abruptly, the circle widened; the lip irised out and disappeared; the gray surrounded the screen and blanked it out, and then it was bright blue, and a curl of cirro-cumulus in one quadrant of the screen.

Metro had promised no cloud over the tactical area, but there was cloud there. Captain Mabry frowned and tapped a tune on the buttons before him; the cirro-cumulus disappeared and a line of gray-white appeared at an angle on the screen. "Horizon," said Mabry. "Labble to make you seasick, Lootenant." He tapped some more and the image righted itself. A faint yellowish stain, not bright against the bright cloud, curved up before them and burst into spidery black smoke. "Oh, they are anxious," said Mabry, sounding nettled. "General, weather has busted it again. Cain't see a thing."

Spiegelhauer bawled angrily, "I'm going to the weather station," and stamped out. Kramer knew what he was angry about. It was not the waste of a bird; it was that he had been made to lose face before the general's aide-de-camp. There would be a bad time for the Weather Officer because Kramer had been there that day.

The telemetering crew turned off their instruments. The whining eighteen-inch reel that was flinging tape across a row of fifteen magnetic heads, recording the picture the spy-bird took, slowed and droned and stopped. Out of instinct and habit Kramer pulled out his rough diary and jotted down *Brig. Spiegelhauer—Permits bad wea. sta. situation?* But it was little enough to have learned on a flight to Kiska, and everything else seemed going well.

Captain Mabry fetched over two mugs of hot cocoa. "Sorry," he said. "Cain't be helped, I guess."

Kramer put his notebook away and accepted the cocoa.

"Beats U-2in'," Mabry went on. "Course, you don't get to see as much of the country."

Kramer could not help a small, involuntary tremor. For just

a moment there, looking out of the sky-bird's eyes, he had imagined himself actually in the air above yute territory and conceived the possibility of being shot down, parachuting, internment, the Blank Tanks, "Yankee! Why not be good fellow? You *proud* you murderer?"

"No," Kramer said, "you don't get to see as much of the country." But he had already seen all the yute country he ever wanted.

Kramer got back in the elevator and descended rapidly, his mind full. Perhaps a psychopath, a hungry cat or a child would have noticed that the ride downward lasted a second or two less than the ride up. Kramer did not. If the sound echoing from the tunnel he walked out into was a bit more clangorous than the one he had entered from, he didn't notice that either.

Kramer's mind was occupied with the thought that, all in all, he was pleased to find that he had approached this close to yute territory, and to yute Blank Tanks, without feeling *particularly* afraid. Even though he recognized that there was nothing to be afraid of, since, of course, the yutes could not get hold of him here.

Then he observed that the door Mabry opened for him led to a chamber he knew he had never seen before.

They were standing on an approach stage and below them forty-foot rockets extended downward into their pit. A gantry-bridge hung across space from the stage to the nearest rocket, which lay open, showing a clumsily padded compartment where there should have been a warhead or an instrument capsule.

Kramer turned around and was not surprised to find that Mabry was pointing a gun at him. He had almost expected it. He started to speak. But there was someone else in the shadowed chamber, and the first he knew of *that* was when the sap struck him just behind the ear.

It was all coming true: "Yankee! Why not be honest man? You *like* to murder babies?" Kramer only shook his head. He knew it did no good to answer. Three years before he had answered. He knew it also did no good to keep quiet; because he had done that, too. What he knew most of all was that nothing was going to do him any good because the yutes had him now, and who would have thought Mabry would have been the one to do him in? They did not beat him at this point, but then they did not need to. The nose capsule Mabry had thrust him into had never been designed for carrying passengers. With ingenuity Kramer could only guess that Mabry had contrived to fit it with parachutes and water-tight seals and flares so the yute gunboat could find it in the water and pull out their captive alive. But he had taken 15- and 20-G accelerations, however briefly. He seemed to have no serious broken bones, but he was bruised all over. Secretly he found that almost amusing. In the preliminary softening up the yutes did not expect their captives to be in physical pain. By being in pain he was in some measure upsetting their schedule. It was not much of a victory but it was all he had.

Phase Two was direct questioning: What was Ripsaw exactly? How many divisions? Where located? Why had Lieutenant General Grote spent so much time with Lieutenant General Clough? When Mary Elizabeth Grote, before her death, entertained the Vietnamese UNESCO delegate's aunt in Sag Harbor, had she known her husband had just been passed over for promotion to brigadier? And was resentment over that the reason she had subsequently donated twenty-five dollars to a mission hospital in Laos? What were the Bering Straits rendezvous points for missile submarines supporting Ripsaw? Was the transfer of Lieutenant Colonel Carolyn S. Bucknell from Message Center Battalion C.O. to Mess Officer a cover for some CIC complexity? What air support was planned for D plus one? D plus two? Did Major Somebody-or-other's secret drinking account for the curious radio intercept in clear logged at 0834 on 6 October 1985? Or was "Omobray for my eadhay" the code designation for some nefarious scheme to be launched against the gallant, the ever-victorious forces of Neo-Utilitarianism?

Kramer was alternately cast into despondency by the amount of knowledge his captors displayed and puzzled by the psychotic irrelevance of some of the questions they asked him. But most of all he was afraid. As the hours of Phase Two became days, he became more and more afraid–afraid of Phase Three–and so he was ready for Phase Three when the yutes were ready for him.

Phase Three was physical. They beat the living be-hell out of First Lieutenant John Kramer, and then they shouted at him and starved him and kicked him and threw him into bathtubs filled half with salt water and half with shaved ice. He was in constant pain. But he didn't think much about the pain. What he thought about was what came next. For the bad thing about Phase Three was Phase Four.

He remembered. First they would let him sleep. Then they would wake him up and feed him quickly, and bandage his worst bruises, and bandage his ears with cotton tampons, and bandage his eyes, and bandage his mouth, so he couldn't bite his tongue, and bandage his arms and legs, so he couldn't move them or touch them together . . .

And then the short superior-private who was kicking him while he thought all this stopped and talked briefly to a noncom. The two of them helped him to a mattress and left.

Ten hours later he was back in the Blank Tanks.

Sit back and listen. What do you hear?

Perhaps you think you hear nothing. You are wrong. You discount the sound of a distant car's tires, or the crackle of metal as steam expands the pipes. Listen more carefully to these sounds; others lie under them. From the kitchen there is a grunt and hum as the electric refrigerator switches itself on. You change position; your chair creaks, the leather of your shoes slip-slides with a faint sound. Listen more carefully still and hear the tiny roughness in the main bearing of the electric clock in the next room, or the almost inaudible hum of wind in a television antenna.

In the Blank Tanks a man hears nothing at all.

The pressure of the tampons in the ear does not allow stirrup to strike anvil; teeth cannot touch teeth, hands cannot clap, he cannot make a noise if he tries to, or hear it if he did.

That is deafness. The Blank Tanks are more than deafness. In them a man is blind, even to the red fog that reaches through closed eyelids. There is nothing to smell. There is nothing to taste. There is nothing to feel except the swaddling cloths, and through time the nerve ends tire and stop registering this constant touch.

Kramer was ready for the Blank Tank and did not at once panic. He remembered the tricks he had employed before. He swallowed his own sputum and it made a gratifying popping sound in his inner ear; he hummed until his throat was raw and gasped through flaring nostrils until he became dizzy. But each sound he was able to produce lasted only a moment. He might have dropped them like snowflakes onto wool. They were absorbed and they died.

It was actually worse, he remembered tardily, to produce a sound because you could not help but listen for the echo and no echo came. So he stopped.

In three years he *must* have acquired some additional resources, he thought. Of course. He had! He settled down to construct a crossword puzzle in his head. Let 1 Across be a tropical South American bird, *hoatzin*. Let 1 Down be a medieval diatonic series of tones, *hexachord*. Let 2 Down be the Asiatic wild ass, or *onagin*, which might make the first horizontal word under 1 Across be, let's see, E–N– . . . well, why not the ligature of couplets in verse writing, or *enjambment*. That would make 3 Down– He began to cry, because he could not remember 1 Across.

Something was nagging at his mind, so he stopped crying and waited for it to take form, but it would not. He thought of General Grote, by now surely aware that his aide had been taken; he thought of the consternation that must be shuddering through all the tentacles of Ripsaw. It was not actually going to be so hard, he thought pathetically, because he didn't actually have to *hold out* against the Blank Tanks, he only had to *wait*. After D day, or better, say D plus 7, it wouldn't much matter what he told

The Quaker Cannon _____ *151*

them. Then the divisions would be across. Or not across. Breakthrough or failure, it would be decided by then and he could talk.

He began to count off Ripsaw's division officers to himself, as he had so often seen the names on the morning reports. Catton of the XLIst Armored, with Colonels Bogart, Ripner and Bletterman. M'Cleargh of the Highland & Lowland, with Brigadiers Douglass and McCloud. Leventhal of the Vth Israeli, with Koehne, Meier and–he stopped, because it had occurred to him that he might be speaking aloud. He could not tell. All right. Think of something else.

But what?

There was nothing dangerous about sensory deprivation, he lied. It was only a test. Nobody was hurting him. Looked at in the right way, it was a chance to do some *solid* thinking like you never got time for in real life–strike that. In *outside* life. For instance, what about freshing up on French irregular verbs? Start with *avoir*. Tu as, vous avez, nous avons. Voi avete, noi abbiamo, du hast . . . Du hast? How did that get in there? Well, how about poetry?

It is an ancient Mariner, and he stops the next of kin.
The guests are met, the feast is set, and sisters under the
   skin
Are rag and bone and hank of hair, and beard and glittering
   eye.
Invite the sight of patient Night, etherized under the sky.
I should have been a ragged claw; I should have said 'I love
   you';
But–here the brown eyes lower fell–I hate to go above you.
If Ripsaw fail and yutes prevail, what price Clough's
   Quaker cannon?
So Grote–

Kramer stopped himself, barely in time. Were there throat mikes? Were the yutes listening in?

He churned miserably in his cotton bonds, because, as near

as he could guess, he had probably been in the Blank Tank for less than an hour. D day, he thought to himself, praying that it was only to himself, was still some six weeks away and a week beyond that was seven. Seven weeks, forty-nine days, eleven hundred and seventy-six hours, sixty-six thousand minutes plus. He had only to wait those minutes out. What about the diary? And then he could talk all he wanted. Talk, confess, broadcast, anything, what difference would it make then?

He paused, trying to remember. That furtive thought had struggled briefly to the surface but he had lost it again. It would not come back.

He tried to fall asleep. It should have been easy enough. His air was metered and the CO_2 content held to a level that would make him torpid; his wastes catheterized away; water and glucose valved into his veins; he was all but *in utero*, and unborn babies slept, didn't they? Did they? He would have to look in the diary, but it would have to wait until he could remember what thought it was that was struggling for recognition. And that was becoming harder with every second.

Sensory deprivation in small doses is one thing; it even has its therapeutic uses, like shock. In large doses it produces a disorientation of psychotic proportions, a melancholia that is all but lethal; Kramer never knew when he went loopy.

IV

He never quite knew when he went sane again, either, except that one day the fog lifted for a moment and he asked a WAC corporal, "When did I get back to Utah." The corporal had dealt with returning yute prisoners before. She said only: "It's Fort Hamilton, sir. Brooklyn."

He was in a private room, which was bad, but he wore a maroon bathrobe, which was good–at least it meant he was in a hospital instead of an Army stockade. (Unless the private room meant he was in the detention ward of the hospital.)

Kramer wondered what he had done. There was no way to tell,

at least not by searching his memory. Everything went into a blurry alternation of shouting relays of yutes and the silence of the Blank Tanks. He was nearly sure he had finally told the yutes everything they wanted to know. The question was, when? He would find out at the court-martial, he thought. Or he might have jotted it down, he thought crazily, in the diary.

Jotted it down in the . . . ?

Diary!

That was the thought that had struggled to come through to the surface!

Kramer's screams brought the corporal back in a hurry, and then two doctors who quickly prepared knockout needles. He founght against them all the way.

"Poor old man," said the WAC, watching him twitch and shudder in unconsciousness. (Kramer had just turned forty.) "Second dose of the Blank Tanks for him, wasn't it? I'm not surprised he's having nightmares." She didn't know that his nightmares were not caused by the Blank Tanks themselves, but by his sudden realization that his last stay in the Tanks was totally unnecessary. It didn't matter what he told the yutes, or when! They had had the diary all along, for it had been on him when Mabry thrust him in the rocket; and all Ripsaw's secrets were in it!

The next time the fog lifted for Kramer it was quick, like the turning on of a light, and he had distorted memories of dreams before it. He thought he had just dreamed that General Grote had been with him. He was alone in the same room, sun streaming in a window, voices outside. He felt pretty good, he thought tentatively, and had no time to think more than that because the door opened and a ward boy looked in, very astonished to find Kramer looking back at him.

"Holy heaven," he said. "Wait there!"

He disappeared. Foolish, Kramer thought. Of course he would wait. Where else would he go?

And then, surprisingly, General Grote did indeed walk in.

"Hello, John," he said mildly, and sat down beside the bed,

looking at Kramer. "I was just getting in my car when they caught me."

He pulled out his pipe and stuffed it with tobacco, watching Kramer. Kramer could think of nothing to say. "They said you were all right, John. Are you?"

"I . . . think so." He watched the general light his pipe. "Funny," he said. "I dreamed you were here a minute ago."

"No, it's not so funny; I was. I brought you a present."

Kramer could not imagine anything more wildly improbable in the world than that the man whose combat operation he had betrayed should bring him a box of chocolates, bunch of flowers, light novel or whatever else was appropriate. But the general glanced at the table by Kramer's bed.

There was a flat, green-leather-covered box on it. "Open it up," Grote invited.

Kramer took out a glittering bit of metal depending from a three-barred ribbon. The gold medallion bore a rampant eagle and lettering he could not at first read.

"It's your D.S.M.," Grote said helpfully. "You can pin it on if you like. I tried," he said, "to make it a Medal of Honor. But they wouldn't allow it, logically enough."

"I was expecting something different," Kramer mumbled foolishly.

Grote laughed. "We smashed them, boy," he said gently. "That is, Mick did. He went straight across Polar Nine, down the Ob with one force and the Yenisei with another. General Clough's got his forward command in Chebarkul now, loving every minute of it. Why, I was in Karpinsk myself last week–they let me get that far–of course, it's a rest area. It was a brilliant, bloody, back-breaking show. Completely successful."

Kramer interrupted in sheer horror: "Polar *Nine?* But that was the cover–the Quaker cannon!"

General Grote looked meditatively at his former aide. "John," he said after a moment, "didn't you ever wonder why the card-sorters pulled you out for my staff? A man who was sure to crack in the Blank Tanks, because he already had?"

The room was very silent for a moment.

"I'm sorry, John. Well, it worked—had to, you know; a lot of thought went into it. Novotny's been relieved. Mick's got his biggest victory, no matter what happens now; he was the man that led *the* invasion."

The room was silent again.

Carefully Grote tapped out his pipe into a metal wastebasket. "You're a valuable man, John. We traded a major general to get you back."

Silence.

Grote sighed and stood up. "If it's any consolation to you, you held out four full weeks in the Tanks. Good thing we'd made sure you had the diary with you. Otherwise our Quaker cannon would have been a bust."

He nodded good-by and was gone. He was a good officer, was General Grote. He would use a weapon in any way he had to, to win a fight; but if the weapon was destroyed, and had feelings, he would come around to bring it a medal afterward.

Kramer contemplated his Distinguished Service Medal for a while. Then he lay back and considered ringing for a Sunday *Times*, but fell asleep instead.

Novotny was now a sour, angry corps commander away off on the Baltic periphery because of him; a million and a half NAAARMY troops were dug in the heart of the enemy's homeland; the greatest operation of the war was an unqualified success. But when the nurse came in that night, the Quaker cannon—the man who had discovered that the greatest service he could perform for his country was to betray it—was moaning in his sleep.

ELEMENTARY by Laurence M. Janifer and Michael Kurland

This story, like our own "Prose Bowl" which concludes the anthology, offers a satirical look at the writing biz—specifically, here, that singular (and not altogether lovable) group of individuals known as literary agents. In the introduction to "Elementary" in Impossible?, *his 1968 collection, Larry Janifer writes that it was conceived as an all-out joke on his and Michael Kurland's mutual agent. The agent, however, responded with neither laughter nor an invitation to "fold it five ways and put it where the moon don't shine," as Dick Cavett once suggested to Norman Mailer on national TV; said agent responded instead by submitting the story to* The Magazine of Fantasy & Science Fiction *and in due course sending the collaborators a check, less his standard ten-percent commission. Who, then, Janifer wonders, is the joke really on?*

Who indeed.

Laurence M. Janifer (b. 1933) has published several science fiction novels, most notable among them You Sane Men *(1964), later reissued as* Bloodworld, *and many short stories. His collaborative credits include another story with Michael Kurland and one with Donald E. Westlake; three novels with the late S.J. Treibich; and three humorous novels with Randall Garrett—*That Sweet Little Old Lady, Out Like a Light, *and* Occasion for Disaster, *all under the name of "Mark Phillips" and all published first in* Astounding *and later in book form by Pyramid.*

Michael Kurland (b. 1938) has also published several novels and short stories in the field; Transmission Error *(1970),* Pluribus *(1975), and* The Whenabouts of Burr *(1975) are three of his best longer works. Collaboratively, he has done one novel with Chester Anderson and has written short stories with*

Richard Lupoff and, in the mystery field, with one of your editors. In addition to his writing, he recently founded, with Alva Rogers, his own science fiction publishing company, Pennyfarthing Press.

ELEMENTARY

By Laurence M. Janifer and Michael Kurland

"Excellent!" I cried.
"Elementary," said he.
—*The Crooked Man,* by John H. Watson, M. D.

The two men stood side by side, each holding a small revolver. Both revolvers were smoking slightly. One of the men was named Blake, the other Ewing. Blake had a beard, as befit a successful author. Ewing, a comparative novice, was thinking about starting a small moustache. Behind the desk, Hamish Seul'homme stared blankly back, the two bullet-holes hardly bleeding at all, his seated figure barely disarranged.

"You know," Ewing said in a quiet tone, "he looks peaceful."
"As still as death," Blake said. "He never liked clichés."
"He used to cut them from my manuscripts," Ewing said.
"And mine," Blake said softly. "Sometimes he called up to complain."

"Well, that's all over with now," Ewing said.

"Done with, you mean," Blake said. "All done with."

Ewing accepted the correction in silence. Another second passed while both gazed in a satisfied fashion on the body of Hamish Seul'homme.

"Literary agents," Ewing said at last, "will learn a lesson from this."

"Not to mention," Blake added, "detective-story writers. Perhaps we ought to get busy."

"By all means," Ewing said. Carefully, both men checked the office for traces of their habitation, but there were few. Ewing picked up a small shred of lint which had fallen on the cork-tiled floor from the pocket of his suede jacket. Blake retrieved a stray beard-hair which had caught somehow in the desk-blotter.

"We'll need a new agent," Ewing said.

"I suppose so," Blake said sadly. "But perhaps the next one will be different. They can't all be like Seul'homme, can they?"

"They all seem to be," Ewing said. "I've heard a lot of writers talking about their agents–"

"I know," Blake said. "It's a terrible world." He sighed. "But perhaps this death will teach them. Perhaps they will learn to reform."

"Stop returning our best stories," Ewing said.

"Stealing our plots for other writers," Blake added.

"Refusing us advances," Ewing said.

"Taking two-hour lunches," Blake finished, "on *our ten percents.*"

Now, carefully, they went to the door of the suite of offices. All the lights were turned out and, as Ewing knelt to begin work on the cork tiling, Blake swung open the door soundlessly. In the dim corridor lighting the letters shone:

HAMISH SEUL'HOMME
LITERARY REPRESENTATIVE
OFFICES IN NEW YORK. LONDON, PARIS,
ROME, SAN FRANCISCO, HONOLULU, MUNICH, TOKYO,

RIO DE JANEIRO AND ATHENS
"THE FRIENDLY AGENCY"
BY APPOINTMENT ONLY

Blake barely gave them a glance. His steely eyes roved the corridor for a second in silence. Then he whispered: "There's nobody around."

"Good," Ewing said. He had pried up a small section of flooring, and was panting slighty. "Got the key?"

Blake searched in his pockets. "Right here," he said at last. "It got stuck in my notebook." He produced it. Ewing took it with a gloved hand and inserted it in the lock from the inside. From another pocket, Blake produced a pencil, which Ewing put through the hole at the top of the key.

"You're sure they won't miss the key?" Ewing said.

"They don't even know it exists," Blake said. "I took a wax impression of *his* key six months ago. This is the result. Even then, I could see this moment coming."

"Far-sighted of you," Ewing commented admiringly.

"Nothing at all," Blake said. "After a while you develop a sense for these matters."

Ewing now attached a long string to the key, leading it round the door to the outside. In the corridor, he too looked round for a second.

"No one at all," he said. "You'd think there would be people working late."

"America's going downhill," Blake said regretfully. "They don't take pride in their jobs any more."

"True," Ewing said. "Sad, but true."

The door was closed. From the outside, Ewing now inserted a long metal ruler which just fit under the bottom of the door. Working by touch, he slid the ruler under the cork tiling and then lifted the tiling up by angling the ruler. At last he held the ruler steady.

"Got it?" Blake asked curtly.

"Got it," Ewing replied.

Blake began work on the string—first turning the key inside to lock the door, then jerking the key out so that it fell to the empty floor, while Ewing pushed the cork tiling still farther out of its way. With the tiling gone, the key fit easily under the door as Blake led it out on its string, and the pencil came along after only a short struggle.

Ewing let the cork tiling drop, and both men heard the thunk as it fell back into place and adhered, thanks to the quick-drying cement with which he had spread its underside.

Blake pocketed key and pencil: Ewing took as his share the string and the ruler. A second of silence went by.

"You know," Ewing said, "I want to say that I'm proud to be associated with you in an enterprise like this."

"You've been a great help," Blake said. "I could never have done it alone."

"I'm grateful you think so," Ewing said.

"I wonder," Blake began after a few seconds. "Who do you think will find him?"

"His secretary, probably," Ewing said. "She never liked me."

"Nor me," Blake said. "Used to tell me Seul'homme was out when I wanted an advance."

"Me too."

Quite suddenly, they heard footsteps around a corner of the hall.

"Well," Blake said, "we'd better be going."

"Right-oh," Ewing replied. They headed for the automatic elevators.

"You know," Ewing said as they stepped aboard, "I can't think that anyone will miss him."

"A literary agent?" Blake said with a little laugh. "Don't be silly, young man. Of course nobody will miss him. The office will be closed—that's all. And that snip of a secretary will have to find a new job." He paused. "Perhaps we ought to stop by tomorrow and express suitable surprise," he said, "but hardly regret. No one could expect us to show regret."

Elementary

"Quite," Ewing said. He had recently had some success with a series of mysteries set in New Scotland Yard.

At three o'clock the following afternoon, Blake stepped out of the automatic elevator and started down the corridor, Ewing the obligatory few feet behind. At the door of the Hamish Seul'homme offices, both stopped.

"There's no one inside," Ewing said, shocked.

"Don't be silly," Blake said. "Probably they're all in Seul'homme's private offices, trying to figure out what happened."

"A locked room," Ewing murmured. "A perfect locked room."

Blake turned the door handle. The door opened.

"You see?" he said as he stepped inside.

The secretary looked up from her desk inside the outer door. "Oh," she said. "You." She noticed Ewing behind Blake after a second, but said nothing more.

"Is he in, Ursula?" Blake asked.

The secretary sniffed audibly. "I'll check, if you really need to see him," she said.

"Please do," Ewing said, with a slight frown.

The secretary did a few clicking things with her switchboard, and then turned back to the two authors. "He's in," she said. "And he'll see you, though I'm sure I don't know why."

Now frankly puzzled, Blake and Ewing made their way across the familiar tiled floor to the interior office, and pushed open the door.

"Well, boys," Hamish Seul'homme said cheerfully, "always glad to see a few of my hard-working authors. Lucky you caught me—I'm just back from lunch and I have an appointment with some movie starlets. What's new?"

Phillips, a rotund man who seemed to take up enough room for any two average human beings, stirred in his chair. "Normal enough," he wheezed fatly. "I suppose every writer's had the experience. I know I did, once, with my agent."

Blake and Ewing leaned forward eagerly. "But this is different–" Ewing began.

"Yes," Blake cut in. "We called you over here because we can't understand what happened. Both of us remember the murder–the actual murder–so it can't have been a dream."

"But it was," Phillips said. "It always is. I remember when I murdered my agent–a most convincing dream. And going to see him the next afternoon was a shock, believe me. To sleep, perchance to dream . . ." He sighed. Phillips had the unfortunate habit of lapsing into quotation on almost no provocation, which gave him an air at once learned and unoriginal. "But you get over it, boys," he said. "Believe me, you get over it."

"I tell you–" Ewing began.

"Of course, all this is in confidence?" Blake asked suddenly.

"Of course," Phillips said massively. "I shall be as silent as the grave–ha-ha–the grave into which you put your agent."

"Because we intend to try again," Blake said. "Do you know what he's done? He's agreed to let Spanish rights to my books go for twenty-eight dollars each!"

"And he didn't even bother to argue with the publishers who returned my latest book!" Ewing added.

"Don't blame you in the least," Phillips said. "Murder most foul . . the only thing for an agent. But don't worry about that dream."

"But it couldn't have been–" Ewing began.

"Whatever you say," Blake added smoothly. "And–if you ever need help in any little job of your own–"

"Oh, I gave that all up years ago," Phillips said. "Love thy fellow man, you know, and all that."

Blake and Ewing shook their heads. "Surely," Blake said, "you're carrying love a little too far?"

"I mean, after all," Ewing added. "An *agent*."

At eleven o'clock the next evening, the floor which held the Hamish Seul'homme offices was deserted, except for the dead body of Hamish Seul'homme, and the fairly lively ones of Blake and Ewing.

"It's lucky you could convince him to stay late," Ewing said. "Yesterday and now today."

"I told him I wanted to discuss a new agency contract," Blake said wearily. "That always gets them."

"But was yesterday a dream?" Ewing asked. "Or what?"

"You got me," Blake said inelegantly. "But today–this time we know for sure."

"Right," Ewing said.

"And it's a good thing, at that," Blake said. "That locked-room idea was fancy, but it would never work. Suppose the tiling fell back a little off center–first thing the cops would notice. Or scratches in the lock from the way we pulled the key out. Even our gloves must have left smudges here and there. They'd realize it was two of us–and then they'd have us. We're the only two who came up there together."

"But this time–" Ewing began.

"This time they won't know how many there were," Blake said. "Seul'homme has three shots in him, from three different guns–and then there's all this."

His gesture covered the contents of the open valise, which were spread out on the floor of the suite. Several grimy caps from the city's second-hand-clothing stores, a pile of old and muddy shoes from various places, some crumpled copies of tabloid newspapers, a length of iron pipe and other such items lay scattered before them.

"A gang murder," Ewing said. "It's a great idea."

"Right," Blake said. Rapidly, the two men began making footprints with the muddy shoes, footprints toward the body and away from it, back to the front door. There the shoes were wiped clean with the tabloid sheets, which were left crumpled in a corner.

"Gee, boss," Ewing said, "this gimmick works swell."

"Sure does, kid," Blake said. "A h— of a lot better than the other notion."

"This is the real stuff," Ewing said admiringly.

Blake tracked one more pair of shoes dizzily to the door. "That oughta wrap it up, kid," he said. "Let's blow."

"Sure-mike," Ewing said. "You're the boss."

"You're d— tootin' I am," Blake said with satisfaction. The valise was repacked, leaving the caps, the iron pipe, and suchlike clues scattered in the office. Both men stepped silently out into the empty hallway.

Suddenly there was the sound of footsteps.

"Cheese it, the cops," Ewing muttered hoarsely.

"We'll scram," Blake said. "We'll take it on the lam."

In the elevator, he turned to his younger parnter. "Do you know," he said, "that Seul'homme once told me I had no grasp of criminal lingo?"

"Shocking," Ewing said sadly. "But that's all over with now."

Afternoon rolled round, correctly on schedule, and at three o'clock Blake and Ewing stood once more before the Hamish Seul'homme offices. "Again?" Ewing murmured.

"They're all inside, that's all," Blake returned, but without real conviction.

The sight of Seul'homme's secretary, when he opened the door, was hardly even a shock.

"Well?" she said nastily. "What do you want this time?"

"Is–" Blake began. "Is–"

"Yes, he's in," the secretary said. "Why don't you go home and write, instead of bothering him all the time?"

Ewing said: "But–" and stopped.

There didn't seem anything else to say.

That night, in Blake's apartment, both men sat, morose, confused and determined.

"Something's gone wrong," Blake said.

"There's something awfully strange here," Ewing said.

"We killed him," Blake said. "Twice. I remember it distinctly."

"And I," Ewing said.

Elementary

"A locked-room murder, and a gang murder," Blake said.
Ewing frowned. "Didn't the gang murder come first?" he asked.
"The locked room first," Blake said. "Classic tradition. Then the romantic."
"What's next?" Ewing asked.
"We can't go on murdering him forever," Blake said. "We've got to figure out what's gone wrong."
Ewing nodded sadly. "You know," he said, "I wouldn't even mind being caught, not as much as I mind this."
"It is sort of eerie," Blake said.
"Let's have one more try, though," Ewing said. "Maybe we'll be able to figure the whole thing out this time."
"Another gang murder?"
Ewing shrugged. "Well, why not?" he asked.
"Repetitious," Blake said. "Besides, it's so complicated. And tiring. And I'm sure the police would have traced back our clues to the second-hand shops and such."
"Come to think of it," Ewing said slowly, "what happened to the clues? Someone must have taken them away . . ."
"It's a plot," Blake said.
Ewing nodded. "It's supposed to be a plot," he said. "But it's supposed to be *our* plot."
"Someone," Blake said, "is revising us."
"Seul'homme," Ewing said instantly.
"But we killed him," Blake said.
"Maybe he's wearing a bullet-proof vest," Ewing said. "Maybe he's playing with us."
"That could be it," Blake said. "Still . . ."
A silence fell. Both authors sat thinking deeply. After a time Blake looked up. Ewing gazed at him attentively.
"Yes?" the younger man said at last.
"Even a bullet-proof vest," Blake said, "would do little good after a fall from Seul'homme's office window."
"On the thirty-second floor," Ewing said. "Wonderful! Amazing!"

Blake shrugged, stroking his beard. "Elementary," he said casually.

Coming up in the elevator, somewhat boredly, the next night, the two authors carried no tools. Only a small sheet of paper, folded over, rested in Blake's inside jacket pocket.

"Of course, you'll copy it over on Seul'homme's typewriter," Ewing said.

"Of course," Blake said. "But it doesn't do to run these things out first-draft. A really good suicide note requires careful revision." He patted his pocket. "If I say so myself, I came up with some fine touches here and there," he added.

"Oh, very fine indeed," Ewing said. "That bit about not being able to live with his conscience after all the terrible things he's done to authors—"

"And I must admit you helped with the phrasing here and there," Blake put in.

"Oh, now, really," Ewing said, abashed. "Anyone would have done the same."

The elevator let them off, and they walked quietly down the corridor to the familiar door. Blake opened it with his gloved hand.

"Come in!" Hamish Seul'homme said cheerily. "Come right in."

The two authors took a step forward, then another. "Stand where you are!" Blake commanded, drawing his gun.

Ewing drew his own. Facing them, Hamish Seul'homme smiled.

Then, for both authors, everything went black.

"I'm seeing double," Blake whispered. "Whatever hit me on the head has affected my brain."

"Mine, too," Ewing said. "I see two of them."

Sprawled in chairs, loosely tied, both authors confronted their enemy.

"But we are twins," the two Hamish Seul'hommes said. Each

of them was holding one of the revolvers with which Blake and Ewing had planned to back Seul'homme to the window. "In a way," the two added.

"But–" Blake began.

"You can't–" Ewing said.

The two Hamish Seul'hommes sighed. "Authors," they said. "No imagination, no intellect, no power of reason. And we give them ninety percent of our money. Ridiculous!" They waved the guns negligently and sighed again.

"You're–you're a corporation of identical beings," Blake stammered. "From an alien planet. And you've come to conquer Earth, but you–"

"Silly," the two Seul'hommes chided.

"It's hypnotism," Ewing said. "You've managed to hypnotize us into believing that there are two of you, so that–"

"Inane," the Seul'hommes said.

"All right," Blake conceded after a glance at his despondent partner. "We give up. What are you?"

"We," the two Seul'hommes said, "are an agent. We have been known as ten-per-centers–why should it surprise you that there are ten of us–each in one of our main offices?"

"But–" Blake began. "But–"

"We have a country estate," the two Seul'hommes said. "All agents have country estates. You must have noticed that. Yet they are always in the city. Have you never wondered why we maintain a country place?"

"Well," Ewing began. "I–"

"Crude," the Seul'hommes said. "Lacking in imagination. Brutish and stupid." They smiled. "It is on our estates, naturally," they said, "that we grow new ones. Just like every other agent. Ten active parts at a time–with ten per cent for each. And a new supply coming up."

"You mean we really did–" Blake said.

"Kill us?" the Seul'hommes said. "Of course. And, to be frank, it's getting to be a bore. We decided to stop it. You two are much more stubborn than most authors. Most of them seem easily enough convinced that they have experienced no more than a particularly vivid dream."

"Like Phillips," Ewing said in a hushed voice.

Blake turned a steely gaze on his companion. "No names!" he hissed.

"Oh, we know about Phillips," the Seul'hommes said blandly. "As a matter of fact, he knows about us as well–though he knows it wouldn't do for him to mention the fact."

"Not even–" Ewing began.

"Not even to another author," the Seul'hommes said. "Exactly so." They chuckled in unison, a horrible sound. "Of course, his agent–all ten of him–has made it worth his while."

Blake took a deep breath. "And now," he said bravely, "you're going to kill us?"

"Good Lord, no!" the Seul'hommes cried. "Kill an author? My God, man, how would we live?"

"Aha," Blake said cleverly. "Then you need us, too."

"Can't get along without us," Ewing said.

The Seul'hommes merely nodded. "Of course," they said. "But we're going to swear you to silence. Can't let the word get out, you know."

Blake and Ewing looked at each other. "Writers," Blake said at last, *"deserve* to know."

"It's the least we can do," Ewing added.

The Seul'hommes merely waited. Blake thought of saying: "Aha," again, but a lone "Aha," all by itself, somehow lacked elegance. Or even meaning, he thought.

"It's an impasse," Ewing said at last. "You can't kill us, and you can't let us live."

"Writers," the Seul'hommes said to each other, sadly. "Always that triumphant leap at the obvious." They sighed. "No subtlety," they said. "No intellect. No depth."

"Now, wait a minute–" Blake began.

The Seul'hommes raised one hand each. "Consider," they said. "We will not dispute your feelings toward agents. After all, that's none of our concern." They sniggered. "But your feelings toward other writers–this idiotic *loyalty* . . ."

It was Ewing's turn to say: "Now, wait a minute–"

"What have other writers ever done for you?" the Seul'hommes asked. "Stolen your plots, taken up space in magazines you want to write for, anticipated all your best ideas–why, however you feel about agents, can't you see that it's other writers you really ought to dislike?"

There was a little silence. At last Blake, as senior, spoke.

"Well," he said, "if you put it that way–"

"Writers become editors, as well," the Seul'hommes said. "And anthologists. Why, if it weren't for other writers, you could publish anything you liked, anywhere. You'd have no problems at all."

Ewing nodded decisively. "Let them fend for themselves," he said. "I don't see why we should do a thing for them."

"If necessary," Blake added, "we'll even mislead them. They deserve misleading."

The Seul'hommes smiled. "Perfectly proper," they said with satisfaction. "And now that you've decided to join us–" Blake and Ewing winced slightly, but remained firm–"we really ought to help you out, as well."

"Help us out?" Blake asked.

"Exactly," the Seul'hommes said. "Haven't you ever noticed how a few writers can provide enough material–enough stories and books–to flood even today's markets? A mystery writer or two here, a science-fiction writer there, a humorist, a novelist–all making enormous sums of money on sheer production."

Ewing stared. "What do you mean?" he asked in a whisper.

The Seul'hommes shrugged. "It's very simple," they said. "You've heard critics talk about the way a writer has grown. What did you think they meant?"

"Grown?" Blake said.

"Of *course*," the Seul'hommes said. "How much work do you think ten of you could do?"

THE LOOLIES ARE HERE by Ruth Allison and Jane Rice

Collaborations between two women, unlike those between two men, are rare in science fiction (as are non-marital collaborations between a man and a woman). The reason for this may have something to do with certain differences in literary outlook. When male writers get together, particularly in situations where a large quantity of liquid refreshment is available, they tend to discuss two things at great length: fiction ideas and money. This in turn tends to trigger the collaborative urge. Female writers, on the other hand, don't seem to feel the need to share plots, nor do they seem to enjoy getting companionably squiffed together; they prefer, in a sober and industrious fashion, to do their own work and thus receive all *the money instead of just half. Which ought to tell the two of us something but probably won't.*

Anyhow, "The Loolies Are Here" is one of the few two-woman collaborations in the field and we're pleased to present it here. As Damon Knight wrote on the occasion of its publication in the first of his Orbit *anthologies, "Men who read this story invariably laugh; women, however, especially those with small children, weep."*

We know little in the way of biographical information about either Ruth Allison or Jane Rice. What we do know: Ms. Rice has been publishing science fiction and fantasy since the early forties, when such stories as "The Crest of the Wave" and "The Refugee" appeared in the late-lamented Unknown; *other short work has graced the pages of* Astounding *and* The Magazine of Fantasy & Science Fiction, *as well as such slick magazines as* Ladies' Home Journal, Cosmopolitan, *and* Charm. *Ms. Allison appears to pursue fiction-writing as an avocation, mostly in partnership with Ms. Rice; she is married and the mother of five sons.*

THE LOOLIES ARE HERE
By Ruth Allison and Jane Rice

They are. I've seen one. He (it?) was standing in the washbasin in our bathroom, during an electrical storm, in the middle of the night. He was about a foot high in his bare feet and he had a whiskery face and he smiled at me . . . slowly. I don't care to dwell on it. They have more teeth than we do–or *something*, and this one was wearing a little pockety-looking garment somewhat on the order of a shoemaker's apron. He must have been able to see in the dark because he was reading a threatening note I had written milord and scotch-taped *firmly* to the mirror.

In case you're thinking what I think you're thinking, the answer is–No, I don't. Nor am I subconsciously fulfilling a psychological need. I am the mother of four small boys and I need a loolie like milord needs a coat hanger caught in the lawnmower.

Anyhow, to the inevitable queries–Why are they called loolies? Where do they come from, et cetera?–I can only reply through a mouthful of clothespins, I haven't time to bat this over the head with a rolled-up research paper. I guess they're called loolies for the same reason that brownies are called brownies. It is their name. Maybe they come from the same place. Et cetera. Wherever that is. However and where*as* a brownie is a good-natured goblin who performs helpful services at night (that's what I need, begod, a reliable brownie, with an eyeshade and some counterfeiting equipment) a loolie will leave you lop-legged. And probably already he has. I'm not sure a loolie is a goblin either.

No matter. Think back. Do you own a listless, slump-shouldered voltage-starved appliance that brightens, clicks its dials, and does a sexy Flamenco the minute the repair truck turns into the driveway? Does your gravel sprout grass, your lawn nourish moles, and your iced tea get cloudy? Do your paper bags jump out of the cupboard at you when you've got your eggbeater full of runny so that you get splaat all over? Are your children behaving like subversives in the employ of a foreign power? Are your groceries being delivered with the cans on top of the grapes on top of the potato chips? Does someone whom you haven't seen since your pink tulle and corsage days–such as an old Sigma Chi beau–drop in from Paris en route to the Orient when you've just returned from a catfish fry at Thick Lake and are going with your tongue hanging out looking like doodledy squat? Do drawers stick? Gutters runneth over? Sheets split down the middle? What always makes three too many of those floorboard screeks you hear in the dark? Where are your car keys? (Wanna bet?)

That's enough for a sample. Try them for size. If they fit, Welcome to the Club. The password is May Day and don't say you weren't warned. Another thing, pay attention to what your wee ones jabber at you when you find the sink stopped up, the ceiling leaking milk, and the baby licking the flyswatter. Let me be a lesson to you. I didn't listen and now I wear a size Gulp dress and my house is shrinking. Your motto should be WATCH OUT, out thy hoe handle uprise and whack thee in thy teeth.

If you're the It Can't Happen Here type, get down on the kitchen floor where everything else usually is and hunt for eeny-weeny footprints. Act at once. The neck you save may be your own, honey. I learned the hard way, with a stray roller skate as my Cinderella slipper (a typical loolie ploy) and an ironing board for a partner. Recognizing this prone situation as a seldom-come-by pooprtunity*, I rested a spell. Which is how I saw the footprints.

When I was a new bride I would've thought MICE but I have realized that mice ain't much, comparatively speaking, and that eeeeek don't solve nuthin'. Therefore I merely shifted onto one elbow and ruminated hmmmmm. If I dipped snuff I'd've dipped some.

The prints were too large for mice. And they all had fairly human-looking toes, which is how human toes generally look. Was a lost doll walking around the neighborhood trying to beam in on Ma-Ma? Considering what-all dolls do nowadays this idea

*This is *not* a typographical error.

The Loolies Are Here

wasn't far-fetched. Could it be a baby robot, for that matter? Or, a ditto Martian, a very likely possibility. Perhaps it was loolies. Maybe it was–

. . . loolies . . .

! and ? Suppose loolies weren't scapegoats invented by our imaginative progeny? Suppose loolies were the truth? It was idiotic to suppose that loolies had painted our car wheels, when I had collared the syndicate white-handed, but suppose loolies were the *Master*minds. Lor' luv a duck . . .

A succession of past events blipped across my inner eye, like the fruit on a slot machine. The Great Sugar Fight and Toothpaste Squirt. The company's-coming, big, old-fashioned Thanksgiving dinner which *dis*interested the company mightily when milord, probing the golden-brown-turkey-dripping-with-delicious-goodness, came up with a soggy wool mitten. The day our offspring sneaked their scraggly, half-grown, spook-footed, purple Easter chickens into the car trunk and we didn't discover the witless, scrawky, whap-flap THINGS until we arrived at our destination, a downtown hotel in Louisville. The day they built the snowman, indoors. The day I was sure I had erected an impregnable barricade to defend a freshly varnished floor when here they came, huffing and puffing, to show me how thistledown worked.

And what about weevils in the flour. Cobwebs overnight. Holes in socks. All those long lost, tenor, *s'wahoo ol' buddy* buddies milord finds at Homecomings, and places. And all those ol' midnight invitations for beckon and eggsh at our housh while I weigh my chances of beating the rap on a murder charge.

Y'know something? An all-woman jury would be a cinch. They wouldn't bother to leave the box. They would simply continue to knit one, purl two as they murmured in unison, "Justifiable homicide." Their modish foreman (not a grease spot on her, not one bead of sweat) would stand and say, "Your Honor . . . we find the defendant . . NOT THE LEAST BITTY BIT GUILTY." Pandemonium. Judge pounds gavel, to no avail. Jury pounds prosecuting attorney. Snake dance forms . . . flambeaux . . . floats. . . bunting . . . banners . . .

loudspeakers . . . *Allison Rice for President!* A prominent (size 42, D cup) society matron climbs up on the Helen Hayes Theatre marquee and does the split. Huzzah! Huzzah! Wall Street and ticker tape . . . Pennsylvania Avenue . . . the Inaugural Ball . . . and there, beside me, in the spotlight, my family. Milord has just met a long-lost, *tattooed* buddy. Our children have been eating dirt. The smallest is holding a one-eyed alley cat with a bad case of mange. They are showing a prominent society matron a bottle of spit they've saved up. They espy Lady Bird (a Mrs. Lady Bird Jackson who is famous for her salt-rising bread) and wave and yell for her to come watch how they can piddle-puddle through a knothole. I confront them with the footprints. Loolies? My voice booms over the microphones. There is a skitter of amusement. A widening sputter of mirth. A surge, a roar of jelly-belly laughter. I am horrified to discover I am the sole lady present who is not wearing a topless evening gown. The scene mercifully fades. . . .

Let's see. Where–

Ah, *there* you are. What are you doing way over there? Never mind, let us hurry on, past milord's theory that the loolie prints could've been made by any of the following: turtles, hamsters, cats, kittens, dogs, frogs, hoptoads, rabbits, a salamander with a short tail, or large mice. I make no comment except to remark that at least he doesn't think they're mine.

As traps are taboo (too many fingers and toes–260½ to be exact, counting everyone) I left nightly saucers of milk for the loolies. Cookies. The latest issue of *House Beautiful.* I tried appealing to their sense of fun with a rubber lizard and a Hallowe'en nose. Please be informed that hope will get you nowhere. Our cat produced a litter of seven female kittens, and litter is the one right word, believe me. Our dog had an encounter with a skunk and, subsequently, terrorized the whole neighborhood by acting like an animal out of Mythical Beasts. We went through measles, mumps, green apples, a rash of dents and blown fuses and more baby rabbits and vacuum cleaner trouble. And have you ever, when getting the wash ready, emptied a child's *sock* and found yourself holding something terrible with a bite out of it?

Next, I "hexed." If you must know, I wrote "loolies" in pig Latin on the inside of a peanut-butter sandwich and ate it for lunch. It tasted clean, and good, and true. Yet, within twenty-four hours I was back on the *s'wahoo ol' buddy* circuit, and there was a whole quartet of the aforementioned s.o.b.s and one of them had a guitar. If you think I put up with this hootenanny nonsense you win first prize, two pounds of beckon and a dozen eggsh.

And then, out of the Slough of Despond, came the midnight storm. It was a doozy. One of those torrential, lightning-ripped, rumble, BLAM things, black as cats one second and livid fluorescent green the next. Did the children rouse, frightened and seeking comfort? No. Did Milord awaken to batten down the hatches and protect his nearest and dearest from loose electricity? No. 'Twas I, Minnie the Mermaid (no Ho-Daddy, she!) who crossed the Rubicon without so much as a flashlight (the battery was dead).

Oh, pioneers! I used to think I'd have made a splendid settler woman. Brave. Intrepid. Dauntless. The Indians would have named me Little Bright Rattlesnake. I know, now, I'd have been a dud. For, when I pussyfooted into the bathroom for a towel to mop wet windowsills with and, BLAM, saw the loolie . . . had an Indian been handy he could have lifted my scalp right off my head, slick as a whistle, without benefit of tomahawk–that's how high my hair rose and how loose I was all the way up from my knees . . , as I vainly flicked the light switch.

From my knees down I was pure steel piston and I was out in the kitchen in nothing flat, desperately trying light switches en route and making thin keening noises as I snatched up suitable weapons.

Armed, I took a deep breath and started back, an inch at a time, keeping close to the walls like they do in the movies. Quietly. Quietly. The storm slammed and glittered about the house but Little Bright Rattlesnake slipped silently–the lights came on suddenly and I screamed.

Milord appeared in the hallway, sleepy and disheveled. "What——" he began, and stopped. I think at that moment he'd have traded me in for a used Edsel.

Behind him the bathroom was brilliantly lit, and empty. The note on the mirror was gone. He'd never believe me. Never in the wide world.

"I , . . uh . . . thought I heard something," I explained, lamely.

"You did," he said, eyeing my broom, and long-handled barbecue fork, and me. "Thunder."

Let us, for politeness' sake, lower the curtain here and raise it again the following morning. *This* morning, to be exact. Visualize, if you will, the sunny kitchen with its limp rained-on curtains, and me staring bug-eyed and whopper-jawed at the name *Chauncey* written in strawberry jam on the refrigerator door.

I realize *why* the loolie's strange attire. I wonder numbly what *else* he may have pocketed. The note on the mirror arises Phoenix-like in my mind.

Dearest *Chauncey:*
Someone who uses barbershop hair tonic used my hairbrush. Pray tell, could it be you? How would you like to be snatched baldheaded?
Love and kisses,
Guess Who

As you have no doubt surmised, Chauncey is milord's middle name which he keeps under such careful guard that even Agent 007 couldn't spring it. Well, I thought, it was out now. I could almost see the graffiti on the sidewalk, the locker room floor at the club, the office bulletin board . . .

Hastily, I soaped a sponge and wiped the refrigerator door, and none too soon, for milord burst into the kitchen as if shot from guns. His expression was deathly, his voice a knell.

"Honey," he intoned in accents of DOOM, "I'm . . . I'm getting bald!"

The Loolies Are Here _____ *177*

MURPHY'S HALL by Poul and Karen Anderson

Husband-and-wife collaborative teams are also uncommon in science fiction (although in other areas of literature they are less rare; the mystery field has had several, more than any other type of writing except, perhaps, for general nonfiction). The most famous pair in s-f, of course, is Henry Kuttner and C. L. Moore; though much of their work in the forties and fifties appeared under their individual by-lines, or under a variety of pseudonyms, a great percentage of it was written in partnership. The field's only other collaborating spouses of note are Walt and Leigh Richmond, Spider and Jeanne Robinson, and Poul and Karen Anderson. (Another well-known couple, Leigh Brackett and Edmond Hamilton, were married for many years but for reasons of their own never wrote anything together.)

The Anderson collaborations have all been short stories, most of them science fiction with an infrequent crime piece; "Murphy's Hall," which was first published in the second of five original anthologies edited by Robert Hoskins, Infinity 2, *is one of the most recent. It is also a considerable departure in style and approach for both writers—a curious story which appears to be about the failure of man in space but which is actually a celebration of human achievement and space exploration; and which, at the same time, is a mocking comment on certain so-called "New Wave" writers and techniques (one of those writers no doubt being one of us).*

Poul Anderson (b. 1926) has been involved in several other joint efforts, including the "Hoka" series with Gordon R. Dickson; and his first published story, as previously noted, was a collaboration with F. N. Waldrop ("Tomorrow's Children," Astounding, July 1947). *Karen Anderson, unlike her prolific husband, has limited her own non-collaborative output to a few short stories and to poetry. Her sonnet "Henry Kuttner: In Memoriam," which appeared in* The Magazine of Fantasy & Science Fiction *shortly after Kuttner's death in 1958, strikes us as being the finest poem ever to come out of the field.*

MURPHY'S HALL

By Poul and Karen Anderson

This is a lie, but I wish so much it were not.

Pain struck through like lightning. For an instant that went on and on, there was nothing but the fire which hollowed out his breast and the body's animal terror. Then as he whirled downward he knew:

Oh, no! Must I leave them already?

Only a month, a month.

Weltall, verweile doch, du bist so schoen.

The monstrous thunders and whistles became a tone, like a bell struck once which would not stop singing. It filled the jagged darkness, it drowned all else, until it began to die out, or to vanish into the endless, century after century, and meanwhile the night deepened and softened, until he had peace.

But he opened himself again and was in a place long and high. With his not-eyes he saw that five hundred and forty doors gave onto black immensities wherein dwelt clouds of light. Some of the clouds were bringing suns to birth. Others, greater and more distant, were made of suns already created, and turned in majestic Catherine's wheels. The nearest stars cast out streamers of flame, lances of radiance; and they were diamond, amethyst, emerald, topaz, ruby; and around them swung glints which he knew with his not-brain were planets. His not-ears heard the thin violence of cosmic-ray sleet, the rumble of solar storms, the slow patient multiplex pulses of gravitational tides. His not-flesh shared the warmth, the blood-beat, the megayears of marvelous life on uncountable worlds.

Six stood waiting. He rose. "But you–" he stammered without a voice.

"Welcome," Ed greeted him. "Don't be surprised. You were always one of us."

They talked quietly, until at last Gus reminded them that even here they were not masters of time. Eternity, yes, but not time. "Best we move on," he suggested.

"Uh-huh," Roger said. "Especially after Murphy took this much trouble on our account."

"He does not appear to be a bad fellow," Yuri said.

"I am not certain," Vladimir answered. "Nor am I certain that we ever will find out. But come, friends. The hour is near."

Seven, they departed the hall and hastened down the star paths. Often the newcomer was tempted to look more closely at something he had glimpsed. But he recalled that, while the universe was inexhaustible of wonders, it would have only the single moment to which he was being guided.

They stood after a while on a great ashen plain. The outlook was as eerily beautiful as he had hoped–no, more, when Earth, a blue serenity swirled white with weather, shone overhead: Earth, whence had come the shape that now climbed down a ladder of fire.

Yuri took Konstantin's hand in the Russian way. "Thank you," he said through tears.

But Konstantin bowed in turn, very deeply, to Willy.

And they stood in the long Lunar shadows, under the high lunar heaven, and saw the awkward thing come to rest and heard: "Houston, Tranquillity Base here. The Eagle has landed."

Stars are small and dim on Earth. Oh, I guess they're pretty bright still on a winter mountaintop. I remember when I was little, we'd saved till we had the admission fees and went to Grand Canyon Reserve and camped out. Never saw that many stars. And it was like you could see up and up between them—like, you know, you could *feel* how they weren't the same distance off, and the spaces between were more huge than you could imagine. Earth and its people were just lost, just a speck of nothing among those cold sharp stars. Dad said they weren't too different from what you saw in space, except for being a lot fewer. The air was chilly too, and had a kind of pureness, and a sweet smell from the pines around. Way off I heard a coyote yip. The sound had plenty of room to travel in.

But I'm back where people live. The smog's not bad on this rooftop lookout, though I wish I didn't have to breathe what's gone through a couple million pairs of lungs before it reaches me. Thick and greasy. The city noise isn't too bad either, the usual growling and screeching, a jet-blast or a burst of gunfire. And since the power shortage brought on the brownout, you can generally see stars after dark, sort of.

My main wish is that we lived in the southern hemisphere, where you can see Alpha Centauri.

Dad, what are you doing tonight in Murphy's Hall?

A joke. I know. Murphy's Law: "Anything that can go wrong, will." Only I think it's a true joke. I mean, I've read every book and watched every tape I could lay hands on, the history, how the discoverers went out, further and further, lifetime after lifetime. I used to tell myself stories about the parts that nobody lived to put into a book.

The crater wall had fangs. They stood sharp and grayish white in the cruel sunlight, against the shadow which brimmed the bowl. And they grew and grew. Tumbling while it fell, the spacecraft had none of the restfulness of zero weight. Forces caught nauseatingly at gullet and gut. An unidentified loose object clattered behind the pilot chairs. The ventilators had stopped their whickering and the two men breathed stench. No matter. This wasn't an Apollo 13 mishap. They wouldn't have time to smother in their own exhalations.

Jack Bredon croaked into the transmitter: "Hello, Mission Control . . . Lunar Relay Satellite . . anybody. Do you read us? Is the radio out too? Or just our receiver? God damn it, can't we even say goodbye to our wives?"

"Tell 'em quick," Sam Washburn ordered. "Maybe they'll hear."

Jack dabbed futilely at the sweat that broke from his face and danced in glittering droplets before him. "Listen," he said. "This is Moseley Expedition One. Our motors stopped functioning simultaneously, about two minutes after we commenced deceleration. The trouble must be in the fuel feed integrator. I suspect a magnetic surge, possibly due to a short circuit in the power supply. The meters registered a surge before we lost thrust. Get that system redesigned! Tell our wives and kids we love them."

He stopped. The teeth of the crater filled the entire forward window. Sam's teeth filled his countenance, a stretched-out grin. "How do you like that?" he said. "And me the first black astronaut."

They struck.

When they opened themselves again, in the hall, and knew where they were, he said, "Wonder if he'll let us go out exploring."

Murphy's Halt? Is that the real name?

Dad used to shout, "Murphy take it!" when he blew his temper. The rest is in a few of the old tapes, fiction plays about spacemen, back when people liked to watch that kind of story. They'd say when a man had died, "He's drinking in Murphy's Hall." Or he's dancing or sleeping or frying or freezing or whatever it was. But did they really say "Hall"? The tapes are old.

Nobody's been interested to copy them off on fresh plastic, not for a hundred years, I guess, maybe two hundred. The holographs are blurred and streaky, the sounds are mushed and full of random buzzes. Murphy's Law has sure been working on those tapes.

I wish I'd asked Dad what the astronauts said and believed, way back when they were conquering the planets. Or pretended to believe, I should say. Of course they never thought there was a Murphy who kept a place where the spacefolk went that he'd called to him. But they might have kidded around about it. Only was the idea, for sure, about a hall? Or was that only the way I heard? I wish I'd asked Dad. But he wasn't home often, these last years, what with helping build and test his ship. And when he did come, I could see how he mainly wanted to be with Mother. And when he and I were together, well, that was always too exciting for me to remember those yarns I'd tell myself before I slept, after he was gone again.

Murphy's Haul?

By the time Moshe Silverman had finished writing his report, the temperature in the dome was about seventy, and rising fast enough that it should reach a hundred inside another Earth day. Of course, water wouldn't then boil at once; extra energy is needed for vaporization. But the staff would no longer be able to cool some down to drinking temperature by the crude evaporation apparatus they had rigged. They'd dehydrate fast. Moshe sat naked in a running river of sweat.

At least he had electric light. The fuel cells, insufficient to operate the air conditioning system, would at least keep Sofia from dying in the dark.

His head ached and his ears buzzed. Occasional dizziness seized him. He gagged on the warm fluid he must continually drink. *And no more salt,* he thought. *Maybe that will kill us before the heat does, the simmering, still, stifling heat.* His bones felt heavy, though Venus has in fact a somewhat lesser pull than Earth; his muscles sagged and he smelled the reek of his own disintegration.

Forcing himself to concentrate, he checked what he had written, a dry factual account of the breakdown of the reactor. The next expedition would read what this thick, poisonous inferno of an atmosphere did to graphite in combination with free neutrons; and the engineers could work out proper precautions.

In sudden fury, Moshe seized his brush and scrawled at the bottom of the metal sheet: "Don't give up! Don't let this hellhole whip you! We have too much to learn here."

A touch on his shoulder brought him jerkily around and onto his feet. Sofia Chiappellone had entered the office. Even now, with physical desire roasted out of him and she wetly agleam, puffy-faced, sunken-eyed, hair plastered lank to drooping head, he found her lovely.

"Aren't you through, darling?" Her tone was dull but her hand sought his. "We're better off in the main room. Mohandas' punkah arrangement does help."

"Yes, I'm coming."

"Kiss me first. Share the salt on me."

Afterward she looked over his report. "Do you believe they will try any further?" she asked. "Materials so scarce and expensive since the war—"

"If they don't," he answered, "I have a feeling—oh, crazy, I know, but why should we not be crazy?—I think if they don't, more than our bones will stay here. Our souls will, waiting for the ships that never come."

She actually shivered, and urged him toward their comrades.

Maybe I should go back inside. Mother might need me. She cries a lot, still. Crying, all alone in our little apartment. But maybe she'd rather not have me around. What can a gawky, pimply-faced fourteen-year-old boy do?

What can he do when he grows up?

O Dad, big brave Dad, I want to follow you. Even to Murphy's . . . Hold?

Director Saburo Murakami had stood behind the table in the commons and met their eyes, pair by pair. For a while silence had pressed inward. The bright colors and amateurish figures in the mural that Georgios Efthimakis had painted for pleasure–beings that never were, nymphs and fauns and centaurs frolicking beneath an unsmoky sky, beside a bright river, among grasses and laurel trees and daisies of an Earth that no longer was–became suddenly grotesque, infinitely alien. He heard his heart knocking. Twice he must swallow before he had enough moisture in his mouth to move his wooden tongue.

But when he began his speech, the words came forth steadily, if a trifle flat and cold. That was no surprise. He had lain awake the whole night rehearsing them.

"Yousouf Yacoub reports that he has definitely succeeded in checking the pseudovirus. This is not a cure; such must await laboratory research. Our algae will remain scant and sickly until the next supply ship brings us a new stock. I will radio Cosmocontrol, explaining the need. They will have ample time on Earth to prepare. You remember the ship is scheduled to leave at . . . at a date to bring it here in about nine months. Meanwhile we are guaranteed a rate of oxygen renewal sufficient to keep us alive, though weak, if we do not exert ourselves. Have I stated the matter correctly, Yousouf?"

The Arab nodded. His own Spanish had taken on a denser accent, and a tic played puppetmaster with his right eye. "Will you not request a special ship?" he demanded.

"No," Saburo told them. "You are aware how expensive anything but an optimum Hohmann orbit is. That alone would wipe out the profit from this station–permanently, I fear, because of financing costs. Likewise would our idleness for nine months."

He leaned forward, supporting his weight easily on fingertips in the low Martian gravity. "That is what I wish to discuss today," he said. "Interest rates represent competition for money. Money represents human labor and natural resources. This is true regardless of socioeconomic arrangements. You know how desperately short they are of both labor and resources on Earth. Yes, many billions of hands–but because of massive poverty, too few

Murphy's Hall

educated brains. Think back to what a political struggle the Foundation had before this base could be established.

"We know what we are here for. To explore. To learn. To make man's first permanent home outside Earth and Luna. In the end, in the persons of our great-grandchildren, to give Mars air men can breathe, water they can drink, green fields and forests where their souls will have room to grow." He gestured at the mural, though it seemed more than ever jeering. "We cannot expect starvelings on Earth, or those who speak for them, to believe this is good. Not when each ship bears away metal and fuel and engineering skill that might have gone to keep *their* children alive a while longer. We justify our continued presence here solely by mining the fissionables. The energy this gives back to the tottering economy, over and above what we take out, is the profit."

He drew a breath of stale, metallic-smelling air. Anoxia made his head whirl. Somehow he stayed erect and continued:

"I believe we, in this tiny solitary settlement, are the last hope for many remaining in space. If we are maintained until we have become fully self-supporting, Syrtis Harbor will be the seedbed of the future. If not—"

He had planned more of an exhortation before reaching the climax, but his lungs were too starved, his pulse too fluttery. He gripped the table edge and said through flying rags of darkness: "There will be oxygen for half of us to keep on after a fashion. By suspending their other projects and working exclusively in the mines, they can produce enough uranium and thorium so that the books at least show no net economic loss. The sacrifice will . . . will be . . . of propaganda value. I call for male volunteers, or we can cast lots, or— Naturally, I myself am the first."

—That had been yesterday.

Saburo was among those who elected to go alone, rather than in a group. He didn't care for hymns about human solidarity; his dream was that someday those who bore some of his and Alice's chromosomes would not need solidarity. It was perhaps well she had already died in a cinderslip. The scene with their children had been as much as he could endure.

He crossed Weinbaum Ridge but stopped when the dome-cluster was out of sight. He must not make the searchers come too far. If nothing else, a quick duststorm might cover his tracks, and he might never be found. Someone could make good use of his airsuit. Almost as good use as the alga tanks could of his body.

For a time, then, he stood looking. The mountainside ran in dark scaurs and fantastically carved pinnacles, down to the softly red-gold-ocher-black-dappled plain. A crater on the near horizon rose out of its own blue shadow like a challenge to the deep purple sky. In this thin air–he could just hear the wind's ghostly whistle–Mars gave to his gaze every aspect of itself, diamond sharp, a beauty strong, subtle, and abstract as a torii gate before a rock garden. When he glanced away from the shrunken but dazzling-bright sun, he could see stars.

He felt at peace, almost happy. Perhaps the cause was simply that now, after weeks, he had a full ration of oxygen.

I oughtn't to waste it, though, he thought. He was pleased by the steadiness of his fingers when he closed the valve.

Then he was surprised that his unbelieving self bowed over both hands to the Lodestar and said, *"Namu Amida Butsu."*

He opened his faceplate.

That is a gentle death. You are unconscious within thirty seconds.

–He opened himself and did not know where he was. An enormous room whose doorways framed a night heaven riotous with suns, galaxies, the green mysterious shimmer of nebulae? Or a still more huge ship, outward bound so fast that it was as if the Milky Way foamed along the bow and swirled aft in a wake of silver and planets?

Others were here, gathered about a high seat at the far end of where-he-was, vague in the twilight cast by sheer distance. Saburo rose and moved in their direction. Maybe, maybe Alice was among them.

But was he right to leave Mother that much alone?
I remember her when we got the news. On a Wednesday, when

I was free, and I'd been out by the dump playing ball. I may as well admit to myself, I don't like some of the guys. But you have to take whoever the school staggering throws up for you. Or do you want to run around by yourself (remember, no, don't remember what the Hurricane Gang did to Danny) or stay always by yourself in the patrolled areas? So Jake-Jake does throw his weight around, so he does set the dues too high, his drill and leadership sure paid off when the Weasels jumped us last year. They won't try that again–we killed three, count 'em, three! –and I sort of think no other bunch will either.

She used to be real pretty, Mother did. I've seen pictures. She's gotten kind of scrawny, worrying about Dad, I guess, and about how to get along after that last pay cut they screwed the spacefolk with. But when I came in and saw her sitting, not on the sofa but on the carpet, the dingy gray carpet, crying– She hung onto that sofa the way she'd hung on Dad.

But why did she have to be so angry at him too? I mean, what happened wasn't his fault.

"Fifty billion munits!" she screamed when we'd started trying to talk about the thing. "That's a hundred, two hundred billion meals for hungry children! But what did they spend it on? Killing twelve men!"

"Aw, now, wait," I was saying, "Dad explained that. The resources involved, uh, aren't identical," when she slapped me and yelled:

"You'd like to go the same way, wouldn't you? Thank God, it almost makes his death worthwhile that you won't!"

I shouldn't have got mad. I shouldn't have said, "Y-y-you want me to become . . . a desk pilot, a food engineer, a doctor . . . something nice and safe and in demand . . . and keep you the way you wanted he should keep you?"

I better stop beating this rail. My fist'll be no good if I don't. Oh, someday I'll find how to make up those words to her.

I'd better not go in just yet.

But the trouble *wasn't* Dad's fault. If things had worked out right, why, we'd be headed for Alpha Centauri in a couple of years. Her and him and me– The planets yonderward, sure, they're the real treasure. But the ship itself! I remember Jake-Jake telling me I'd be dead of boredom inside six months. "Bored aboard, haw, haw, haw!" He really is a lardbrain. A good leader, I guess, but a lardbrain at heart–hey, once Mother would have laughed to hear me say that– How could you get tired of Dad's ship? A million books and tapes, a hundred of the brightest and most alive people who ever walked a deck–

Why, the trip would be like the revels in Elf Hill that Mother used to read me about when I was small, those old, old stories, the flutes and fiddles, bright clothes, food, drink, dancing, girls sweet in the moonlight. . .

Murphy's Hill?

From Ganymede, Jupiter shows fifteen times as broad as Luna seen from Earth; and however far away the sun, the king planet reflects so brilliantly that it casts more than fifty times the radiance that the brightest night of man's home will ever know.

"*Here* is man's home," Catalina Sanchez murmured.

Arne Jensen cast her a look which lingered. She was fair to see in the goldenness streaming through the conservatory's clear walls. He ventured to put an arm about her waist. She sighed and leaned against him. They were scantily clad–the colony favored brief though colorful indoor garments–and he felt the warmth and silkiness of her. Among the manifold perfumes of blossoms (on plants everywhere to right and left and behind, extravagantly tall stalks and big flowers of every possible hue and some you would swear were impossible, dreamlike catenaries of vines and labyrinths of creepers) he caught her summery odor.

The sun was down and Jupiter close to the full. While the terraforming project was going rapidly ahead, as yet the satellite had too little air to blur vision. Tawny shone that shield, emblazoned with slowly moving cloud-bands that were green, blue, orange, umber, and with the jewel-like Red Spot. To know that a single one of the storms raging there could swallow Earth whole added majesty to beauty and serenity. A few stars had the brilliance to pierce that luminousness, down by the rugged horizon. The gold poured soft across crags, cliffs, craters, glaciers, and the machines that would claim this world for man.

Outside lay a great quietness, but here music lilted from the ballroom. Folk had reason to celebrate. The newest electrolysis plant had gone into operation and was releasing oxygen at a rate fifteen percent above estimate. However, low-weight or no, you got tired dancing–since Ganymedean steps took advantage, soaring and bouding aloft–mirth bubbled like champagne and the girl you admired said yes, she was in a mood for Jupiter watching–

"I hope you're right," Arne said. "Less on our account–we have a good, happy life, fascinating work, the best of company–than on our children's." He squeezed a bit harder.

She didn't object. "How can we fail?" she answered. "We've become better than self-sufficient. We produce a surplus, to trade to Earth, Luna, Mars, or plow directly back into development. The growth is exponential." She smiled. "You must think I'm awfully professorish. Still, really, what can go wrong?"

"I don't know," he said. "War, overpopulation, environmental degradation–"

"Don't be a gloomy," Catalina chided him. The lambent light struck rainbows from the tiara of native crystal that she wore in her hair. "People can learn. They needn't make the same mistakes forever. We'll build paradise here. A strange sort of paradise, yes, where trees soar into a sky full of Jupiter, and waterfalls tumble slowly, slowly down into deep-blue lakes, and birds fly like tiny bright-colored bullets, and deer cross the meadows in ten-meter leaps . . . but paradise."

"Not perfect," he said. "Nothing is."

"No, and we wouldn't wish that," she agreed. "We want some discontent left to keep minds active, keep them hankering for the stars." She chuckled. "I'm sure history will find ways to make them believe things could be better elsewhere. Or nature will–Oh!"

Her eyes widened. A hand went to her mouth. And then, frantically, she was kissing him, and he her, and they were clasping and feeling each other while the waltz melody sparkled and the flowers breathed and Jupiter's glory cataracted over them uncaring whether they existed.

He tasted tears on her mouth. "Let's go dancing," she begged. "Let's dance till we drop."

"Surely," he promised, and led her back to the ballroom.

It would help them once more forget the giant meteoroid, among the many which the planet sucked in from the Belt, that had plowed into grim and marginal Outpost Ganymede precisely half a decade before the Martian colony was discontinued.

Well, I guess people don't learn. They breed, and fight, and devour, and pollute, till:

Mother: "We can't afford it."

Dad: "We can't not afford it."

Mother: "Those children–like goblins, like ghosts, from starvation. If Tad were one of them, and somebody said never mind him, we have to build an interstellar ship . . . I wonder how you would react."

Dad: "I don't know. But I do know this is our last chance. We'll be operating on a broken shoestring as is, compared to what we need to do the thing right. If they hadn't made that breakthrough at Lunar Hydromagnetics Lab, when the government was on the point of closing it down– Anyway, darling, that's why I'll have to put in plenty of time aboard myself, while the ship is built and tested. My entire gang will be on triple duty."

Mother: "Suppose you succeed. Suppose you do get your precious spacecraft that can travel almost as fast as light. Do you imagine for an instant it can–an armada can ease life an atom's worth for mankind?"

Dad: "Well, several score atoms' worth. Starting with you and Tad and me."

Mother: "I'd feel a monster, safe and comfortable en route to a new world while behind me they huddled in poverty by the billions."

Dad: "My first duty is to you two. However, let's leave that aside. Let's think about man as a whole. What is he? A beast that is born, grubs around, copulates, quarrels, and dies. Uh-huh. But sometimes something more in addition. He does breed his occasional Jesus, Leonardo, Bach, Jefferson, Einstein, Armstrong, Olveida–whoever you think best justifies our being here–doesn't he? Well, when you huddle people together like rats, they soon behave like rats. What then of the spirit? I tell you, if we don't make a fresh start, a bare handful of us free folk whose descendants may in the end come back and teach–if we don't, why, who cares whether the two-legged animal goes on for another million years or becomes extinct in a hundred? Humanness will be dead.''

Me: "And gosh, Mother, the fun!"
Mother: "You don't understand, dear."
Dad: "Quiet. The man-child speaks. He understands better than you."
Quarrel: till I run from them crying. Well, eight or nine years old. That night, was that the first night I started telling myself stories about Murphy's Hall?
It *is* Murphy's Hall. I say that's the right place for Dad to be.

When Hoo Fong, chief engineer, brought the news to the captain's cabin, the captain sat still for minutes. The ship thrummed around them; they felt it faintly, a song in their bones. And the light fell from the overhead, into a spacious and gracious room, furnishings, books, a stunning photograph of the Andromeda galaxy, an animation of Mary and Tad; and weight was steady underfoot, a full gee of acceleration, one light-year per year per year, though this would become more in shipboard time as you started to harvest the rewards of relativity . . . a mere two decades to the center of this galaxy, three to the neighbor whose portrait you adored. . . . How hard to grasp that you were dead!

"But the ramscoop is obviously functional," said the captain, hearing his pedantic phrasing.

Hoo Fong shrugged. "It will not be, after the radiation has affected electronic parts. We have no prospect of decelerating and returning home at low velocity before both we and the ship have taken a destructive dose."

Interstellar hydrogen, an atom or so in a cubic centimeter, raw vacuum to Earthdwellers at the bottom of their ocean of gas and smoke and stench and carcinogens. To spacefolk, fuel, reaction mass, a way to the stars, once you're up to the modest pace at which you meet enough of those atoms per second. However, your force screens must protect you from them, else they strike the hull and spit gamma rays like a witch's curse.

"We've hardly reached one-fourth c," the captain protested. "Unmanned probes had no trouble at better than ninety-nine percent."

"Evidently the system is inadequate for the larger mass of this ship," the engineer answered. "We should have made its first complete test flight unmanned too."

"You know we didn't have funds to develop the robots for that."

"We can send our data back. The next expedition–"

"I doubt there'll be any. Yes, yes, we'll beam the word home. And then, I suppose, keep going. Four weeks, did you say, till the radiation sickness gets bad? The problem is not how to tell Earth, but how to tell the rest of the men."

Afterward, alone with the pictures of Andromeda, Mary, and Tad, the captain thought: *I've lost more than the years ahead. I've lost the years behind, that we might have had together.*

What shall I say to you? That I tried and failed and am sorry? But am I? At this hour I don't want to lie, most especially not to you three.

Did I do right?

Yes.

No.

O God, oh, shit, how can I tell? The moon is rising above the soot-clouds. I might make it that far. Commissioner Wenig was talking about how we should maintain the last Lunar base another few years, till industry can find a substitute for those giant molecules they make there. But wasn't the Premier of United Africa saying those industries ought to be forbidden, they're too wasteful, and any country that keeps them going is an enemy of the human race?

Gunfire rattles in the streets. Some female voice somewhere is screaming.

I've got to get Mother out of here. That's the last thing I can do for Dad.

After ten years of studying to be a food engineer or a doctor, I'll probably feel too tired to care about the moon. After another ten years of being a desk pilot and getting fat, I'll probably be outraged at any proposal to spend my tax money–

–except maybe for defense. In Siberia they're preaching that strange new missionary religion. And the President of Europe has said that if necessary, his government will denounce the ban on nuclear weapons.

The ship passed among the stars bearing a crew of dead bones. After a hundred billion years it crossed the Edge–not the edge of space or time, which does not exist, but the Edge–and came to harbor at Murphy's Hall.

And the dust which the cosmic rays had made began to stir, and gathered itself back into bones; and from the radiation-corroded skeleton of the ship crept atoms which formed into flesh; and the captain and his men awoke. They opened themselves and looked upon the suns that went blazing and streaming overhead.

"We're home," said the captain.

Proud at the head of his men, he strode uphill from the dock, toward the hall of the five hundred and forty doors. Comets flitted past him, novae exploded in dreadful glory, planets turned and querned, the clinker of a once living world drifted by, new life screamed its outrage at being born.

The roofs of the house lifted like mountains against night and the light-clouds. The ends of rafters jutted beyond the eaves, carved into dragon heads. Through the doorway toward which the captain led his crew, eight hundred men could have marched abreast. But a single form waited to greet them; and beyond him was darkness.

When the captain saw who that was, he bowed very deeply. The other took his hand. "We have been waiting," he said. The captain's heart sprang. "Mary too?"

"Yes, of course. Everyone."

Me. And you. And you. And you in the future, if you exist. In the end, Murphy's Law gets us all. But we, my friends, must go to him the hard way. Our luck didn't run out. Instead, the decision that could be made was made. It was decided for us that our race–among the trillions which must be out there wondering what lies beyond their skies–is not supposed to have either discipline or dreams. No, our job is to make everybody nice and safe and equal, and if this happens to be impossible, then nothing else matters.

If I went to that place–and I'm glad that this is a lie–I'd keep remembering what we might have done and seen and known and been and loved.

Murphy's Hell.

FACES FORWARD by Jack Dann and George Zebrowski

As in previous decades, the seventies has had its share of new collaborative teams. The most successful, of course, is that of Larry Niven and Jerry Pournelle with the three major novels mentioned in the general introduction. (Oddly, while both Niven and Pournelle are prolific writers of short stories they have never done one together; if they had it would have appeared in these pages.) Other partners of note are Gregory Benford and Gordon Eklund, Piers Anthony and Robert Margoff, and Jack Dann and George Zebrowski. (Your editors may or may not also qualify as partners of note in the seventies. Depends on who you talk to. Our wives think so, if nobody else does.)

Jack M. Dann and George Zebrowski (both b. 1945) have done only a few stories together, but all of them have been of high quality. Individually, Dann is the author of Starhiker (1976) and Junction (1979), has another science fiction novel in progress and a short-story collection scheduled out from Doubleday, and has co-edited anthologies with Zebrowski and with Gardner Dozois; Zebrowski has published two s-f novels, The Omega Point and Starweb, and one collection, and recently published a long novel, Macrolife, which had been in progress since 1972. In addition to his tandem work with Dann, he has collaborated on stories with Pamela Sargent.

"Faces Forward" originally appeared in Dystopian Visions, a Roger Elwood anthology published almost invisibly by Prentice-Hall in 1975 (no paperback edition). In its deft and chilling offhandedness, in its grace and control, it seems to us to be one of the finest if least-known science fiction short-shorts of this odd and troubled decade.

FACES FORWARD
By Jack Dann and George Zebrowski

It's just a job. I know I should have looked for something better, but times are bad. And what could I do? Be a shoe salesman or a delivery boy? But anything would be better than this.

So I sit and watch the ugly people browse through the magazines. They all have greasy faces and greasy hair and they probably smell. The store smells from onions, anyway.

A greaser drops two faggot magazines on the counter and tries not to look at me. I stare at the top of his head, burning the fear of God into his fetid brain. He should spend his money on a new suit. But he wants filth, just like the others. They all slink around the filth magazines, hands in greasy pockets, eyes downcast,

Because they know I know. And God knows. The hardness in their pants and their unholy thoughts are blasphemy. And the people walking past, on their way home from a day's work, know also. They look in the window and then turn their heads.

I turn around and smile at them, paying no attention to a callow boy twitching before my counter, waiting to pay for a vicarious thrill.

"Wake up, buster. Hey fat man, how about my change?" The callow youth is gone. Or did he step out the door and step back in, changed by thirty years in time? The man in front of me looks like me. His lips curl in a snarl, and I feel the hatred inside, uncoiling like a snake, slipping into my arms, then into my brain, whispering.

And I hate myself more than I could hate my image.

I think of time, tedious corrupting time, fiery time taking me endlessly ahead; my names are different, but I am the same.

Fin de siècle–a century running out like poison wine, red wine, thick with additives. There. It's gone. The next hundred years begin. Row on row of new bottles, filled with . . . what?

With filth. Only the packages have changed, and the names.

But the magazines are still here, behind shock fields and sensor lights. Handy-randies and telefactape machines gleam in the back room, exotic machinery to substitute for flesh. New weapons to use against flesh.

Outside, the crowds are drunk. They wander around in the yellow thoughtfog, pulled this way and that by the best or most delicious or strongest thoughtstrands.

The door slides open and a crowd bursts into the store. I ignore them. Their beadblankets can glow, their falsefaces can mimic me and smirk as they like, I'll ignore them. They are just undercity filth who lust only for synthetic flesh and machines.

"Come in, come in," I shout to them finally. They will not leave. They are intent on trying to drown me in their scum. But I swim with God. My stare withers them.

I am different from them. I am better. If I could leave this place, this job, this time, I would pray and meditate on life and goodness. And keep away from this filth.

"The machine doesn't work," screams a young girl who should be home with her family.

"Good," I whisper. I think of starships swimming through the dark light-years to newer, greener worlds, where all centuries are just beginning, where wide-eyed children play, ignorant of what lies within their bodies, the iron fist of endings hiding in their minds, which one day will break their youthful worlds to dust.

They are smashing everything. It's only a question of time before they reach this block. The slaughter-funhouse and campo-casino have been melted, the people inside mere discolorations in the shiny metal.

My soundsensors are turned on full. I can hear the crowd screaming in the street, righteously killing and dismembering the pleasurepeople. So let them. They are right. It has been a long time coming. Take us.

I'll be spared. But I hate the waiting. This is such a small store, and it has become difficult to breathe. They must have reached the purification plant. So what to do? Stare at the machine, the illicit pleasure builder, and think about what will be.

I'm growing tired and bored. My hands look larger to me than they should. And my nails are discolored from drugdip.

But who can sleep? I could turn off the soundsensors, but . . . The noise is constant now, a groaning punctuated by strident lustscreams.

And with tired eyes–the air is so close–I watch the side of the store melt into a rainbow. I scream but my throat is gravel. Three faces appear before me; I'll wake up soon and turn off the sensors.

I get up and go outside into the street.

Everyone is gone. It's hard to breathe. The light is getting dimmer. Then I see them walling up the neighborhood, bricking it up to die. I run to the end of the block, but I'm too late. The last stone is set. They have all gone but me. I was too late to get out. I slept too long in my thoughtfog. The ones who live above, below and side, have blotted us out.

I run back to the store and tick on the telefac what has happened; but the tape goes nowhere. My words are frozen.

The nerves to the rest of the world have been cut.

The family is getting married. A dozen daughters, kept pure by exclusive use of surrogate animals, will join now in holy-chain-lock with a dozen daddies.

A wedding.

Two chain families. The quick-witted head-father smiles. The daughters will be with family tonight, at home, safe from the bricked-up cancer a hundred stories below.

Shower burst.

None living can know my face. Identities, minds, and hearts change like colors in a glass. Who am I today?

What does it matter? My face is still flesh, still bone and tissue. Let me be Lisa, the bald daughter of the Citizen Leader. The one with the flared nose and synthomouth that parts her long face. The one who smells.

But what wonderful smells: musk, pyhrr, sweetsweat–all the odors of lust and love. So I can smell myself, pretend that I'm

the tease, the teaser, the teased.
Out of the box. It's done. Let them look at me, let Lisa's proud nowfather disclaim me. I can do what I like for the duration. It's the rule. I am Lisa. Lisalisalisa. I love you, I love your smell, your touch, your quaking voice, your toothless smile–who needs food?
All I need is a reflection. But it's not enough. Touching yourself, even discovering new curves and bone structures, is always the same. Lisalisa's probably under by now. She can't be seen until I'm through. That's the law.
"Well," says the Citizen Leader, "you might as well join the household. You know the rules."
Yes, I know, I know. I'll stay for a week, but my skin is already beginning to sag and I'm still not complete. Perhaps I should have waited for Lisa.
She wouldn't sag.

Ventricular contractions. My heart is swollen with candy juices, congealing into thick honey. In a few moments it will set, and my heart will be made of rock candy.
What a world to live in. So I'm in love. A constant state of mind. Why not? Everything is verdant, grown green and orange and stippled for effect. Clouds scud past and I make up animals and shapes to see inside them.
Stop lying, you green-crusted sleeper. The room is small and clean and brightly lit. It's all machine; there's no flesh here, just crystal and wire and plastiglass and shiny metal. Where am I? There's no place to go. No arms to slit my imaginary throat. No mouth or lung to promote a human scream.
What matter? The only rule is that I must be alone. But I want flesh.
What a world to live in. So I'm in love. A . . .

An incandescent wire glows in the night, branching in a billion directions, reaching into the forever of a trillion soft brains. Energy flows through the arteries, whispering in the undernight of the worlds, bringing a little of whatever, something of nothingness, a small amount of nameless things. Negative graces bestowed by an electric generator.

Solipsis. Lone-Alone.
A man, so-called, is sitting in a chair.
Me.
The others, a myriad or more, face me. Their faces are masks, their hearts are hard.
I am a virgin. I am all virgins. They are filth, used.
They flood me. Their minds enter mine and marvel. My innocence is their pleasure. I am ecstatic music in their brains. My brain is sodomized. They teach me the word, they make me feel its meaning. They are strong. They grasp. They take. They leave.
The mindgate closes.
Now it's my turn. The gate opens. I enter their diseased wastes. They are old, alone, barren, dirty, different from me. Incomparable landscapes. Dingy shapes crouching in blue light. Black shapes rearing under red suns.
My pleasure swells. The suns bleed. I wallow. My body remains pure, unspoiled, a glacier of white infinities.
I am a virgin. That's my job.
I cry out and die.
Nothing stands in their way.
They start again.

In the corner of the world my eye sees the superimposed calendar clock. Outside it's 2251, Anno Domini. The hold cannot be broken.
Kyrie Eleison.

PROSE BOWL by Bill Pronzini and Barry N. Malzberg

The central idea for this novelette emerged over a few vodkas in the Pronzini living room in August 1978 ("hey, what if writers competed like professional athletes?"/"well, what if they *were* professional athletes?" etc.). It started out as a slight, funny satire on writers and sports clichés and was first-drafted that night at 1200 words. Dried out and solemn the next day, however, we realized that we had tied into material far more personal and complicated than a party joke, and that it demanded a lot more wordage and a lot more effort.

So we proceeded to do it in its present form, which is still satire but, from where we sit, not slight and not quite so funny after all. You want to know what it's like to be, in the words of Jack Woodford, "a professional fiction racketeer"? This is it, folks. We are all of us, to one degree or another, Rex Sackett and The Cranker.

Bill Pronzini (b. 1943) is the author of eighteen novels to which he will admit and over 200 short stories and articles; he is mostly regarded as a mysterist but does not think of himself as anything other than an unadjectival writer. Barry N. Malzberg (b. 1939) is the author of fifty novels to which he will admit and over 200 short stories and articles; he is mostly regarded as a science-fictionist but does not think of himself as anything other than an unadjectival writer. Together we have edited three science fiction anthologies and written 30 short stories and three suspense novels, with a fourth novel in progress (the first of our novels, *The Running of Beasts*, Putnam, 1976, was a moderate commercial success; we won't discuss the other two). In other collaborations, one of us has co-authored novels and/or stories and co-edited anthologies with a number of writers, including Collin Wilcox and Joe Gores; the other of us has written jointly in science fiction with Kris Neville and Harry Harrison, and co-edited anthologies with Edward L. Ferman.

As a work of "Literature" (we fiction racketeers always tack on the quote marks when we use the big L), "Prose Bowl" may well be the best of all our collaborations together and apart. Who knows? If so, credit Doctor Smirnoff.

PROSE BOWL
By Bill Pronzini and Barry N. Malzberg

Standing there at midfield in the Coliseum, in front of a hundred thousand screaming New-Sport fans and a TriDim audience estimated at thirty million, I felt a lot of different emotions: excitement, pride, tension, and maybe just a touch of fear. I still couldn't believe that I was here–Rex Sackett, the youngest ever to make it all the way through the playoffs to the Prose Bowl. But I'd done it, and if I cleared one more hurdle I would be the new world champion.

Just one more hurdle.

I looked across the Line at the old man. Leon Culp, better known as The Cranker. Fifty-seven years old, twenty million words in a career spanning almost four decades. Twice defeated in the quarter-finals, once defeated in the semi-finals two years ago. His first time in the Prose Bowl too, and he was the sentimental favorite. I was just a kid, an upstart; by all rights, a lot of the scribes had been saying, I didn't deserve to be here at my age. But the odds-makers had made me a 3-2 favorite because of my youth and stamina and the way I had handled my opponents in the playoffs. And because there were also a lot of people who felt The Cranker couldn't win the big ones; that he depended too much on the Fuel now; that he was pretty near washed up and had made it this far only because of weak competition.

Maybe all of that was true, but I wasn't so sure. Leon Culp had always been my idol; I had grown up reading and studying him, and in his time–and despite his misfortune in past Prose Bowl races–he was the best there was. I'd been in awe of him when I was a wet-behind-the-ears kid in the Junior Creative Leagues and I was still a little in awe of him now.

It wasn't that I lacked confidence in myself. I had plenty of confidence, and plenty of desire too; I wanted to win not only for myself and the $100,000 championship prize, but for Sally, and for Mort Taylor, the best agent in the business, and most of all for Mom and Dad, who had supported me during those first five lean years when I was struggling in the semi-pros. Still, I couldn't seem to shake that sense of nervous wonder. This wasn't any ordinary pro I was about to go up against. This was The Cranker.

It was almost time for the Face-Off to begin. The P.A. announcer introduced me first, because as the youngest of the contestants I was wearing the visitor's red, and I stepped out and waved at the packed stands. There was a chorus of cheers, particularly from over in G Section where Sally and Mort and the folks were sitting with the Sackett Boosters. The band struck up my old school song; I felt my eyes dampen as I listened.

When the announcer called out The Cranker's name, the cheers were even louder–but there were a few catcalls mixed in too. He didn't seem to pay any attention either way. He just stood without moving, his seamed old face set in stoic determination. In his blue uniform jersey, outlined against the hot New Year's Day sky, he looked bigger than he really was–awesome, implacable. Unbeatable.

Everybody stood up for the national anthem. Then there was another uproar from the fans–I'd never imagined how deafening it could get down here on the floor of the Prose Bowl–and finally the Head Editor trotted out and called us over for the coin flip. I called Tails in the air, and the coin fell to the turf and came up Tails. The Head Editor moved over to me and patted my shoulders to indicate I'd won the toss; the Sackett Boosters bellowed their approval. Through all of this Culp remained motionless and aloof, not looking at me or the Head Editor or anything else, it seemed.

We went back to the Line and got ready. I was becoming more and more tense as the Face-Off neared; the palms of my hands were slick and my head seemed empty. What if I couldn't think of a title? What if I couldn't think of an opening sentence?

"Be cool, kid," Mort Taylor had told me earlier. "Don't try to force it. The words'll come, just like they always have."

The Cranker and I stood facing each other, looking at the huge electronic scoreboards at opposite ends of the field. Then, out of the corner of my eye, I saw the Head Editor wave his red starting flag at the Line Editor; and in the next instant the two plot topics selected by the officials flashed on the board.

A. FUTURISTIC LOVE-ADVENTURE
B. MID-TWENTIETH-CENTURY DETECTIVE

I had five seconds to make my choice. Both of the topics looked tough, but this was the Prose Bowl and nothing came easy in the championship. I made an arbitrary selection and yelled out "Plot B!" to the Head Editor. He unfurled his white flag with the letter B on it, and immediately the P.A. announcer's voice boomed, "Rex Sackett chooses Plot B!"

The crowd broke into thunderous applause; the sound of it was like a pressure against my eardrums. I could feel my pulse racing in hard irregular rhythm and my stomach was knotted up. I tried not to think about the thirty million people watching me on the TriDim closeups.

The Line Editor's claxon went off.

The Cranker and I broke for our typewriters. And all of a sudden, as I was sliding into my chair, I felt control and a kind of calm come into me. That was the way it always was with me, the way it always was with the great ones, Mort had said: No matter how nervous you were before the start of a match, once the horn sounded your professionalism took over and you forgot everything except the job you had to do.

I had a title even before I reached for the first sheet of paper beside the typewriter, and I had the first sentence as soon as I rolled the sheet into the platen. I fired out the title–THE MICAWBER DIAMOND–jabbed down the opening sentence and the rest of the narrative hook, and was into the second paragraph before I heard Culp's machine begin its amplified hammering across the Line.

A hundred thousand voices screamed for speed and continuity. The Cranker's rooting section and the Sackett Boosters made the most noise; I knew Sally would be leading the cheers on my side and I had a sharp mental image of her in her red-and-white sweater with the big S on the front. Sweet, wonderful Sally. . . .

I hunched forward, teeth locked around the stem of my old briar, and drove through two more paragraphs of stage-setting. End of page one. I glanced up at the south-end scoreboard as I ripped the sheet out of the platen and rolled in a new one. SACKETT 226, CULP 187. I laid in half a page of flashback, working the adjectives and the adverbs to build up my count, powered through eight lines of descriptive transition, and came into the first passage of dialogue. Up on the board, what I was writing appeared in foot-high electronic printout, as if the words were emblazoned on the sky itself.

SAM SLEDGE STALKED ACROSS HIS PLUSH OFFICE, LEAVING FOOTPRINTS IN THE THICK SHAG CARPET LIKE ANGRY DOUGHNUTS. VELDA VANCE, ALLURINGLY BEAUTIFUL SECRETARY TO SLEDGE AND CHANDLER INVESTIGATIONS, LOOKED UP IN ALARM. "SOMEBODY MURDERED MILES CHANDLER LAST NIGHT," SLEDGE GRITTED TO HER, "AND STOLE THE

MICAWBER DIAMOND HE WAS GUARDING."

It was solid stuff, I knew that. Not my best, but plenty good enough and just what the fans wanted. The sound of my name echoing through the great stadium put chills on my back.

"*Sackett! Hack it! Sackett, hack it! Sackett hack it Sackett hack it Sackett hack it!*"

I finished the last line on page two and had the clean sheet into the machine in two seconds flat. My eyes found the scoreboard again as I pounded the keys: SACKETT 529, CULP 430. Hundred-word lead, but that was nothing in this early going. Without losing speed or concentration, I sneaked a look at what The Cranker was punching out.

THE DENEBIAN GREEN-BEAST CAME TOWARD HER, MOVING WITH A CURIOUSLY FLOWING MOTION, ITS TENTACLES SWAYING IN A SENSUAL DANCE OF ALIEN LUST. SHE STOOD FROZEN AGAINST A RUDDER OF ROCK AND STARED AT THE THING IN HORROR. THE UNDULATING TENTACLES REACHED TOWARD HER AND THE GREEN WAVES OF DAMP WHICH THE BEAST EXUDED SENT SHUDDERS THROUGH HER.

God, I thought, that's top-line prose. He's inspired, he's pulling out all the stops.

The crowd sensed it too. I could hear his cheerleaders chanting, almost drowning out the cries from my own rooters across the way.

"*Come on, Culp! Write that pulp!*"

I was in the most intense struggle of my life, there was no doubt about that. I'd known it was going to be rough, but knowing it and then being in the middle of it were two different things. The Cranker was a legend in his own time; when he was right no one had his facility, his speed, his edge with the cutting transitions, his ability to produce under stress. If he could maintain pace and narrative drive, there wasn't a writer on earth who could beat him–

SACKETT 920, CULP 894.

The score registered on my mind and I realized with a jolt that my own pace had slacked off: Culp had cut my lead by more than half. That was what happened to you when you started worrying about your opponent and what he was doing. I could hear Mort's voice again, echoing in my memory: "The pressure will turn your head, kid, if you let it. But I don't think it will. I think you're made of the real stuff; I think you've got the guts and the heart."

THE ANGER ON MICAWBER'S FACE MELTED AWAY LIKE SOAP IN A SOAP DISH UNDER A STREAM OF HOT DIRTY WATER.

I jammed out that line and I knew I was back in the groove, beginning to crank near the top of my form. The sound of my machine climbed to a staccato pulse. Dialogue, some fast foreshadowing, a string of four adjectives that drew a burst of applause from the Sackett Boosters. I could fell my wrists starting to knot up from the strain and there was pain in my left leg where I'd pulled a hamstring during the semi-final match against the Kansas City Flash. But I didn't pay any attention to that; I had written in pain before and I wasn't about to let it bother me now. I just kept firing out my prose.

Only I wasn't gaining back any of my lead, I saw then. The foot-high numerals read SACKETT 1163, CULP 1127. The Cranker had hit his stride too and he was matching me word for word, sentence for sentence.

SHE HAD NO MORE STRENGTH LEFT TO RUN. SHE WAS TRAPPED NOW, THERE WAS NO ESCAPE. A SCREAM BURST FROM HER THROAT AS THE BEAST BOUNDED UP TO HER AND DREW HER INTO ITS AWFUL CLUTCHES, BREATHING GREEN FUMES AGAINST HER FACEPLATE. IT WAS GOING TO WORK ITS WILL ON HER! IT WAS GOING TO DO UNSPEAKABLE THINGS TO HER BODY!

"Culp, Culp, Culp!"

THE NIGHT WAS DARK AND WET AND COLD AND THE RAIN FELL ON SLEDGE LIKE A MILLION TEARS FROM A MILLION LOST LOVES ON A MILLION WORLDS IN A MILLION GALAXIES.

"*Sackett, Sackett, Sackett!*"

Sweat streamed into my eyes, made the numerals on the board seem smeared and glistening: SACKETT 1895, CULP 1857. I ducked my head against the sleeve of my tunic and slid a new sheet into the machine. On the other side of the Line, The Cranker was sitting straight and stiff behind his typewriter, fingers flying, his shaggy head wreathed in cigarette smoke. But he wasn't just hitting the keys, he was *attacking* them–as if they, not me, were the enemy and he was trying to club them into submission.

I reached back for a little extra, raced through the rest of the transition, slammed out three paragraphs of introspection and five more of dialogue. New page. More dialogue, then another narrative hook to foreshadow the first confrontation scene. New page. Description and some cat-and-mouse action to build suspense.

AS HE WAITED IN THE DARK ALLEY FOR THE GUY WHO WAS FOLLOWING HIM, SLEDGE'S RIGHT HAND ITCHED AROUND THE GUN IN HIS POCKET. HE COULD FEEL THE OLD FAMILIAR RAGE BURNING INSIDE HIM, MAKING HIS BLOOD BOIL LIKE WATER IN A KETTLE ON THE OLD WOOD-BURNING STOVE IN HIS OLD MAN'S FOURTH-FLOOR WALKUP IN

My typewriter locked. I heard the cheering rise to a crescendo; two hundred thousand hands commenced clapping as the Line Editor's horn blared.

End of the first quarter.

SACKETT 2500, CULP 2473.

I leaned back in my chair, sleeving more wetness from my face, and took several deep breaths. The Cranker had got to his feet. He stood in a rigid posture, a fresh cigarette between his lips, and squinted toward the sidelines. His Seconds were already on the field, running toward him with water bucket and a container of Fuel.

My own Seconds reached me a short time later. One of them extended Fuel, but even though my mouth was dry, sandy, I shook my head and gestured him away. Mort and I had agreed that I should hold off on the Fuel as long as possible; it was part of the game plan we had worked out.

By the time I finished splashing water on my face and toweling off, there was less than a minute of the time-out left. I looked over at G Section. I couldn't pick Mom and Dad out of the sea of faces, or Sally or Mort either, but just knowing they were there was enough.

I took my place, knocked dottle out of the briar, tamped in some fresh tobacco, and fired it. My mind was already racing, working ahead–a full four sentences when Culp sat down again and the Head Editor raised the red starting flag.

Claxon.

THE OLD NEIGHBORHOOD. THE FOLLOWER HAD SOMETHING TO DO WITH HIS PARTNER'S MURDER AND THE THEFT OF THE DIAMOND, SLEDGE WAS SURE OF THAT. HE WAS GOING TO GET SOME ANSWERS NOW, ONE WAY OR ANOTHER.

And I was off, banging my machine at the same feverish pace of the first period. I cut through a full page of action, interspersing it with dialogue, drawing it out; the scene was good for another 500 words, at least. Twelve pages down and the thirteenth in the typewriter. My quality level was still good, but when I glanced up at the board I saw that The Cranker was once again cranking at the top of his form.

BUT EVEN WHILE SHE WAS CLINGING TO THE STAR-FLEET CAPTAIN WHO HAD SAVED HER LIFE, SHE FELT A STRANGE SADNESS. THE GREEN-BEAST HAD BEEN DISINTEGRATED AND WAS NOTHING MORE NOW THAN A PUDDLE OF GREEN ON THE DUSTY SANDS OF DENEB, LIKE A SPLOTCH OF PAINT ON AN ALIEN CANVAS. THE HORROR WAS OVER. AND YET . . . AND YET, DESPITE HER REVULSION, THE THING HAD STIRRED SOMETHING DEEP AND PRIMITIVE INSIDE HER THAT SHE WAS ONLY JUST BEGINNING TO UNDERSTAND.

"Culp, Culp–crank that pulp!"

My lead had dwindled to a mere twelve words: the scoreboard

read SACKETT 3359, CULP 3347. The Cranker was making his move now, and he was doing it despite the fact that I was working at maximum speed.

The feeling of tension and uncertainty began to gnaw at me again. I fought it down, concentrated even more intensely, punching the keys so hard that pain shot up both wrists. Fresh sweat rolled off me; the hot sun lay on the back of my neck like a burning hand.

SLEDGE SNARLED, "YOU'LL TALK, ALL RIGHT!" AND SWATTED THE GUY ACROSS THE HEAD WITH HIS FORTY-FIVE. THE GUY REELED AND STAGGERED INTO THE WET ALLEY WALL. SLEDGE MOVED IN ON HIM, TRANSFERRING THE GUN TO HIS LEFT HAND. HE HIT THE FOLLOWER A SECOND TIME, HIT HIM IN THE MOUTH WITH A HAND LIKE A FIST

The Head Editor's whistle blew.

And my typewriter locked, jamming my fingers.

Penalty. Penalty!

My throat closed up. I snapped my head over toward the sidelines and saw the ten-second penalty flag waving–the green-and-black one that meant "Phrasing Unacceptable." The crowd was making a magnified sound that was half excited, half groaning; I knew the TriDim cameras would have homed in on me for a series of closeups. I could feel my face reddening. First penalty of the match and I had let it happen to me.

But that wasn't the worst part. The worst part was that it was going to cost me the lead: The Cranker's typewriter was still clattering on at white heat, churning out words and sentences that flashed like taunts on the board.

I counted off the seconds in my mind, and when the Head Editor's flag dropped and my machine unlocked I flailed the keys angrily, rewriting the penalty sentence: HE HIT THE FOLLOWER A SECOND TIME, HIT HIM IN THE MOUTH WITH A HAND LIKE A CEMENT BLOCK. But the damage had been done, all right. The board told me that and told everyone else too.

Prose Bowl _____ *211*

CULP 3899, SACKETT 3878.

The penalty seemed to have energized The Cranker, given him a psychological lift; he was working faster than ever now, with even more savagery. I felt a little wrench of fear. About the only way you could beat one of the greats was to take the lead early on and hold it. Once an experienced old pro like Culp got in front, the advantage was all his.

A quote dropped into my mind, one I'd read a long time ago in an Old-Sports history text, and it made me shiver: "Going up against the best is a little bit like going up against Death."

I had my own speed back now but my concentration wasn't as sharp as it had been before the penalty; a couple of times I hit the wrong keys, misspelled words and then had to retype them. It was just the kind of penalty-reaction Mort had warned me against. "Penalties don't mean a thing," he'd said. "What you've got to watch out for is worrying about them, letting them dam up the flow or lead you into another mistake."

But it wasn't Mort out here in the hot Prose Bowl sun. It wasn't Mort going head-to-head against a legend. . . .

The amplified sound of Culp's machine seemed louder than my own, steadier, more rhythmic. Nervously, I checked the board again. His stuff was coming so fast now that it might have been written by one of the experimental prose computers instead of a pulpeteer.

SHE LOOKED OUT THROUGH THE SHIP'S VIEW SCREEN AT THE EMPTY SWEEP OF SPACE. BEHIND HER SHE COULD HEAR THE CAPTAIN TALKING TO THE BASE COMMANDER AT EARTH COLONY SEVEN, RELAYING THE INFORMATION ABOUT THE SHUTTLE-SHIP CRASH ON DENEB. "ONLY ONE SURVIOR," HE WAS SAYING. YES, SHE THOUGHT, ONLY ONE SURVIVOR. BUT I WISH THERE HADN'T BEEN ANY. IF I'D DIED IN THE CRASH TOO, THEN I WOULDN'T HAVE BEEN ATTACKED BY THE GREEN-BEAST. AND I WOULDN'T BE FEELING THESE STRANGE AND TERRIBLE EMOTIONS, THIS SENSE OF UNFULFILLMENT AND DEPRIVATION.

Some of the fans were on their feet, screaming *"Cranker! Cranker!"*

CULP 4250, SACKETT 4196.

I felt lightheaded, giddy with tension; but the adrenaline kept flowing and the words kept coming, pouring out of my subconscious and through the mind-haze and out into the blazing afternoon–nouns, verbs, adjectives, adverbs. Don't let him gain any more ground, I kept urging myself. Stay close. Stay close!

SLEDGE FOLLOWED THE FAT MAN THROUGH THE HEAVY DARKNESS ALONG THE RIVER. THE STENCH OF FISH AND MUD AND GARBAGE WAFTED UP FROM THE OILY BLACK WATER AND SLAPPED HIM ACROSS THE FACE LIKE A DIRTY WET TOWEL. HE DIDN'T KNOW WHERE THE FAT MAN WAS LEADING HIM, BUT I FELT SURE IT

Whistle.

Lock.

Penalty.

I looked up in disbelief and saw the Head Editor waving the purple-and-gold penalty flag that signified "Switched Tense." A smattering of boos rolled down around me from the stands. My eyes flicked to the board, and it was true, I had slipped out of third person and into first–an amateur's mistake, a kid's blunder. Shame made me duck my head; it was as if, in that moment, I could feel concentrated waves of disgust from the sixty million eyes that watched me.

The ten seconds of the penalty were like a hundred, a thousand. Because all the while The Cranker's machine ratcheted onward, not once slowing or breaking cadence. When my typewriter finally unlocked I redid the sentence in the proper tense and plunged ahead without checking the score. I didn't want to know how far behind I was now. I was afraid that if I did know, it would make me reckless with urgency and push me into another stupid error.

My throat was parched, raw and hot from pipe smoke, and for the first time I thought about the Fuel. It had been a long time since I'd wanted it in the first half of a Face-Off, but I wanted it now. Only I couldn't have it, not until halftime, not without taking a disastrous 20-second Fuel penalty. There had to be less than 600 words left to the end of the quarter, I told myself; I could hold out that long. A top-line pro could do 600 words no matter what the circumstances. A top-line pro, as The Cranker himself had once said, could do 600 words *dead*.

I forced myself to shut out everything from my mind except the prose, the story line. Old page out of the platen, new page in. Old page out, new page in. Speed, speed, but make sure of the grammar, the tense, the phrasing. Still a full 5000 words to go in the match. Still an even chance for a second-half comeback.

THE INTERIOR OF THE WAREHOUSE WAS DANK AND MUSTY AND FILLED WITH CROUCHING SHADOWS LIKE A PLATOON OF EVIL SPIRITS WAITING TO LEAP ON HIM. THEN THERE WAS A FLICKER OF LIGHT AT THE REAR AND IT TOLD SLEDGE THE FAT MAN HAD SWITCHED ON A SMALL POCKET FLASH. GUN IN HAND, HE CREPT STEALTHILY TOWARD THE

My machine locked again.

I jerked my head up, half-expecting to see a penalty flag aloft for the third time. But it wasn't a penalty; it was halftime at last. The Line Editor's horn blew. The Cranker's cheering section was chanting *"Culp, Culp, Culp!"*

I had to look at the board then, at the score shining against the sky, and I did: CULP 5000, SACKETT 4796.

Some of the tension drained out of me and I sat there feeling limp, heavy with fatigue. The joints in my fingers were stiff; there was a spot of blood on the tip of my right forefinger where the skin had split near the nail. But the score was all that mattered to me at that moment, and it wasn't as bad as I'd feared. Only 204 words down. I had made up larger margins than that in my career; I could do it again.

Across the Line, Culp was on his feet and staring down at the turf with eyes that gleamed and didn't blink. He wasn't quite so imposing now, strangely. His back was bowed and his hands looked a little shaky–as though he were the one who was trailing by 204 words and facing an uphill battle in the second half.

When I pushed back my own chair and stood up, a sudden sharp pain in my tender hamstring made me clutch at the table edge. I was soaked in sweat and so thirsty I had trouble swallowing. But I didn't reach for the Fuel when my Seconds appeared; in spite of my need I didn't want to take any while I was out here, didn't want to show The Cranker and the crowd and the TriDim audience that I needed it. In the locker room, yes. Just another few minutes.

Two of Culp's Seconds began escorting him off the field toward the tunnel at the south end; he was hanging onto his Fuel container with both hands. I waved away my people and hobbled toward the north tunnel alone.

Fans showered me with roses and confetti as I came into the tunnel. That was a good sign; they hadn't given up on me. The passageway was cool, a welcome relief from the blazing sun, and empty except for the two guards who were stationed there to keep out fans, New-Sport reporters, and anyone else who might try to see me. The Prose Bowl rules were strict: Each of the contestants had to spend halftime alone, locked in his respective locker room without typewriter or any other kind of writing tools. Back in '26, the year of the Postal-Rate Riots, a pro named Penny-A-Word Gordon had been disqualified for cheating when officials found out another wordsmith, hired by Gordon's agent, had written a fast 1000-word continuation during the break and delivered it to Gordon, who then revised it with a pen, memorized it, and used it to build up an early third-quarter lead. The incident had caused a pretty large scandal at the time and the Prose Bowl people weren't about to let it happen again.

As soon as I came into the locker room the familiar writer's-office odors of sweat, stale tobacco, and spilled Fuel assailed me and made me feel a little better. The Prose Bowl officials were also careful about creating the proper atmosphere; they wanted each of the contestants to feel at home. Behind me the door panel whispered shut and locked itself electronically, but I was already on my way to where the Fuel container sat waiting on the desk.

I measured out three ounces, tossed it off, and waited for it to work its magic. It didn't take long; the last of the tension and most of the lassitude were gone within seconds. I poured out another three ounces, set it aside, and stripped off my sodden uniform.

While I was showering I thought about The Cranker. His performance in the first half had been flawless: no penalties, unflagging speed, front-line prose. Even his detractors wouldn't be able to find fault with it, or even the slightest indication that he was washed up and about to wilt under the pressure.

So if I was going to beat him I had to do it on talent and speed and desire–all on my own. Nothing came easy in this business or in the Prose Bowl; I'd known that all along. You had to work long and hard if you wanted to win. You had to give your all, and try to stay away from the penalties, and hope that you were good enough and strong enough to come out on top.

No, The Cranker wasn't going to beat himself. And I wasn't going to beat myself either.

I stepped out of the shower, toweled dry, bandaged the wound on my right forefinger, put on a clean jersey, and took the rest of my allotted Fuel an ounce at a time. I could feel my confidence building, solidifying again.

The digital clock on one wall said that there were still nine minutes left in the time-out. I paced around, flexing my leg to keep the hamstring from tightening up. It was quiet in there, almost too quiet–and suddenly I found myself thinking how alone I was. I wished Mort were there so we could discuss strategy; I wished the folks and Sally were there so I could tell them how I felt, how self-assured I was.

But even if they were here, I thought then, would it really make a difference? I'd still be alone, wouldn't I? You were always alone in the pros; your parents, your agent, the Editors, the girl you loved, all of them gave you as much help and support as they could–but they weren't pulpeteers and they just didn't know what it was like to go out time after time and face the machine, the blank sheets of paper, the pressures and pain of millions of words and hundreds of Face-Offs. The only ones who did know what it was like were other pros; only your own could truly understand.

Only your own.

The Cranker?

Were we really opponents, enemies? Or were we soul brothers, bound more closely than any blood relatives because we shared the same basic loneliness?

It was an unnerving thought and I pushed it out of my head. I couldn't go out there and face Culp believing we were one and the same. It would be like going up against myself, trying to overcome myself in a contest that no one could ever win. . . .

The door panel unlocked finally, just as the three-minute warning horn blew, and I hurried out of the locker room, down the tunnel past the silent guards and back into the stadium. The last of the marching bands and majorettes were just filing off onto the sidelines. The fans were buzzing, and when they saw me emerge and trot out toward the Line there were cheers and applause and the Sackett band began playing my old school song again.

Culp wasn't there yet. But as I reached the Line and took my position, I heard the roar from the stands intensify and his rooting section set up a chant: *"Cranker! Cranker!"* Then I saw him, coming out of the south tunnel, not running but walking in a loose rapid gait. Halfway out he seemed to stagger just a little, then regained his stride. When he stopped across from me I saw that his eyes were still bright and fixed, like shiny nailheads in a block of old gray wood. I wondered how much Fuel he'd had during the time-out. Not that it mattered; it wouldn't have been enough to make a difference.

The Head Editor walked out carrying his flags. I lit my pipe and Culp fired a cigarette; we were both ready. The crowd noise subsided as the Head Editor raised his red flag–and then surged again as the flag fell and the claxon sounded.

The second half was underway.

My mind was clear and sharp as I dropped into my chair. I

had checked my prose printout, waiting at the Line, and I had the rest of my unfinished halftime sentence and the rest of the paragraph already worked out; I punched it down, followed it with three fast paragraphs of descriptive narrative. Build into another action-confrontation scene? No. I was only at the halfway point in the story line and it would throw my pacing off. I laid in a deft one-line twist, for shock value, and cut away into transition.

"That's it, Sackett! That's how to hack it!"

The approving cheers from the Sackett Boosters and from the rest of the fans were like a fresh shot of Fuel: I could feel my thoughts expanding, settling squarely into the groove. Words poured out of me; phrases, sentences, crisp images. The beat of my typewriter was steady, unrelieved, like a peal of thunder rolling across the hot blue sky.

But it wasn't the only thunder in the Prose Bowl, I realized abruptly. The Cranker's machine was making it too—louder, faster, even more intense. For the first time since the quarter had begun I glanced up at the score.

CULP 6132, SACKETT 5898.

I couldn't believe it. I had been certain that I was cutting into his lead, that I had closed to within at least 175 words; instead Culp had widened the margin by another 30. The thin edge of fear cut at me again, slicing through the confidence and that feeling of controlled power I always had when I was going good. I was throwing everything I had at The Cranker here in the third period, and it wasn't good enough–he was still pulling away.

I bit down so hard on the stem of my briar that I felt it crack between my teeth. Keep bearing down, I told myself grimly. Don't let up for a second.

HE WAS STILL THINKING ABOUT THE CASE, TRYING TO PUT THE PIECES TOGETHER, WHEN THE TELEPHONE RANG. IT WAS VELDA. "I'VE BEEN WORRIED ABOUT YOU, SAM," HER SOFT PURRING VOICE SAID, AND ALL AT ONCE HE FELT A BURNING NEED TO SEE HER. SHE WAS THE ONLY PERSON HE COULD TALK TO, THE ONE

PERSON IN THE WORLD WHO UNDERSTOOD HOW HE FELT.

"*Sackett, Sackett!*"

But The Cranker's machine kept on soaring; The Cranker's words kept on racing across the board with relentless speed.

WHEN SHE WAS SURE THE CAPTAIN WAS ASLEEP SHE GOT OUT OF THE BUNK AND PADDED OVER TO WHERE HIS UNIFORM LAY. SHE KNEW WHAT SHE HAD TO DO NOW. SHE ACCEPTED THE TRUTH AT LAST, BECAUSE THE WHOLE TIME SHE HAD BEEN COPULATING WITH THE CAPTAIN HER THOUGHTS HAD BEEN BACK ON DENEB, FULL OF THE SIGHT AND THE SMELL OF GREEN.

"*Culp, Culp, Culp!*"

The lift from the six ounces of Fuel I'd had in the locker room was gone now and the tension was back, binding the muscles in my fingers and shoulders. The sun seemed to be getting hotter, drawing runnels of sweat from my pores, making my head throb. My words were still coming fast, but the images weren't quite as sharp as they'd been minutes ago, the quality level not quite as high. I didn't care. Speed was all that mattered now; I was willing to sacrifice quality for the maintenance of speed.

CULP 6912. SACKETT 6671.

Down by 241 now; The Cranker had gained only seven words in the last 800. But *he* had gained them, not me–I couldn't seem to narrow his lead, no matter what I did. I lifted my head, still typing furiously, and stared across at him. His teeth were bared; sweat glistened like oil on his gray skin. Yet his fingers were a sunlit blur on the keys, as if they were independent creatures performing a mad dance.

CLENCHING THE CAPTAIN'S LASER WEAPON IN HER HAND, SHE MADE HER WAY AFT TO WHERE THE LIFECRAFT WERE KEPT. SHE KNEW THE COORDINATES FOR DENEB. SHE WOULD ORDER THE LIFECRAFT'S COMPUTER TO TAKE HER THERE–TAKE HER TO THE PROMISE OF THE GREEN.

A feeling of desperation came into me. Time was running out; there were less than 500 words left to go in the quarter, less than 3000 left in the match. You could make up 250 words in the fourth period of a Face-Off, but you couldn't do it unless you had momentum. And I didn't have it, I couldn't seem to get it. It all belonged to The Cranker.

The fans continued to shriek, creating a wild counterpoint to the thunder of our machines. I imagined I could hear Mort's voice telling me to hold on, keep cranking, and Dad's voice hoarse from shouting, and Sally's voice saying "You can do it, darling, you can do it!"

CULP 7245, SACKETT 7002.

Holding. Down 245 now but holding.

You can do it, you can do it!

SLEDGE'S EYES GLOWED AS HE LOOKED AT VELDA'S MAGNIFICENT BOSOM. VELDA, THE ONLY WOMAN HE'D WANTED SINCE HIS WIFE LEFT HIM THREE YEARS BEFORE BECAUSE SHE COULDN'T STAND HIS JOB AND THE KIND OF PEOPLE HE DEALT WITH. THE PALMS OF HIS HANDS WERE WET, HOT AND WET WITH DESIRE.

The palms of my hands were hot and wet, but I didn't dare take the time to wipe them dry. Only 150 to go in the quarter now.

HE TOOK HER INTO HIS ARMS. THE FEEL OF HER VOLUPTUOUS BODY WAS EXQUISITE. HE CRUSHED HIS MOUTH AGAINST HERS, HEARD HER MOAN AS HIS HAND CAME UP AND SLID ACROSS THE CURVE OF HER BREAST. "TAKE ME, SAM," SHE BREATHED HUSKILY AGAINST HIS LIPS. "TEAR MY CLOTHES OFF AND GIVE ME YOUR HOT

I tore page twenty-six out of the typewriter, slapped in page twenty-seven.

LOVE. GIVE IT TO ME NOW, SAM!"

SLEDGE WANTED TO DO JUST THAT. BUT SOMETHING HELD HIM BACK. THEN HE HEARD IT–A SOUND OUT IN THE HALLWAY, A FURTIVE SCRABBLING SOUND

LIKE A RAT MAKES. YEAH, HE THOUGHT, A HUMAN RAT. HE LET GO OF VELDA, PULLED OUT HIS FORTY-FIVE, AND SPUN AROUND IN A CROUCH.

My machine locked the instant after I touched the period key; the Line Editor's horn sounded.

The third quarter was over.

I sagged in my chair, only half aware of the crowd noise swelling around me, and peered up at the board. The printout and the numerals blazed like sparks of fire in the sunlight.

CULP 7500, SACKETT 7255.

A deepening fatigue seeped through me, dulling my thoughts. Dimly I saw The Cranker leaning forward across his typewriter, head cradled in his arms; his whole body heaved as if he couldn't get enough air into his lungs. What were the New-Sport announcers saying about him on the TriDim telecast? Did they believe he could maintain his grueling pace for another full quarter?

Did they think I still had a chance to win?

Down 245 with only 2500 left. . . .

Culp took his Fuel sitting down this time, with his head tilted back and his throat working spasmodically. I did the same; I felt that if I stood up my knees would buckle and I would sprawl out like a clown. The game plan called for no more than three ounces at the third-quarter break–none at all if I could hold off–but neither Mort nor I had counted on me being down as far as I was. I took a full six ounces, praying it would shore up my flagging strength, and even then I had to force myself not to make it nine or ten.

Only it didn't do anything for me, as it had at halftime and as it usually did in competition. No lift at all. My mind remained sluggish and the muscles in my arms and wrists wouldn't relax. The only effect it had was to make my head pound and my stomach feel queasy.

With a minute of the time-out left I loaded my pipe, put a match to the tobacco. The smoke tasted foul and made my head throb all the more painfully. I laid the pipe down and did some

Prose Bowl

slow deep-breathing. On his side of the Line Culp was lighting a fresh cigarette off the butt of an old one. He looked shrunken now, at least ten years older than his age of 57—not formidable at all.

You don't awe me anymore, I told him mentally, trying to psych myself up. I can beat you because I'm as good as you are, I'm *better* than you are. Better, old man, you hear me?

He didn't look at me. He hadn't looked at me once during the entire Face-Off.

The Head Editor's red flag went up. I poised my hands at the ready, shaking my head in an effort to clear away some of the fuzziness. The screaming voices of the fans seemed almost hysterical, full of anticipation and a kind of hunger, like animals waiting for the kill.

All right, I thought, this is it.

The red flag dropped and the claxon blared.

ALL RIGHT, SLEDGE THOUGHT, THIS IS IT. HE

And my mind went blank.

My hands started to tremble; body fluid streamed down my cheeks. Think of a sentence, for God's sake! But it was as if my brain had contracted, squeezed up into a tiny clotted mass that blocked off all subconscious connection.

The Cranker's machine was making thunder again.

HE

Nothing.

"Come on, Sackett! Hack it, hack it!"

HE

HE

Block. I was blocked.

Panic surged through me. I hadn't had a block since my first year in the semi-pro Gothic Romance League; I'd never believed it could happen to me in the Bigs. All the symptoms came rushing in on the heels of the panic: feeling of suffocation, pain in my chest, irregular breathing, nausea, strange sounds coming unbidden from my throat that were the beginnings, not the endings of words.

HE

A volley of boos thudded against my eardrums, like rocks of sound stinging, hurting. I could feel myself whimpering; I had the terrible sensation of imminent collapse across my typewriter.

The stuttering roar of Culp's machine ceased for two or three seconds as he pulled out a completed page and inserted new paper, then began again with a vengeance.

A fragment of memory disgorged itself from the clotted mass inside my head: Mort's voice saying to me a long time ago, "To break a block you begin at the beginning. Subject. Object. Noun. Verb. Preposition. Participle. Take one word at a time, build a sentence, and pretty soon the rest will come."

Subject.
Noun. Pronoun.
HE
Verb. Verb.
WENT
HE WENT
Preposition.
TO
HE WENT TO
Object.
THE DOOR AND THREW IT OPEN AND THE FAT MAN WAS THERE, CROUCHED AT THE EDGE OF THE STAIRCASE, A GUN HELD IN HIS FAT FIST. SLEDGE FELT THE RAGE EXPLODE INSIDE HIM. HE DODGED OUT INTO THE HALLWAY, RAISING HIS FORTY-FIVE. THE BIG MAN WOULD FEEL SLEDGE'S FIRE IN HIS FAT PRETTY SOON NOW.

"Sackett, Sackett, Sackett!"

It had all come back in a single wrenching flood; the feeling of mind-shrinkage was gone, and along with it the suffocation, the chest pain, the nausea. But the panic was still there. I had broken the momentary block, I was firing again at full speed, but how much time had I lost? How many more words had I fallen behind?

I was afraid to look up at the board. And yet I *had* to know the score, I had to know if I still had any kind of chance. Fearfully I lifted my eyes, blinking away sweat.

CULP 8015, SACKETT 7369.

The panic dulled and gave way to despair. 650 words down, with less than 2000 to go and The Cranker showing no signs of weakening. Hopeless–it was hopeless.

I was going to lose.

Most of the fans were standing, urging Culp on with great booming cries of his name; they sounded even hungrier now. It struck me then that they wanted to see him humiliate me, pour it on and crush me by a thousand words or more. Well, I wasn't going to give them that satisfaction. I wouldn't be disgraced in front of Mort and my girl and family and thirty million TriDim viewers. I wouldn't quit.

In a frenzy I pounded out the last few lines on page thirty, ripped it free and replaced it. Action, action–draw the scene out for at least three more pages. Adjectives, adverbs, similes. Words. Words.

SLEDGE KICKED THE FAT MAN IN THE GROIN AND SENT HIM TUMBLING DOWN THE STAIRS LIKE A BROKEN SCREAMING DOLL, SCREAMING OUT THE WORDS OF HIS PAIN.

Agony in my head, in my leg, in my wounded forefinger. Roaring in my ears that had nothing to do with the crowd.

CULP 8566, SACKETT 7930.

Gain of 20–twenty words! I wanted to laugh, locked the sound in my throat instead, and made myself glance across at Culp. His body curved into a humpbacked C, fingers hooked into claws, expression of torment on his wet face: the strain was starting to tell on him too. But up on the board, his prose still pouring out in letters as bright as golden blood.

SHE WAS SO TIRED AS SHE TRUDGED ACROSS THE DUSTY SANDS OF DENEB, SO VERY TIRED. BUT SHE HAD TO GO ON, SHE HAD TO FIND THE GREEN. THE BRIGHT GREEN, THE BEAUTIFUL GREEN, IT SEEMED

AS IF THERE HAD NEVER BEEN ANYTHING IN HER LIFE EXCEPT THE SEARCH AND THE NEED FOR THE GREEN.

I imagined again the urgent cries from Sally, from Mom and Dad: "Don't give up, Rex! There's still hope, there's still a chance!" Then they faded, and everything else seemed to fade too. I was losing all track of time and place; I felt as if I were being closed into a kind of vacuum. I couldn't hear anything, couldn't see anything but the words, always the words appearing like great and meaningless symbols on the paper and in the sky. It was just The Cranker and me now, alone together in the stadium. Winning and losing didn't even matter any more. All that mattered was the two of us and the job we were compelled to do.

Finished page out, new page in.

THE FAT MAN SAT BLEEDING AGAINST THE WALL WHERE SLEDGE'S SLUGS HAD HURLED HIM. HE WAS STILL ALIVE BUT NOT FOR LONG. "ALL RIGHT, SHAMUS," HE CROAKED, "I'M FINISHED, IT'S BIG CASINO FOR ME. BUT YOU'LL NEVER GET THE DIAMOND. I'LL TAKE IT TO HELL WITH ME FIRST."

Carriage return, tab key.

The board:

CULP 8916, SACKETT 8341.

And The Cranker's prose still coming, still running:

THE BEAST LOOMED BEFORE HER IN THE THICKET AND SHE FELT HER HEART SKIP A BEAT. SHE FELT DIZZY, AS IF SHE WOULD FAINT AT ANY SECOND. I CAN'T GO THROUGH WITH THIS, SHE THOUGHT. HOW CAN I GO ON LIKE THIS? I NEED

Culp's machine stopped chattering then, as if he had come to the end of a page. I was barely aware of its silence at first, but when five or six seconds had passed an awareness penetrated that it hadn't started up again. The noise from the stands seemed to have shifted cadence, to have taken on a different tenor; that penetrated too. I brought my head up and squinted across the Line.

The Cranker was sitting sideways in his chair, waving frantically at the sidelines. And as I watched, one of his Seconds came racing out with a container of Fuel. The Head Editor began waving his blue-and-yellow flag.

Fuel penalty. Culp was taking a 20-second Fuel penalty.

It was the first crack in his rigid control–but I didn't react to it one way or the other. The crack was too small and it had come too late: a 20-second penalty at this stage of the game, with the score at 8960 to 8419, wouldn't make any difference in the outcome. It might enable me to cut the final margin to 400 or less but that was about all.

I didn't watch The Cranker take his Fuel this time; I just lowered my head and kept on punching, summoning the last reserves of my strength.

"Culp, Culp–give us the pulp!"

As soon as the chant went up from his rooters I knew that the penalty time was about to elapse. I raised my eyes just long enough to check the score and to see The Cranker hunched over his typewriter, little drops of Fuel leaking down over his chin like lost words.

CULP 8960, SACKETT 8536.

His machine began to hammer again.

The illusion that I was about to collapse returned, but it wasn't the result of another block; it was just exhaustion and the terrific mental pressure. My speed was holding and the words were still spewing out as I headed into the final confrontation scene. They seemed jumbled to me, incoherent, but there was no lock and no penalty flag.

SLEDGE KNEW THE UGLY TRUTH NOW AND IT WAS LIKE A KNIFE CARVING PIECES FROM THE FLESH OF HIS PSYCHE. HE KNEW WHO HAD THE MICAWBER DIAMOND AND WHO HAD HELPED THE FAT MAN MURDER HIS PARTNER.

Thirty-five pages complete and thirty-six in the typewriter.

CULP 9333, SACKETT 8946.

Less than 700 words to go. The Prose Bowl was almost over.

Just you and me, Cranker, I thought. Let's get it done.
More words rolled out–fifty, a hundred.
And all at once there was a collective gasping sound from the crowd, the kind of sudden stunned reaction you hear in a packed stadium when something unexpected has happened. It got through to me, made me straighten up.
The Head Editor's brown-and-orange penalty flag, the one that meant "Confused Narrative," was up and semaphoring. I realized then that The Cranker's machine had gone silent. My eyes sought the board and read his printout in disbelief.
"I WANT YOU," SHE SAID TO THE CREATURE, "I WANT YOU AS THE SHORES OF NEPTUNE WANT THE RESTLESS PROBING SEAS AS THE SEAS WANT THE DEPTHS GARBAGE GARBAGE
I kept staring at the board, still typing, my subconscious vomiting out the words of my prose. I couldn't seem to grasp what had happened; Culp's words made no sense to me. Some of the fans were booing lustily. Over in G Section, the Sackett Boosters began chanting with renewed excitement.
"Do it, Rex! Grind that text!"
The Cranker was just sitting there behind his machine with a strange, stricken look on his face. His mouth was open, his lips moving; it seemed as if he was talking to himself. Babbling to himself?
I finished page thirty-six, pulled it out blindly, and reached for another sheet of paper. Just as I brought it into the platen, Culp's machine unlocked and he hit the keys again.
But not for long.
I CAN'T WRITE THIS SHIT ANY MORE
Lock into silence. Penalty flag.
I understood in that moment, as the crowd and the TriDim viewers understood: The Cranker had broken under the pressure, the crack had become a crevasse and collapsed his professional control. I had known it to happen before, but never in the Prose Bowl. And never to a pulpeteer who was only a few hundred words from victory.

CULP 9449, SACKETT 9228.

The penalty flag came down.

GARBAGE

And the flag came back up and the boos echoed like mad epithets in the hot afternoon.

Culp's face was contorted with emotion, wet with something more than sweat–something that could only be tears. He was weeping. The Cranker was *weeping*.

A sense of tragedy, of compassion touched me. And then it was gone, erased by another perception of the radiant numerals on the board–CULP 9449, SACKETT 9296–and a sudden jolt of discovery, belated by fatigue. I was down by only 150 words now; if The Cranker didn't recover at the end of this penalty, if he took yet another one, I would be able to pull even.

I could still beat him.

I could still win the Prose Bowl.

"IT WAS YOU ALL ALONG, VELDA," SLEDGE HAMMERED AT HER. "YOU SET MILES UP FOR THE FAT MAN. NOBODY ELSE BESIDES ME AND MICAWBER KNEW HE WOULD BE GUARDING THE DIAMOND THAT NIGHT, AND MICAWBER'S IN THE CLEAR."

Penalty flag down.

ALL GARBAGE

Penalty flag up.

Virgin paper into my typewriter. Words, sentences, paragraphs. Another half-page completed.

SHIT, The Cranker's printout said.

A rage of boos. And screams, cheers, from G Section.

SACKETT 9481, CULP 9449.

I'd caught up, I'd taken the lead. . . .

VELDA REACHED INSIDE THE FRONT OF HER DRESS, BETWEEN HER MAGNIFICENT BREASTS. "YOU WANT THE DIAMOND?" SHE SCREAMED AT HIM. "ALL RIGHT, SAM, HERE IT IS!" SHE HURLED THE GLITTERING STONE AT HIM, THEN DOVE SIDEWAYS TO HER PURSE AND YANKED OUT A SMALL PEARL-HANDLED AUTO-

MATIC. BUT SHE NEVER HAD THE CHANCE TO USE IT. HATING HER, HATING HIMSELF, HATING THIS ROTTEN PAINFUL BUSINESS HE WAS IN, SLEDGE FIRED TWICE FROM THE HIP.

"Sackett, hack it! Sackett, hack it!"

More words. Clean page. More words.

SACKETT 9702, CULP 9449.

The Cranker was on his feet, stumbling away from his machine, stumbling around in circles on the lonely field, his hands clasped to his face, tears leaking through his shaky old fingers.

TEARS LEAKED FROM SLEDGE'S EYES AS HE LOOKED DOWN AT WHAT WAS LEFT OF THE BEAUTIFUL AND TREACHEROUS VELDA LYING ON THE FLOOR. ALL HE WANTED TO DO NOW WAS TO GET OUT OF THERE, GO HOME TO SALLY, NO, SALLY HAD LEFT HIM A LONG TIME AGO AND THERE WAS NOBODY WAITING AT HOME ANY MORE. HE WAS SO TIRED HE COULDN'T THINK STRAIGHT.

Two of Culp's Seconds had come out on the grass and were steadying him, supporting him between them. Leading him away.

New page, old words. A few more words.

SLEDGE SENT THE CAR SLIDING QUICKLY THROUGH THE COLD WET RAIN, ALONG THE MEAN STREETS OF THE JUNGLE THAT WAS THE CITY. IT WAS ALMOST OVER NOW, ALMOST FINISHED. HE NEEDED A LONG REST AND HE DIDN'T KNOW IF HE COULD GO ON DOING HIS JOB EVEN AFTER HE'D HAD IT, BUT RIGHT NOW HE DIDN'T CARE. HE JUST DIDN'T CARE.

Pandemonium in the stands.

Word count at 9985.

AND SAM SLEDGE, AS LONELY AND EMPTY AS THE NIGHT ITSELF, DROVE FASTER TOWARD HOME.

THE END.

The claxon sounded.

Above the din the amplified voice of the P.A. announcer began shouting, "Final score: Rex Sackett 10,000, Leon Culp 9449.

Rex Sackett is the new Prose Bowl champion!"

Fans were spilling out of the stands; Security personnel came rushing out to throw a protective cordon around me. But I didn't move. I just sat and stared up at the board.

I had won.

And I didn't feel anything at all.

The Cranker was waiting for me in my locker room.

I still wasn't feeling anything when my Seconds delivered me to the door, ten minutes after the final horn. What was inside my head was a great big blank. I didn't want to see anybody while I had that emptiness–not the New-Sport reporters and the TriDim announcers who would be waiting at the victory press conference. Not even Sally, or Mom and Dad, or Mort, even though I knew how proud and eager they must be.

I told the Seconds and the two tunnel guards that I wanted to be alone for a few minutes, that everything was fine but I just wanted to clean up before I talked to anyone. Then I went into the locker room, waited until the door panel whisked shut, and hurried over to the container of Fuel. I had three ounces poured out and in my hand when Culp came out of the back alcove.

"Hello, kid," he said.

I stared at him. His sudden appearance had taken me by surprise and I couldn't think of anything to say.

"I came over under under the stands after they took me off," he said. "One of the guards is a friend of mine and he let me in. You mind?"

A little shakily, I took some of the Fuel. It helped me find my voice. "No," I said, "I don't mind, Cranker."

"Leon," he said. "Just plain Leon Culp. I'm not The Cranker any more."

"Sure you are. You're still The Cranker and you're still the best there is, no matter what happened today. A legend. . . ."

He laughed–a hoarse, humorless sound. He'd had a lot more Fuel before coming over here, I could see that. Still, he looked better than he had on the field, more composed, back in control again.

He said, "Legend? There aren't any legends, kid. Just pros, good and bad. And the best of us are remembered only as long as we keep on winning, stay near the top. Nobody gives a damn about the has-beens and the losers."

"The fans could never forget you–"

"The fans? Hell, you heard them out there when the pressure got to me and I lost it in the stretch. Boos, nothing but boos. It's just a game to them. You think they understand what it's like for us inside, the loneliness and the pain? You think they understand it's not a game for us at all? No, kid, the fans know I'm finished. And so does everybody else in the business."

"You're not finished," I said. "You'll come back again next season."

"Don't be naive. My agent's already called it quits and there's not another ten-percenter who'll touch me. Or a League Editor either. I'm through in the pros, kid."

"But what'll you do?"

"I don't know," he said. "I never saved any of the money; I'm almost as broke now as when I started thirty-five years ago. Maybe I can get a job coaching in one of the Junior Leagues–anything that'll buy bread and Fuel. It doesn't matter much, I guess."

"It matters to me."

"Does it? Well, you're a pro, you understand the way it is. I figured you might."

There seemed to be a thickness in my throat; I swallowed against it. "I understand," I said.

"Then let me give you a little advice. If you're smart, this will be your last competition too. You've got the prize money; invest it right and you can live on it for the rest of your life, you'll never have to write another line. Go out a winner, kid, because if you don't maybe someday you'll go out just like me."

He raised a hand in a kind of awkward salute and shuffled over to the door panel.

"Cranker–wait."

He turned.

"What you typed out there at the end, about the stuff we do

being garbage. Did you really mean it?"

A small bitter smile curved his mouth. "What do you think, kid?" he said, and turned again and went out into the tunnel. The panel slid shut behind him and he was gone.

I sat down in front of the Fuel container. But I didn't want any more of it now; I didn't need it. The emptiness was gone. I could feel again, waves of feeling.

I knew now why I had been so hollow when the Face-Off ended; talking to The Cranker had made me admit the truth. It wasn't because of exhaustion, as I'd wanted to believe. It was because everything he'd said about the business I had intuited myself on the field. And it was because of the insight I'd had at halftime–that The Cranker and I were soul brothers, and in going up against him I was going up against myself; that beating him would be, and *was*, a little like beating myself.

But there was something else too, the most important thing of all. Culp was the one who had broken under the pressure, yet it could just as easily have been Rex Sackett. Could still be Rex Sackett in some other match, some other Prose Bowl–typing GARBAGE GARBAGE and then stumbling around on a lonely field, weeping.

Go out a winner, kid, because if you don't maybe someday you'll go out just like me.

I had already made a decision; I didn't even need to think about it. Sally and my parents would be the first ones I'd tell, then Mort, and after that I would make an official announcement at the press conference.

It was all over for The Cranker and all over for me too.

This would be my last Prose Bowl.

SELECTED BIBLIOGRAPHY

Following is a short list of important collaborative novels in science fiction, as well as a few additional short stories of interest which, for various reasons, could not be included here.

Novels

Garrett, Randall and Laurence M. Janifer. *Supermind*. Pyramid, 1960.
Garrett, Randall and Robert Silverberg. *The Dawning Light*. Avalon, 1957.
Kuttner, Henry and C. L. Moore. *Fury*. Gnome Press, 1947.
———. *Mutant*. Ballantine, 1953.
———. *Tomorrow and Tomorrow/The Fairy Chessman*. Gnome Press, 1948.
Pohl, Frederik and C. M. Kornbluth. *Gladiator-at-Law*. Ballantine, 1954.
———. *The Space Merchants*. Ballantine, 1953.
———. *Wolfbane*. Ballantine, 1957.

Short Stories

Clifton, Mark and Alex Apostolides. "Crazy Joey." *Astounding*, 1953.
Ellison, Harlan and Ben Bova. "Brillo." *Analog*, 1970.
Ellison, Harlan and Samuel R. Delaney. "The Power of the Nail." *Amazing*, 1968.
Ellison, Harlan and Theodore Sturgeon. "Runesmith." *Fantasy & Science Fiction*, 1970.
Kuttner, Henry and C. L. Moore. "Vintage Season." *Astounding*, 1946.
———. "Two-Handed Engine." *Fantasy & Science Fiction*, 1955.
Pohl, Frederik and C. M. Kornbluth. "The Meeting." *Fantasy & Science Fiction*, 1972.
Pronzini, Bill and Barry N. Malzberg. "On Account of Darkness." *Fantasy & Science Fiction*, 1977.

PRO   SHARED TOMORROWS: SCIENCE FICTION
       IN COLLABORATION

ST. ALBERT LIBRARY
4 GLENVIEW CRESCENT
ST. ALBERT, ALTA. T8N 0G2